Her *Scottish Groom*

Ann Stephens

ZEBRA BOOKS
KENSINGTON PUBLISHING CORP.
http://www.kensingtonbooks.com

ZEBRA BOOKS are published by

Kensington Publishing Corp.
119 West 40th Street
New York, NY 10018

All Kensington titles, imprints, and distributed lines are available at special quantity discounts for bulk purchases for sales promotion, premiums, fund-raising, educational, or institutional use.

Special book excerpts or customized printings can also be created to fit specific needs. For details, write or phone the office of the Kensington Special Sales Manager: Attn. Special Sales Department. Kensington Publishing Corp., 119 West 40th Street, New York, NY 10018. Phone: 1-800-221-2647.

Zebra and the Z logo Reg. U.S. Pat. & TM Off.

ISBN-13: 978-1-4201-0868-2
ISBN-10: 1-4201-0868-9

First Printing: March 2011

10 9 8 7 6 5 4 3 2 1

Printed in the United States of America

NEVER BEEN KISSED

A quizzical smile played about his mouth. "We could remedy some of your ignorance tonight." Her eyes opened wide as he slid his hands around her waist to pull her closer. Before she could protest, he brushed his lips over hers.

She gasped as a shiver ran down her spine. Taking advantage of it, he pressed his mouth gently but firmly onto hers. Vague awareness of the textured embroidery of his robe entered her mind as her fingers kneaded his shoulders. Heavy muscles shifted under her hands as he pulled her closer.

As he deepened the kiss, her focus centered on the sensation of their mouths slanting over each other. When his tongue slid between her lips, she opened farther, seeking to explore it with her own. He gave a muffled sigh that aroused a warm tingle in her nipples and between her legs.

Then she was free. Fearing her legs would give way, she clung to his arms and stared up at him. Finding her voice, she asked, "Did I do something wrong?"

"No!" He seemed as shaken as she. His chest rose and fell in heavy breaths, and his eyes had darkened to green. He stared down at her with frightening intensity. "You've never kissed before?"

She shook her head, not understanding why he asked. He did not enlighten her. Instead he gently stroked her cheek. "You did nothing wrong at all, sweetheart."

Also by Ann Stephens

TO BE SEDUCED

Published by Kensington Publishing Corporation

For Paul,
my real life hero,
and the heroines we raised

ACKNOWLEDGMENTS

Kim S. & Lizzie, I value your ability to point out my mistakes and sharpen my writing more than I can say. And I value your friendship even more. To Gerry, thanks for providing an example of the courage needed to follow your dreams.

Chapter 1

May 1875

Tonight called for some act of rebellion, no matter how insignificant. Diantha Quinn crept across the thick Aubusson carpet, her way lit by the lamp she carried.

The soft wool tickled her bare feet as the dancing light illuminated a room she had come to loathe. Swags of burgundy velvet draped the solid mahogany four-poster bed and the ornately carved mirror over the vanity. Combined with the gilding splashed on furniture and knickknacks, they lent the room an air both sumptuous and oppressive.

She picked up her quilted wrapper, uttering a small noise of distaste. Although her mother adored the garment's vivid apple green color, the shade gave her own skin a sickly cast.

The alternative of stepping out of her bedroom wearing only her nightgown did occur to her. She managed a small smile at the thought of her family's collective horror should she do so. However, considerations of modesty and good breeding aside, drafts filled the halls of her family's New York City mansion even in May. She sighed and tied the corded sash around her waist. After sliding her feet into an equally garish pair of slippers, she approached her door and turned the handle.

When she cracked it open, the footman drowsing against the corridor wall opposite startled to attention. "Now, miss, you know your father's orders. You're to stay in your room till it's time for you to dress tomorrow." Despite the sympathy in his voice, he took a purposeful step toward her.

"Eoghan, I've spent the last week imprisoned in here. Please, I just want to go to the library and read." She hoped the use of his real name would soften the young servant's heart.

Eoghan, who had been rechristened Edward because Mrs. Quinn feared appearing too Irish, crossed his arms. "Like you said you were going to visit Mrs. Schuyler last month and nearly got all the way to the railway station before they caught you?"

Diantha shuddered at the reminder of her abortive escape attempt and its aftermath. The servant's voice softened.

"Miss, I feel bad for you, I truly do. But your father says he'll send me back to Ireland if I let you get away. You know I can't chance that."

"I know." The twenty-year-old footman, older than she by only a year, had confided that most of his earnings went home to his mother in County Tyrone. Her father ordered his household with the same ruthlessness that characterized his business dealings. It was not an idle threat.

"I promise I'll come back. You have my word." A

grimace twisted her face. "Besides, as my parents pointed out last month, I have no other choice."

How odd to see pity in the eyes of a stripling whose yearly wages did not equal the cost of one of her hats. The boy sighed.

"You'd better, or I'll be hauled aboard the next packet to Belfast." He cleared his throat. "You know, miss, Lord Rossburn isn't a bad sort. For a Scot, anyway."

"The difficulty is that I'm going to be his wife, not his maid." She muttered the words to herself as she made her way down the corridor. A flash of bitterness coursed through her. "Servants can give notice if they're unhappy. I'll be tied to him till I die."

She stared moodily ahead of her. Lord Rossburn had been a complete stranger last summer. Tomorrow she would marry him in a ceremony orchestrated to bring her parents into the inner circle of New York society.

The whisper of her nightclothes echoed ahead of her along the hall to the marble stairway. Faces painted by European masters gazed unseeing out of ornate frames as the glow of her lamp passed. The flicker of light on the statues her father collected lent the impression of movement. As a girl, the illusion had terrified her, but tonight she kept her eyes fixed straight ahead.

Even the thirteenth-century French gargoyles guarding the top of the grand staircase failed to unnerve her now. Her older brothers had named them Buster and Willie. During her childhood, the boys had prevented her from wandering the halls

after bedtime by assuring her that the stone carvings
came to life and roamed through the mansion.

Her siblings anticipated the prospect of her marriage to a lord as enthusiastically as her parents did.
They took no pains to hide their delight at her engagement, and often spoke of the cachet of claim-
ing a British peer as a brother-in-law.

She had tried, cautiously, to correct them once.
She recalled the occasion with painful clarity. The
Quinns had dined *en famille* that evening, a rare oc-
currence.

"I don't believe he thinks of himself as British."
As she and her fiancé had yet to converse privately
during their courtship, she could not be sure of
this, but she did notice he bristled slightly when referred to as an Englishman.

They sat in the pool of light shed by a single
chandelier over their table. On either side of them,
two other tables stretched the length of the immense room, their far ends lost in the shadows.
Enormous antique tapestries lined the room, their
age-dulled colors enhancing the gloomy atmosphere.

"Of course he does, the British have been united
for a hundred and seventy years." James, the elder,
helped himself to a generous slice of layer cake.

"Besides, he doesn't complain about it." Thomas
took a last swallow of vintage Bordeaux and handed
his glass to a waiting footman. "Not that he'll dare
gripe if he wants to get his hands on any of our
money. Right, Father?"

Harold Quinn tore his attention away from his

plate long enough to glare at his younger son. "I'm not dead yet, boy. I earned my own fortune and I'll damned well decide who gets it when I'm dead and gone." His jowls quivered. "Not that I can see any business advantage whatever in marrying my daughter off to some overbred dandy."

In all fairness, Diantha did not think his lordship remotely dandified or effeminate, but chose not to venture her opinion.

"Mr. Quinn, we discussed the matter thoroughly when we agreed to Diantha's engagement. Kindly stop speaking in such a vulgar manner, all of you!" Still tall and slim after fifty years and three children, with only a few strands of silver in her dark blond hair, Amalthea Helford Quinn's fragile beauty belied a will every bit as unyielding as her husband's. Noticing the piece of cake in front of her daughter, she rang the small silver bell at her right hand.

"Edward, Miss Quinn does not care for dessert. Please take it away."

"Mama, I should very much like to have some this evening. Could I not eat just a small piece?" She gazed longingly at the chocolate-frosted confection Eoghan whisked out from under her fork.

"Do not contradict me, young lady. If I let you eat everything you wanted, you'd swell up like a hot air balloon." The words caused a wave of heat to mount slowly into Diantha's cheeks. No matter how hard she tried, she could never live down her mother's disappointment in having borne a daughter who did not match her own beauty.

"For heaven's sake, Mally, there's nothing wrong with the girl's figure." Her grandmother, the one person in the family unafraid of her daughter's temper, patted her lips with a damask napkin. "I certainly never treated you like that growing up." The old woman winked across the table at Diantha, signifying the arrival of a slice of cake in her room later that evening.

Diantha dared a small smile of thanks while her parents were distracted.

"I never had the opportunity to marry a peer of the realm. Although I have had a very satisfactory life with Mr. Quinn." Her mother inclined her head toward her spouse.

As the two regularly engaged in sharp disagreements, she and her brothers had glanced at each other and sought for another subject to discuss.

Diantha pattered down the steps into the darkened entrance hall. The scent of burning oil drifted from the lamp in her hand as she passed the ballroom, already decorated and set up with tables and chairs for three hundred. She did not bother to look inside. Mama had arranged the decorations without consulting her.

Since that conversation with her family, she had suffered through a series of humiliating meetings with her husband-to-be. Forbidden to utter more than the barest commonplaces, she had listened, eyes downcast, while her mother arranged every detail of the wedding and reception. Her parents had even planned their honeymoon trip aboard the flagship of her father's shipping line.

Worse, Mrs. Quinn, in an attempt to secure attention for the splendid match, had permitted several pieces of Diantha's trousseau to be examined by society writers from a popular journal. After exclaiming over the exquisite creations ordered from Worth of Paris, they published descriptions of several items.

Diantha had wanted to sink with shame when she read a detailed account of her embroidered underclothes. The article sparked one of the few times she protested to her parent.

"No one I know has ever had such intimate intrusion into their weddings!" She had shaken the paper in accusation.

Her mother rebuked her sharply. "Stop crying, you stupid girl! Society has closed its doors to this family for twenty-five years. Well, this will make them sit up and take notice."

"I hardly think they're going to be impressed because my corset-covers are embroidered with a flower-and-leaf pattern." The remark earned her a box on the ear, but in her agitation Diantha had not cared.

She had tried to escape the single time they left her unwatched, but failed. Wedding arrangements continued. To the gratification of her father, Astors, Belmonts, and numerous other names from select clubs accepted their invitations.

So tonight she engaged in the only act of defiance she could think of. Slipping into her father's darkened study, she retrieved a small key from its place under his inkstand and opened the inlaid wood liquor cabinet. Her brothers had taken Lord Rossburn out for a last spree this evening. Therefore she would have one of her own.

She supposed they were visiting the establishment of a Madam Sweet. From whispered conversations between James and Thomas, she gathered gentlemen obtained the services of loose women there. She occasionally wondered just what those services entailed, but knew better than to ask.

After examining each bottle, she picked up one and read the label aloud.

"COGNAC XO IMPERIAL.." She poured the dark amber liquid into a cut-crystal snifter and sipped cautiously. It burned going down her throat, but not unpleasantly. In fact, the warmth in her stomach felt very nice indeed in the chilly room.

She filled the bulbous container nearly to the brim. Papa and her brothers often drank several glasses over the course of an evening.

Removing a book on architecture from her father's bookshelf, she settled into an overstuffed wing chair and opened it to a chapter on the Georgian era.

Then she started to weep softly.

James Quinn needed to go on a slimming regimen. Kieran Rossburn held the portly young man up while his younger brother fumbled to unlock the door. "Why not ring for a servant?" His irritation roused his burden from his stupor.

"Father considers drinking and debauchery a waste of good money. So every single time we go out for a bit of fun"—his future brother-in-law indicated the front door of the Fifth Avenue mansion with a sweeping gesture that nearly pulled Kieran off his feet—"the old goat locks the door on us at midnight. We have to let ourselves in as if we still lived over the shop."

"Damned unreasonable, if you ask me." Beside them, Thomas looked over his shoulder from where he struggled with the key. It fell to the top step with a cold ping. "Missed again. You don't think he changed the locks, do you?"

"Highly unlikely." His lordship's patience evaporated as the young man stooped to pick up the key and failed.

"Stand up and hold this." He shoved James into his brother's arms and retrieved the key from its resting place. Seconds later, he opened the door and guided the inebriated pair to a Louis Quinze settle. Groping his way in the dark to a switch, he turned up the gas-lit chandelier overhead.

"Say, you can't do that!" Thomas stood up in protest and promptly collapsed back onto the settle. "The gas isn't supposed to be lit after Father goes to bed." Ignoring him, Kieran tugged vigorously at a bellpull.

"I do not care in the least what your father does or does not permit. And after tomorrow, I shall be free to tell him so myself."

"That's what you think, old boy." James gave a snort of laughter, or perhaps contempt. "Harold Quinn never gives up a groat without a fight. If you want to live off his money, you dance to his tune."

Kieran regarded the younger man coldly. "My estate brings in an adequate amount for me to live off of, thank you. I would like to remind you that your sister comes as part of a business arrangement with him."

A bleary-eyed footman arrived a few minutes later, struggling into his livery jacket. Consigning Thomas to this unfortunate individual, his lordship hoisted James to his feet and ordered the servant to lead the way to their bedrooms.

As he staggered through what appeared to be miles of hallways, he gave thanks that the Quinn brothers slept in neighboring bedrooms. Bundling the portly young man onto his bed, Kieran gasped for breath and regarded him with a jaundiced eye. Then, without a word, he turned on his heel and left the room.

The evening had been one long alcoholic binge for the Quinns, interrupted only by a visit to Madam Sweet's brothel for what they termed "horizontal refreshments." Kieran, already disgusted with the family he was marrying into, partook sparingly of the alcoholic refreshment and bypassed the women completely. A habitué of elegant salons in London, Paris, and Rome, the tawdry entertainment provided at the house of ill-repute failed to impress him.

Not that he expected more from his fiancée's family. The stench of sweat and cheap perfume from the bordello left a sour tang in his mouth. Hopefully a drink from his future father-in-law's well-stocked liquor supply would overcome it. As he made his way toward the study, he fought back the bile that rose in his throat. His engagement had given him plenty of time to assess the family. Only the need to look after his tenants kept him from bolting this neo-Gothic monstrosity they called a house.

He had approached Harold Quinn the previous summer, when the American had rented a house for his wife and daughter in London. Not only did the man run the most successful passenger ships plying the Atlantic, he retained ownership of his grandfather's fishing fleet. Kieran had approached the magnate in the hope of interesting him in backing the fishermen sailing from Cariford, the one harbor on Rossburn lands. The old man had listened to his proposal in silence, then dismissed him with a promise of an answer within a week.

Striding down the dimly lit marble stairs, Kieran's jaw tightened at the memory. He had had no choice but to agree to Quinn's insolence. Ever since the potato blight had spread from Ireland to Scotland in his father's time, their tenants had struggled to make a living. His father had nearly beggared the family in his attempts to provide for their people. It had taken years for the two of them to increase income from the private demesne to the point where the lord's family could live comfortably off of it. Little extra remained to help the tenants.

Despite the social solecism of an aristocrat engaging in trade or industry, Kieran had determined to start some venture to provide employment for his tenants. His family had been in Scotland since before the Normans had invaded England in 1066, during the reign of Malcolm III, king of Scotland, and the sense of responsibility for their people ran deep in Rossburn blood.

Even so, he had refused to pay Quinn's price the first time the old man informed him what it was.

"You're mad." He had regarded the other man with revulsion.

Quinn's brows beetled. Evidently, the magnate did not hear many blunt assessments of his character.

"Mad or not, boy, that's the offer. You want my

help, you take my daughter." Sitting back behind the large desk in the Mayfair library, he laced his hands over his stomach. "Take it or leave it. It won't be repeated, and don't think you'll get any help from any other businessman on either side of the Atlantic." The corners of his withered lips quirked. "I've put the word out that you're a bad risk."

"What?" Kieran erupted from his chair. "I made sure that proposal was more than fair to any investor. By God, you'll not call me dishonorable, sir."

"Not dishonorable, no." The American regarded his steepled fingers with half-closed eyes. "Let's just say I left out a few details when I discussed your ideas with other men in a position to help you."

"Just enough to make me sound like I don't know what I'm doing." He could not keep himself from adding quietly, "You bastard."

The other man waved the obscenity aside. "Been called worse, with more cause. The price of doing business." His pale blue eyes flicked over Kieran. "Actually, you've got a good mind for a lord." In shock, he realized the American meant what he said. "And you've a lot more gumption than most of your ilk. A man who ain't willing to get his hands dirty hardly deserves to be called one."

"How very flattering, to be sure." The young aristocrat bowed.

Quinn growled. "I'm not interested in your sarcasm. Do you want the deal or not?"

The Scot bowed again. "I shall inform you of my decision within the week, sir." With that, he took his leave, determined to find another way to help his people.

He did not find one. True to his word, Quinn

had poisoned the industrial world against him. At the end of seven days, Kieran had admitted defeat and accepted the American's offer, as well as the hand of Diantha Quinn in marriage.

As he passed through the golden glow of the Sienna marble foyer, he glanced at a portrait of Mrs. Quinn, along with her mother and daughter, which hung on one wall. Typically vulgar display, he snorted to himself. Nevertheless, he paused to study it closely for the first time.

Clearly a piece of self-aggrandizement for the mistress of the house, it featured the three of them in eighteenth-century garb, as if they belonged to a long-established family. Kieran admitted that the artist had done a capital job of capturing the character of his subjects. Mrs. Quinn stood in the center, preening like a peacock as she arranged a vase of flowers. To one side, her mother sat with a piece of embroidery, looking at the viewer with a sardonically arched eyebrow. Kieran smiled in spite of his foul mood. Mrs. Helford's vinegary nature appealed to his sense of humor.

On the other side, a young Diantha handed her mother a few more blossoms, her medium brown hair arranged with a lovelock curling over one shoulder. Although she looked more attractive than in her usual garb, she had clearly not inherited her mother's beauty. He peered closer, for a moment fancying a bleak expression in the dark blue eyes.

The echo of his footsteps abruptly ceased as he stepped from parquet flooring onto the thick strip of carpet leading to Quinn's study. Had the girl proved conversable, he might have borne the situation better. Most of his married friends had barely known their fiancées before marriage either, and they got on tolerably well. Their wives might demonstrate the typical foolishness of their gender, but they did at least carry on conversations of more than one sentence.

Unlike his fiancée, who invariably stared at the floor during their interviews, speaking only to answer questions put to her in a quiet voice. The image of year after dreary year in the company of such a dull creature rose before his eyes. And, dear God, after tomorrow he would have to bed her if he hoped to beget an heir.

"Ugh." He shook his head. He had only agreed to marry the girl. Visiting her bed had not been in the contract he had signed. If worst came to worst, his cousin Barclay could inherit the title after he died. Or rather, Barclay's children could, since he was two years younger than his cousin and heir.

He did not consider Miss Quinn unattractive. True, she would never match her mother's remarkable looks, but her face and figure were well enough. No, it was her spiritless demeanor that repelled him. He opened the study door and stopped dead in his tracks.

To his amazement, the subject of his sour thoughts appeared in front of him. In her nightgown and a hideous bright green wrapper.

"Miss Quinn!"

"Lord Rossburn!" She must have scrambled to her feet when she heard the door open, for she stood stiffly in front of an overstuffed chair. His gaze took in the lamp, the glitter of cut crystal on the small table beside her, and a heavy book of some sort lying half open at her feet.

For once, her eyes met his, wide with guilt. They glittered strangely, and he caught his breath at the realization she had been crying. Doubtless nerves, he thought to himself.

"Forgive me for interrupting, madam." He shifted uncertainly on his feet under her glare.

"Can't you wait till tomorrow to start interfering with me?" She plumped herself back into the chair, curling her legs under her. "You're not my husband yet; I shall do as I please."

He noticed that she formed the words carefully, as if struggling to force them out.

Still somewhat at a loss, his lordship groped for a reply. "I had no notion of disturbing you, Miss Quinn. By all means continue reading." He moved toward the liquor cabinet. "I only wish to drink a cognac before returning to my hotel."

"Well, that is a fortuishus—fortu—" After a few more attempts to pronounce *fortuitous*, she gave up. "It's your lucky night." She held up an empty snifter under his shocked gaze. "Papa keeps his spirits locked up, but I had the same thought. I wager you don't even know where he keeps the key."

Glancing inside the open cabinet, he saw an empty space in the line of crystal decanters. Wrenching his gaze back to his fiancée, he gaped as she held up the missing container.

"I have no idea what this is, but I highly recommend it." She swirled the liquid around its interior, and chuckled, an unexpectedly musical sound. He realized he had never heard her laughter. "It tastes like fire going down, but do you know, I have not felt the least draft for over an hour."

Striding over, he relieved her of the decanter despite her protests. Up close, alcohol-scented breath confirmed Miss Quinn's words. His fiancée had indeed imbibed a good portion of the drink.

He examined the level of cognac remaining. "How much of this have you had?"

"I don't precisely recall." Under his incredulous eyes, she wrinkled her brow as she pondered the question. "I remember bringing the decanter over after my second glass because I kept tripping when I walked over to refill it."

"Never mind." He bit off the words before returning the decanter to its place and shutting the cabinet doors. Seeing the key where the girl had left it in the lock, he turned it, and faced her once more. From her position in the large chair, she regarded him with a puzzled expression.

"Aren't you going to have your drink?" She picked up the snifter again, peering mournfully into its empty bottom.

"You need to get back to your room at once, Miss Quinn." He ignored the mulish expression on her face. "As it is, you shall feel quite wretched tomorrow."

"Ha!" She ejaculated the syllable bitterly. "I shall feel wretched anyway." She shot him an unexpectedly shrewd glance. "So will you."

Thrown off balance for a second time, he resorted to his most formal manner. "I assure you that I shall feel nothing of the sort on such a momentous occasion."

"Stuff!" She straightened in the chair, tensing

her body as though to spring. "You came in here for a drink for the same reason I did."

"And what reason is that?" Wondering if her family had forbidden her to speak for fear of exposing a sharp temper, he braced himself in case she flew at him.

"You don't want to marry me any more than I want to marry you." She did not make a move to attack him, but her accurate assessment of his feelings startled him into taking a step back.

"Whatever gave you that idea?" Never mind that she spoke the truth; one did not betray one's emotional state in public. He paced a few steps to the dark fireplace, dropping his eyes.

"You only like pretty women. Everyone says so." The anger left her voice. "I mean, look at me."

Although not a command, he lifted his eyes and did as she said. Miss Quinn stood once again, regarding him steadily from her place in front of the chair. Even with those appalling nightclothes tied at her waist like a pudding bag, he could detect the slim curves they covered. His gaze lingered on the full breasts that rose and fell with her agitated breathing.

And for the first time he found himself able to examine her face. Brown tendrils gleamed around a firm jaw where they had escaped the thick braid hanging down her back. Her mouth with its full, curved lips hinted at sensuality.

"I have mirrors, you know." Her voice broke into his thoughts. Although slightly slurred, it held nothing but a matter-of-fact acceptance of her appearance. It occurred to him that part of her reticence in their courtship might result from growing up with a beauty for a mother. Certainly they had conversed more in the last quarter of an hour than they had in the months previous.

"Oh dear." She swayed suddenly and clutched at the cushioned chair for support. "The room is tipping!" She stared at him accusingly.

He sighed. Moving toward her, he picked up the book from the floor. It had fallen open at a page detailing the mathematical composition of a Palladian building.

"You were reading this?"

She shrugged, her face closed. "Just thumbing through it." A bitter smile twitched across her lips. "I like to look at the pictures."

He shelved it and returned to her. "Allow me to escort you." Holding out an arm he waited for her to take it.

Instead, she put her hands behind her back and tried to step away from him. Stumbling over a leather-covered hassock, she nearly fell. His hands shot out to catch her and she grabbed onto them with a gasp. Holding her upright, he prayed for patience.

"Apparently I am doomed to assist inebriated members of your family to their bedrooms tonight." As she emitted an outraged shriek, he scooped her into his arms and strode out of the library.

"Put me down!" She struggled to get down for a few minutes, then ceased. "Bother! You're making things spin again!" With a small groan, she buried her head in his shoulder as he strode toward the foyer.

"That's the cognac, not me."

"Really? Why on earth do men drink so much of it, then?" She raised her head for a moment, winced, and let it fall to his shoulder again. A silent laugh shook him. Clearly she was a stranger to spirits. Something inside him relaxed slightly and he chuckled at the absurd situation.

"At least you're easier to carry than your brother." She did not reply, merely linking her arms around his neck. To his surprise, he enjoyed the soft weight of her body. Her chest rose and fell in a deep breath and he wondered if she had fallen asleep. He cautiously set one foot on the bottom step.

He nearly lost his balance as she burrowed her face farther into his neck and inhaled again. "You smell wonderful."

"Thank you. If you don't mind, it would be most helpful if you did not move excessively while I'm going up the stairs."

"Mmmmmmmm." She sighed contentedly, and he had hopes of getting her to her chamber undiscovered. If word of this escapade got out to society, both their reputations would suffer. A moment later, she lifted her head slightly. Risking a quick glance at her face, he saw her staring at the carved banisters with an intent expression.

"Do you know something?" She asked the question in a ringing voice, and he hushed her.

"No, listen to me!"

"Miss Quinn, I beg you not to awaken the servants."

Obligingly, she lowered her voice. "I've always thought those carvings look like something from an overambitious wedding cake."

"An apt observation. Pray be quiet." A sheen of sweat broke out on his brow. While his fiancée weighed considerably less than her brother, he had not carried James up the staircase. His breathing became more labored as he neared the top.

"You sound like my mother. She never wants me to talk either." Kieran felt a flash of sympathy for the woman as his fiancée whispered on. "Do you know, she picked out the banisters herself? In France. And the gargoyles. Hello, boys!" She sang out the greeting and waved at the statues. In the light from the foyer below, he could have sworn the damned things smirked at him.

"They are indeed revolting, but I must ask you to remain silent." Having finally reached the top of the stairs, he set her on her feet and leaned on the nearest gargoyle, gasping for breath.

She stood staring at him, swaying slightly on her feet for several seconds. Then she slowly folded into a pile on the floor, looking up at him in confusion.

At least she remained conscious, he thought grimly. "Right, give me your hand." He took the proffered appendage and pulled her to her feet, none too gently. "'Once more unto the breach.'"

"*Henry the Fifth*, Act Three, Scene One." She nodded sagely as he hefted her into his arms once more. "Do you care for Shakespeare, your lordship?"

"He's tolerable." A low ache began to spread across his back. "You appear to be familiar with him, however. Have you attended the play often?" He rolled his eyes at the ridiculous conversation.

She shook her head. "Oh no! Mother would never let me see one of Shakespeare's plays. They're dreadfully improper." Her voice lowered at last. "She doesn't know I read them. I stole the book from my brothers." She giggled. "That was five years ago and they still haven't noticed it's missing."

"Very clever of you, but we really must not wake up the rest of the house." He whispered in hopes of encouraging her to do the same. At the sight of the footman outside her door, he stopped short. To his alarm, the girl failed to take his subtle hint.

"See, Eoghan, I said I'd be back!" He tried unsuccessfully to hush her. "Do you know, Lord Rossburn hates the banister, too."

The servant met his eyes in horror. "Mary, God, and baby Jesus, I'll be sent back to Belfast for sure."

"Is there a discreet female you can fetch to help get Miss Quinn, er, settled in?"

"Wait here." The stripling scurried off into the shadows.

He eased her back onto her feet, this time sliding an arm around her waist before she collapsed again. He strained to listen for any sign that they had been overheard. Thankfully he heard nothing until the brush of feet on the hall carpet and a circle of candlelight heralded the return of the footman.

His relief vaporized when he recognized Mrs. Helford. She came forward to assist her granddaughter.

"Granny!" His fiancée almost literally fell into her arms. "Lord Rossburn and I were enjoying some cognac in the library!"

The old woman pinned him with a ferocious glare. He held up both hands. "I assure you, madam, when I entered the library in search of refreshment, Miss Quinn was already there. In an advanced state of inebriation, I fear."

She scrutinized him for several seconds before addressing the girl. "Diantha Susanne, is that true?"

She giggled. "I got into Papa's best liquor, and there's nothing he can do about it." She tried to snap her fingers, then stared at her hand in bemusement when she failed. "It did taste odd at first, but I got used to it easily enough. Lovely stuff!"

"I doubt you'll think so in the morning." The dry tone of her grandmother's voice sailed over her head. Mrs. Helford sighed and addressed him.

"I suppose it's a blessing that you found her instead of my fool daughter and her husband." She muttered to herself. "What did they expect, keeping the girl locked up like one of their collections? You there!" The hovering manservant snapped to attention. "Get down to the kitchen and warm a large pot of coffee—you and nobody else. If anyone asks, you're bringing it to me. Bring it here and mind no one catches you."

Nodding, the young man hurried away.

"You can safely turn Diantha over to me, young man." She spoke with the crisp air of a military officer. At the mention of her name, the girl looked up before sagging back onto her shoulder. Alarmed, Kieran reached to relieve the small woman of the burden. She waved his assistance away impatiently.

"You get yourself back to your hotel. I've a great deal of work to do if she's to show up at church unimpaired."

He regarded the pair of them with concern. "I quite understand, madam, but will you not need help getting her into bed?"

Despite the circumstances, the old woman

chuckled. "My late husband weighed nearly two hundred pounds in his prime and I certainly helped him to bed often enough. Now shoo!"

On the short walk to his hotel, Kieran shook his head in disbelief. Despite her condition, he had enjoyed his fiancée's company more in the last hour than he had in the previous six months.

Chapter 2

Accompanied only by James Quinn, his lordship stood attentively before the altar of St. Martin's the next morning. As the moment for the bride's expected arrival came, he joined the assemblage in peering down the long nave to the church doors. Unlike the guests, however, he remained unsurprised at her absence. As much as she had had to drink the night before, he had half expected to receive a note from the Quinns delaying the ceremony.

He should have known better. His prospective mother-in-law had expended too much time, effort, and money on this ceremony to delay it because of the bride's indisposition. The church swam with swags of exotic blossoms in shades of peach and pink. They hung between the arches along the main aisle and fountained up in filigree holders attached to every other pew. Additional vases of blooms rose in waves on the altar steps behind him.

If the woman had crammed any more of the bloody things in, he thought, the entire church would drown in a sea of petals. The vulgar female now sat alone in the front pew on the bride's side, dressed in an elaborate toilette of aquamarine blue satin and lace that suited her coloring admirably. Under ordinary circumstances, she would enjoy her solitary place under the gaze of New York's elite, but she seemed as confused as everyone else as the minutes ticked by. Her fair skin flushed as whispers ran through the crowd and gentlemen surreptitiously consulted their pocket watches.

"Where is the stupid girl?" James muttered the question out of the side of his mouth. From her pew, Mrs. Quinn's glare snapped to him and he subsided. By now, several guests were staring at Kieran, eager to see if the aloof British aristocrat showed any sign of discomfiture.

He merely shifted slightly on his feet and gazed disinterestedly at the choir stall above the back of the church, currently occupied by a boys' choir that served as a fashionable charity. To one side of them stood a tenor who repeatedly patted sweat off the jowls overflowing his formal collar.

Beyond the pillars supporting the stall, he watched the bridesmaids take turns peeking out of the great double doors, no doubt searching for any sign of Miss Quinn's arrival. A flurry of activity ensued when the doors opened, but only the bride's grandmother entered. Duly escorted to the front pew by Thomas, she seated herself. Catching Kieran's eye, she gave a slight nod. A tension in his shoulders he had not noticed earlier eased somewhat.

Several more minutes passed until a faint cry from the crowds lining the streets outside indicated that the bridal coach approached.

The cheers grew louder, reaching a crescendo as

the doors opened to admit the bride and her father. The bridesmaids scrambled into order and waited for the organ to begin the processional. After they duly marched up the aisle, it was Diantha's turn.

She leaned heavily on her father's arm as they slowly made their way toward the altar. It might have been a trick of the light, or perhaps because the creamy shade of the dress did not entirely suit her, but his bride looked quite pale under the sheer veil covering her face. As she reached his side, he realized her skin had a distinct greenish tinge. From that and the desperate grip of her hand on his arm after her father handed her off, he guessed she suffered ill effects from the night before.

The miserable expression on her face reminded him of some of his own early experiments with spirits. Recalling them, he patted her hand sympathetically. He leaned close to the small ear under the fashionable coif. "There now, my dear. We'll get through the day together."

Diantha barely heard him through the hammers pounding in her head. She had a vague memory of wishing to do something outrageous the evening before, and of drinking some of Papa's cognac. She had no recollection of returning to her room even though she had awakened in her own bed.

Her only other memories of the previous night consisted of a few fuzzy images, or perhaps she had dreamed them. In one clear vision Lord Rossburn, very handsome indeed in evening dress, stared down at her with something like amazement. In another, someone smelling of bay and lavender carried her down hall after endless hall. She liked that one very well indeed, and had experienced a severe shock when the arms cradling her so tenderly dissolved into Mama and Granny shaking her awake.

The morning had been a nightmare. On top of marrying his supercilious lordship, she suffered from the worst headache she had ever experienced in her life. Mama's fussing and scolding only made her head and stomach ache more and her eyes had developed an unaccountable sensitivity to light.

As she mounted the steps to the altar, a whiff of the banked roses and jasmine blossoms floated into her nostrils. She supposed she suffered from a severe case of nerves, for even the most pleasant scents made her feel downright ill today. Earlier, her favorite breakfast of an omelette, steaming chocolate, and buttered toast had failed to ease her misery, for everything had smelled and tasted dreadful.

Thankfully Granny understood how she felt. "Send the meal back down, Mally! For heaven's sake, Dina just needs something light in her stomach." She waved the offending food away. "Leave the toast and send up a pot of hot tea for Miss Quinn." When it arrived, she had shooed her daughter and the servants out of the room, and sat with Diantha while she ate and drank. With her stomach partially settled she could face the ordeal of dressing for her wedding. Even so, when she came down the marble stairway, she found her father scowling at the Tiffany pocket watch he carried.

He had looked her up and down and grunted. "You'll do. Now come along, you've made us a quarter of an hour late." Ignoring her cry of agony at stepping into full sunlight, he chivvied her into the waiting carriage.

A sense of unreality now enveloped her as she took Lord Rossburn's arm. He looked stunningly handsome, as always. The severe charcoal gray of his morning suit proved a perfect foil for the dark hair neatly combed back from his forehead. Unlike most fashionable gentlemen, he did not wear a beard. Diantha's female acquaintances had discussed the titillating cleft in his chin at length at the round of teas and balls in their honor.

To her surprise, the cool aqua eyes held an expression of concern as he encouraged her to lean on him. He even spared her a tiny smile. As he led her to kneel before the priest, she reflected glumly that she must look truly dreadful to elicit such concern from her normally aloof fiancé.

The rector, a man whose comfortable view of the Christian faith found favor in high society, pronounced the words of the ceremony almost as though he meant them. Diantha dared a glance at his lordship while he repeated his vows. As usual, the expression on his face was one of bored tolerance. Greatly disheartened, she spoke her own vows in a flat voice scarcely audible to anyone but her groom and the divine. Numbly, she heard them pronounced man and wife.

When he lifted the veil for the kiss, she composed her face into the serene visage she supposed everyone expected of a new bride. His lips left a warm trail on her cheek and lingered near her ear. The hairs on the back of her neck lifted as his soft breath brushed her ear.

"Will you be able to get back down the aisle?"

Disregarding the rector's confused expression, she managed a slight nod.

"Yes, thank you." Her lips remained fixed in a slight smile as she breathed the reply. How he knew of her headache and roiling stomach she did not know, but he sounded more sympathetic than most of her family.

Supported by the arm linked with hers, she tottered back down the aisle. The notes of the recessional boomed out from the organ and choristers so loudly she swore they vibrated inside her skull. Even worse, a crowd of onlookers gathered outside St. Martin's erupted into an enormous cheer as the newlyweds emerged. The noise and bright sun sent colored lights rattling through her brain.

Clinging to her groom's muscular arm, she somehow descended the steps to the coach waiting to drive them back to the Fifth Avenue house for the reception. As they settled opposite one another inside, she closed her eyes and leaned against the squabs.

Her moment of peace shattered as the vehicle set off with a jolt. With a groan her lids lifted. Lord Rossburn gazed out the window at the cheering crowd with a frown.

"I'm sorry." She searched for something else to say, but her mysterious indisposition prevented coherent thought. Fortunately his good breeding came to the rescue.

"Sorry for what?" He spoke with the impeccable courtesy he had used the entire length of their engagement, to her, to her family, to the servants. Such politeness chilled her.

She cleared her throat and mentally cursed the

awkwardness that plagued her in his presence. Tongue-tied, she gestured to the onlookers outside their window. "For this. I have always believed weddings should be private events."

He raised an eyebrow. "I did not hear you say anything about your preference to your mother."

"Whatever would that have accomplished?" Surely he had seen enough of her parent to understand that one did not say "no" to Amalthea Quinn. Contempt flickered in his eyes as he made a noncommittal noise in the back of his throat.

Stung, she persevered. "I am also truly sorry you had to marry without the support of your family and friends."

"Thank you, but my mother has been an invalid since before my father's death and is quite unable to travel. My only other close relatives are my aunt, who looks after her, and my cousin, who acts as my deputy when I am absent from my estate." He shrugged. "Doubtless you will meet my acquaintances when we arrive in London." The implication that his marriage was not important enough to invite them hung unspoken between them.

The rest of the drive passed in silence.

Mercifully, their duties at the reception precluded the need for more conversation between them. Footmen served and removed the elaborate courses of the wedding breakfast, most of which she declined. Thomas pressed her to join Papa's toast to the guests with champagne, ignoring her whispered plea to use water instead. Even the thought of drinking wine increased her headache.

"I prefer that Lady Rossburn refrain from drinking spirits today." Her groom reached over from his place and turned her empty glass upside down on the table.

"Nonsense! Nothing like a champagne toast to liven up a dull gathering!" Her younger brother reached for her glass again, but his lordship did not move his hand.

"My wife declines champagne." He accompanied the civil words with an icy stare. Thomas backed down with an angry mutter. Despite his words in the coach, she threw her new husband a grateful smile and picked up her water goblet. The ice in his eyes melted for a moment. A few minutes later he placed a small piece of broiled chicken on her plate along with a roll and a few pieces of steamed asparagus.

"This might sit better in your stomach." He turned away immediately, but after a cautious nibble, she realized he was right. Nearly as high-handed as her parents, but right.

She lost count of the toasts offered over the course of the afternoon. Thanks to his lordship's intervention, she responded with water, gradually feeling better. Still, the din of voices and music left her wishing to seek refuge in her room. As the light outside the French windows in the ballroom turned to late afternoon gold, her mother quietly signaled that the time had arrived for her to slip upstairs and change out of her wedding gown.

She gulped. In all the preparations for the wedding ceremony, the fact that she would leave with Lord Rossburn had been often mentioned, but not dwelt on.

She opened the bedroom door to find her grandmother waiting along with her maid. As they helped her out of the cream gauze gown and into her wrapper, she stared blindly at her reflection in the mirror. Only after the maid rearranged her hair did she glance at her going-away dress. Her eyes widened in surprise.

"That's not what Mama ordered." She ran a wistful hand over a cerulean blue velvet polonaise. Her fingertips sank into the thick nap, relishing cool softness. The skirt consisted of layers of more velvet and matching taffeta, draped into a bustle.

"I ordered it from Mr. Worth on the sly." The old woman's eyes sparkled wickedly. "I figured as much as your mother ordered, nobody would notice one more." Diantha could not help but smile in spite of her pounding heart.

At last Granny dismissed the woman and took her hands.

"Well, Dina, you're facing what comes to every woman that marries." Her gaze took in Diantha from head to toe before settling on her face. Meeting the old woman's eyes, a faded version of her own, the girl nodded, unsure what to say.

Somewhat to her surprise, the old woman dropped her hands and paced a few steps away before facing her. "This moment is difficult enough even when you're leaving your family for a man or a marriage you want."

"You're the only one I'll miss here." She clapped a hand over her mouth as soon as she had blurted the truth out. To her relief, Granny did not scold her.

"The way you've been hemmed in all your life, that's hardly a surprise." The old woman's voice turned wistful as she moved to the four-poster bed. "You know, I was madly in love with your grandfather when we married. It didn't last, though. I found I couldn't respect a man who ran through the fortune he did, and I raised my daughter to take a far more practical view of matrimony."

She fidgeted with the fringe on the bed curtain, still averting her eyes. "It was a terrible mistake. Your mother married for money, and while she's never regretted it, you and your brothers have all suffered because of it. They grew up into hard, selfish men." She turned and patted Diantha's cheek. "You've been spared that, thank God, but you were never allowed to be alive like your mother and I were."

The girl winced as the wrinkled hands dropped and bit into her flesh under the fashionable dress. They loosened instantly, but her grandmother kept her gaze locked on her face.

"You may not want this marriage, Diantha, but I tell you, the man you've married is three times the man your grandfather was and your father is." The rheumy blue eyes darkened. "You have a chance to find happiness, Dina. Take it."

An angry sob escaped the girl. "How? How, Granny? The man despises me! I bribed the servants to find out about him."

The gray brows rose. "Clever of you, my dear. How did you get the money?"

"I bet James that Tom would get drunk at Mrs. Stewart's ball. But that's beside the point! I found out that his—his—" She took a deep breath. "His mistresses have all been great beauties. With dreadful reputations, but clever."

She waited for Granny to ring a peal over her for speaking of a class of women she should not even know of. Instead the old woman gave a crack of laughter. "Of course, he has other women." Diantha gaped at the blunt words. If Mama ever found out about this conversation, she would have a spasm. "My girl, a man picks out a mistress for the same reason he picks a suit of clothes. He wants something that looks good on him, and he changes them just about as often as he does his coat." She stared hard at her granddaughter. "We're wives, not strumpets. A wife has a permanent place in her husband's life and his home, and this gives her what little power she's got."

"It's not fair." Tears rose to her eyes as she muttered the words.

"Fair or not, that's the path open to us." A hand lifted her chin. Her grandmother's face softened under her regard. "I'd like to see you make more of it than your mother and I did."

Diantha sniffled, then pressed her handkerchief to her eyes. "I'd rather find a different path."

A sly smile tugged at the corner of the old woman's mouth. "You've got more heart and common sense than both your parents combined—maybe you will." Briskly, she turned to gather up an elegant paletot and bonnet obviously designed to match the dress. "But not in the next quarter of an hour. Your mother's expecting you downstairs. And your husband."

The girl clutched at the wrinkled hands. "Granny, I'm scared."

"I know. But the realities of married life aren't the horrors they're made out to be."

As her grandmother embraced her, Diantha wondered if she referred to the mysterious conjugal duties that ladies were not permitted to speak of. They involved a bed, she gathered, and some of her friends described them as very pleasant. But they had not specified the mechanics involved.

"Don't forget about your old granny after you cross the ocean, will you?" Despite her sharp manner, the withered lips trembled and her voice broke.

Diantha swallowed a lump in her own throat and forced herself to smile. "Don't be silly, you know I won't."

They gripped each other tightly on that last walk from her room to face the crowd waiting to see them off. At the head of the stairs, that disorienting sense of unreality descended once again. Her mother's artificial smile matched those of the guests crowding the foyer below. Diantha got the distinct impression that they wanted the bride and groom gone so they could return to the ballroom for more dancing.

"What are you doing in that ensemble?" Her mother hissed the words as she brushed each cheek with cool lips. "I selected the blush pink serge for you to leave in."

Her grandmother sniffed. "That pink monstrosity you picked makes Dina look like an overblown rose. This is a gift from me."

"Neither of you have the least idea of what is fashionable! Blush pink is the *dernier cri,* and Miss Fish wore a blue going-away dress just last month!" Diantha willed herself not to flush with shame. She would not miss her mother's tirades. "How could you do this to me?"

"Fiddlesticks! She looks much prettier in this than that getup you ordered for her." Mama's face turned an alarming shade of red, but she bit her tongue in front of their guests. "And I imagine her husband thinks so too."

Diantha twisted her neck to scan the crowd and instantly felt foolish. He waited for her at the bottom of the steps, one large hand resting on the marble banister. He stared at her with a surprised smile and she tamped down a flash of irritation. She wasn't that plain, for heaven's sake!

Her brow puckered as a vague image of telling him something about the carvings swam into her head. Odd, she must have dreamed it.

Even without the blush serge, she received all the appropriate compliments at the bottom of the stairs, including a kiss on her still ungloved hand from her husband. She freed herself from his grasp, resenting the insincere demonstration. Her mother fawned on his lordship one last time. Some of her brothers' friends shouted a few risqué remarks that left her cheeks burning.

Her father shook his new son-in-law's hand without sparing Diantha a look. "We'll see you tomorrow at the dock. Off you go."

The headache that had plagued her all day returned full force as they were escorted to their coach by the more boisterous elements in the crowd. Looking back, she saw her grandmother at the top of the steps, wiping away tears. Trying to match her husband's stoicism, she took a shaky breath and lifted a hand in farewell.

Her vision blurred as she turned away to go down the steps. She missed her footing once, but saved herself almost immediately by clinging to the firm arm linked with hers.

Tilting her head back, her gaze met her husband's. To her surprise a reassuring smile touched his lips as his fingers interlaced with hers and squeezed gently. Unfortunately, one of the newspaper photographers hired by Amalthea chose that moment to take their picture. She hissed in pain as the blinding light jolted through her aching head.

In seconds, she found herself rushed into the carriage, followed by his lordship. She scarcely had time to seat herself before he banged on the roof to tell the driver to start.

He leaned back and exhaled deeply, as though he had just completed a great task. His eyes flicked a glance at her. "Do you still have a headache?"

She cocked her head at the sympathetic question. "It's quite wretched at the moment, but how did you know I have one?"

His lips twitched and a twinkle appeared in his eyes. "After the amount of cognac you imbibed last night, it would be amazing if you did not."

Distracted by the first sign of warmth she had detected in him, his words did not sink in at first. When they did, she gulped weakly. "You—you *know* about last night?"

"Know about it? My dear girl, please remember who helped you to your bedchamber."

"I beg your pardon?" She regarded him, brows furrowed, for several seconds. Then the odd visions she had had all day fell into place and utter mortification replaced her confused state.

"Oh dear God." She buried her face in her hands. "I cannot imagine what you think of me." She huddled

on the seat, waiting for the explosion of wrath. The
sound of spluttering came from the opposite seat.
Her shoulders tensed. Her new husband's fury had
apparently robbed him of the power of speech. Another, even more horrible thought struck her.

"Does Mama know?" She looked up again as she
spoke, to see her spouse keeled over on the leather
cushions, holding a handkerchief to his mouth
while silent paroxysms shook his body.

"Lord Rossburn!" She took an arm to try to pull
him upright, but he hardly budged. She grasped his
lapels, determined to move him. "Please, you can't
have an apoplexy now! My mother will kill me."

Her entire body went weak with relief when he finally took a gasping breath. Then she stiffened as he
fell to his side again, clutching his stomach as he
fought to catch his breath between gusts of laughter.

"Damme, this is the best joke I've had in a year."

Stunned, she balanced herself and caught her
own breath as further howls of mirth erupted from
him. When she could speak at last, her voice trembled with rage.

"Am I to understand that your lordship found
the situation entertaining?"

Ignoring her frigid tone, he nodded once before
bursting into another round of belly laughs. By the
time he righted himself and mopped the tears from
his eyes with the cambric square, Diantha had re-
sumed her seat once more. Her frigid regard only
served to amuse him further, judging from the suppressed chuckle he gave on meeting her eyes.

"Are we quite finished now?"

He nodded, an insouciant smile still twisting his
lips. She wished she had a book in her reticule to

bury herself in. When his face lost its hauteur, it looked alarmingly friendly. Unnerved, she resorted to sarcasm. "I am so pleased that I amuse your lordship."

"Me too." At her outraged exhalation, the smile expanded into a grin and he settled back against the squabs. "You should be pleased, my dear. Very few ladies have a sense of humor, you know."

"I beg your pardon but we most certainly do!" She sniffed. "However, as a lady, I have not been bred to engage in disgusting displays of—of snorts and shouts."

"Snorts? Really, I must draw the line there." He sat up straighter. "I assure you, gentlemen do not snort."

With his eyes twinkling and a grin twisting his mouth, he did not appear remotely cold or forbidding. She could not resist his teasing. "I beg to differ, my lord, as you decidedly did snort just now. Several times." Only a tiny twitch of her lips marred the dignified delivery. Catching herself succumbing to his charm, she pokered up. "A good view of the docks is coming up on your right. By all means enjoy it."

"Eventually you're going to have to say my name." He lounged in the corner, eyes half closed.

"The opportunity has never arisen before now." She laced and unlaced her fingers in her lap.

"Why are you so uncomfortable with me, Diantha?" He asked the question quietly, but the use of her given name gave it unexpected intimacy. Her head twinged painfully as she struggled to form an answer.

"It's just that I've never been alone with you

before now." She knew how foolish the words were as soon as they left her mouth, and tried to explain. "I've never been alone with any man besides my own flesh and blood. And now we're married, and I am expected to carry on conversations with you in private when I've never had any practice doing so!" She broke off as she remembered another aspect of married life.

"And another thing! How on earth am I supposed to carry out my wifely duties when everyone refuses to enlighten me as to what they are!" She glared at him impersonally. "I haven't the least clue as to what is expected of me, and Mama always tells me I am hopeless in society." She stopped, considering. "Although that is not quite true. I am nervous, of course. But I always earned first marks in deportment when I was at school in Paris."

Her last words barely penetrated Kieran's shocked mind. The only women he had ever heard refer so openly to sexual matters were his mistresses, women he had chosen for their forthright appreciation of the pleasures of the flesh. Of course, they had never waxed indignant on the subject. He repressed another laugh at the sight of his new wife crossly exclaiming at her lack of knowledge.

He considered the possibility that remedying her ignorance in this area might not be the chore he had expected it to be. Milky virgins held no appeal for him, but the flashes of spirit he had seen last night and just now intrigued him.

And for once, she wore something that suited

her. That blue rig she wore did something to make her eyes look deeper, and her skin didn't look so sallow. With her hair pulled back into a glossy chignon at the nape of her neck, she looked quite elegant.

For the first time, he wondered how it must feel to be ordered about so constantly. His family treated their servants better than the Quinns treated their daughter. The image of his sturdy Scottish retainers faced with his mother-in-law's pretentions brought a smile to his face.

The Quinn family yacht ferried them across the Hudson River to New Jersey, where they entered a second carriage, decorated with greens and flowers to match those in the church earlier. Several miles later, they arrived at one of the least fashionable Quinn mansions.

Diantha craned her neck to see Cliff Heights through the avenue of trees lining the drive. Her mother had wanted to build a grand home on Long Island, but her husband, in a rare show of sentiment, selected a location in his home state. She and her brothers had always loved it.

The carriage pulled to a stop. Kieran stepped out, assisting her to the ground before he gazed up at the house. Situated on a hill, it overlooked the Hudson, and beyond it, Manhattan Island.

Beside him, Diantha couldn't hide a grin. "It's quite dreadful isn't it?"

"How many different architectural styles am I

looking at?" He murmured the question under his breath as the butler sailed forward to meet them.

"I counted six once." As she replied, Diantha resigned herself to a tedious speech. She tensed as her husband assumed his usual air of cool hauteur.

She turned her attention to the white-haired servant. After greeting him, she managed to deflect most of his welcome speech and they soon sat down to dinner in a room that would not have looked out of place in a baronial hall in Europe.

Despite Mrs. Quinn's assurance that they would be served only a modest repast, the footmen presented them with julienne soup, followed by stuffed cod and braised goose. Accompaniments consisted of potatoes Marie and carrots in dill sauce. Kieran mentally shook his head at the stupidity of serving a full meal to people who had spent most of the day eating. Across the table, he noticed his bride accepted only token offerings of each dish and hardly touched those.

In the presence of the footmen behind their chairs, the butler and the wine steward, he could hardly ask if she still suffered ill effects from the night before. However, he did take a small risk as he watched her toy with a dish of stewed plums.

"Do you not care for sweets?" So absorbed was she in swirling the fragrant pieces of fruit about that he had to repeat the question.

"Oh!" She focused on him as though remembering he sat across from her. "Forgive me, I must have been in a brown study." She gave him a rueful smile. "My mother will tell you I am all too fond of desserts, sir. I am just not very hungry this evening."

Despite the smile and tranquil tone, she regarded him with an air of nervousness. As she bent to her food once more, he noted the pale lips and trembling fingers. He confirmed his suspicions by nodding to the steward. "I believe I will take a brandy while Lady Rossburn retires."

A harsh clatter rang through the room as the spoon dropped from his wife's fingers into the figured porcelain bowl. She stared at the tablecloth where a splatter of the syrup made a rose-colored splotch on the fine damask. Under his eyes, she collected herself and allowed the footman to pull her chair back from the table.

"If you will excuse me, my lord." With a small curtsey, she followed the footman out of the room, exhibiting all the enthusiasm of one mounting the block to the guillotine.

He watched the dark paneled door close behind her before accepting the proffered snifter. He waved away the bottle. The poor girl had had a devil of a day. He took a deep pull on his glass. No need to keep her in suspense.

Her mother had assigned the master suite to the newlyweds. After they helped her change into her nightgown of satin with lace inserts, the giggling maids brushed out her hair and settled Diantha into her mother's gilded bed. Diantha dismissed them as soon as they finished putting away the velvet traveling dress. Refusing to sit there like a sacrificial lamb, she climbed down to pace the floor in front of the fireplace.

She whirled at the creak of the door, only to find the housekeeper waiting to ask if she needed anything.

Only the carriage. She bit back the words unsaid and assured the woman that she was fine. Raising a single eyebrow, the woman curtsied and left the room. The click of the shutting door echoed in the girl's mind like a tolling bell.

Gripping her hands in front of her stomach, she tried to pull herself together. "Women have survived whatever it is for eons. You will too. Now stop being such a coward."

"I've never thought you cowardly."

Lord Rossburn stood in the connecting doorway between their rooms.

Chapter 3

Diantha swallowed hard and took in his appearance. He shifted on his feet, which she noticed were bare, no doubt the reason she had not heard him enter. Looking up toward his face, the triangle of bare flesh below the hollow of his throat riveted her gaze. She gulped as a wave of warmth suffused her body. His hair had loosened from the brushed back style he had worn it in. For the first time she noticed it had a distinct wave. To her relief, he did not wear a nightcap.

Unable to meet his eyes, she stared at his feet again. Loose trousers of pale silk peeped from under his long robe of claret-colored brocade. Unable to bear the silence any longer, she blurted out the first thing that came to mind.

"You're not wearing a nightshirt." Horrified at her own indelicacy, she tried to stutter an apology.

"I prefer pyjamas." He did not sound angry, and when she dared raise her eyes to his face, he regarded her with a kinder expression than she had ever seen before. "I trust you don't mind?"

She shook her head, afraid she could not speak without squeaking. He indicated a small chair at his side, one of a pair set in front of a curtained window. "May I?"

She nodded. He seated himself and invited her to join him with a wave of his hand. Gingerly taking a place opposite him, she rubbed her arms restlessly. When he cleared his throat, she jumped.

"You're quite nervous aren't you?" She shrugged. He could hardly think otherwise.

"I was thinking that perhaps it would be best to delay, er, physical intimacy until we both get to know one another better."

"Oh, thank God!" She winced again; her poise had completely abandoned her this evening. "Unless your lordship would prefer not to." Mama had made clear that she must accommodate her husband's wishes, at least as long as they did not involve disgracing the Quinn name.

A wide grin burst across his face. "With that response, I'd be a brute to insist on visiting your bed."

"Are you quite sure, my lord?" She felt her face heating with acute embarrassment. Staring down at the patterned rug, she forged ahead. "My married friends lead one to believe that men are excessively fond of engaging in conjugal duties. I would hate to be remiss. Of course, you may prefer not to engage in them with me," she finished in a suffocated voice.

"Diantha, look at me." He leaned forward and enveloped one of her hands in both of his large ones. "I am quite fond of—of conjugal duties, as you call them." For some reason, a chuckle escaped him. "And you are quite a pretty girl, especially in that rig you wore here."

He sobered. "But neither of us will gain any satisfaction if you're frightened or uncomfortable. So we'll wait a few days."

"Oh." She lifted her gaze to meet his. "Does my satisfaction matter too, then?"

"It does to me." She found herself blushing under his scrutiny. When he squeezed her hands and released them, she automatically rubbed them together, feeling inexplicably chilly. He stood. "Shall I ring for a maid before I go?"

"Please, no! They act like they know something I don't. Which is probably true." Glumly, she arose and faced him.

A quizzical smile played about his mouth. "We could remedy some of your ignorance tonight." Her eyes opened wide as he slid his hands around her waist to pull her closer. Before she could protest, he brushed his lips over hers.

She gasped as a shiver ran down her spine. Taking advantage of it, he pressed his mouth gently but firmly onto hers. Vague awareness of the textured embroidery of his robe entered her mind as her fingers kneaded his shoulders. Heavy muscles shifted under her hands as he pulled her closer.

As he deepened the kiss, her focus centered on the sensation of their mouths slanting over each other. When his tongue slid between her lips, she opened farther, seeking to explore his with her own. He gave a muffled sigh that aroused a warm tingle in her nipples and between her legs.

Then she was free. Fearing her legs would give way, she clung to his arms and stared up at him.

Finding her voice, she asked, "Did I do something wrong?"

"No!" He seemed as shaken as she. His chest rose and fell in heavy breaths, and his eyes had darkened to green. He stared down at her with frightening intensity. "You've never kissed before?"

She shook her head, not understanding why he asked. He did not enlighten her. Instead he gently stroked her cheek. "You did nothing wrong at all, sweetheart. But I must say good night now if you want those few days."

With another caress, he let her go and walked to the door.

"Kieran?"

He turned back to her eagerly.

"Thank you for giving me time." A wry laugh escaped him as though someone had played a joke on him.

"Only a few days, remember." His eyes darkened again as they swept over her body. "I'm holding you to that."

He left then. After standing in place for a long minute, Diantha crawled back between the sheets. Compared to her husband's warm body, the sheets felt cold. As she twisted and turned to get comfortable, Diantha realized that she regretted being in bed alone.

Curling onto his side between lavender-scented sheets, Kieran sleepily reflected on the kiss he had just experienced. Intending only to discover her reaction to basic physical contact, both their reactions surprised him. When she had addressed him by name, he had hoped for an invitation to her bed after all.

He shifted restlessly. His sense of the ridiculous appreciated the irony of being thoroughly aroused by a virgin, but that did not ease the ache between his thighs.

Part of his response had to stem from months of near-abstinence. His engagement had necessitated only a few discreet meetings with tactful professionals.

Most men did not take such care to keep their liaisons hidden, of course, but he had no wish to make himself the subject of gossip. Besides, to flaunt a mistress during one's engagement was the height of bad manners.

Before drifting off to sleep, he congratulated himself on such foresight. His bride demonstrated more passion than he had dreamed possible in a sheltered girl. He looked forward to introducing her to more sensual delights, ones that would provide both of them with a great deal of pleasure.

Kieran put his plan into action the next morning. An habitual early riser, he enjoyed a cup of tea and read the *New York Times* front to back before hearing anything through the door to her room.

He tapped lightly before entering, to see his bride grab her robe and hold it in front of her with one hand. The other brushed her loose hair out of her eyes. "Your lordship! What are you doing in here?"

He stifled a sigh. These nervous starts of hers made him jumpy. Hiding his exasperation, he gave her the smile that usually coaxed women into doing as he wished. "I thought we might enjoy breakfast together."

An expression of confusion crossed her face. "I expected we would, sir. Breakfast will be laid out downstairs by the time we're dressed."

"I meant up here. And I thought we were on a Christian name basis after last night." He added a mournful note to the last sentence. She rewarded him by coloring a little.

"If you would prefer it, sir—Kieran." Her shy manner disappeared the next moment. "But Mama and Papa do not allow trays in our rooms. We must go down to breakfast."

"My dear girl, I have no intention of permitting your parents to run my life." He strode to the bellpull and tugged. A maid scurried in a few minutes later. When he ordered two breakfast trays brought up, she gulped and nodded weakly before hurrying back out.

"That should take care of that." He turned to his wife.

"I've only been allowed to eat in my room when I was too ill to stand. Mama will be furious." Having shrugged into her robe, she observed him with a mixture of glee and apprehension.

"Really? My aunt does so on a regular basis, and, of course, my mother seldom comes down to the table." He prowled the room, taking in the overdone decoration.

"Perhaps because they are married ladies." She shrugged, absently rearranging a bouquet of lilacs. "Mama does so occasionally, as well."

"You are married yourself, now." He chuckled at her dazzled expression as he paused near the dressing table.

"So I am!" The morning sun picked out a few caramel highlights in her brown hair as she faced him.

The table held a display of silver-backed brushes arranged on top of an embroidered cover. Moiré fell in stiff folds below the protective cloth. He traced the scrolled monogram on the back of the brushes and slanted a glance at the mirror above the cloth.

Its reflection showed his bride eyeing him nervously. He gestured to the chair at his side. "Would you like me to brush your hair?" She looked as shocked as if he had suggested they swing from the chandelier overhead. "Come, surely I can't be that frightening!"

She shook her head and bit her lip, gazing at the chair longingly. "You're not."

Triumph at so simple a beginning to his wife's seduction pulsed through him. He picked up a brush.

The next instant, she rushed toward him as if he handled a poisonous snake. "Please, sir—Kieran— put that down! Mama intensely dislikes having her things touched." She twitched it out of his hands and replaced it with a care all out of proportion to the act. "I'll be sure and let the housekeeper know." The soft murmur barely reached his ears. "None of the maids will get in trouble that way."

She followed the words with a deep breath which did wonderful things to the lace-covered breasts visible under her wrapper. As she addressed him, he wrested his attention away from them to focus on her face.

"I'll get my own things."

He nodded, still bemused by her outburst. She moved across the room and bent over a leather-covered case. Turning back, she held out a brush and comb of similar quality on the table, but simpler in design.

Taking them, he seated himself on the bed. She took a half step back, but he patted the tousled bed-clothes invitingly. "Perhaps it would be best to avoid the dressing table altogether?"

Slowly approaching, she climbed up and settled herself as though braced for instant flight.

Careful to move slowly, he smoothed the heavy strands down her back before running the bristles through them. She tensed under his palms, but did not move. He had learned long ago that most women enjoyed the rhythmic sensation of having their hair brushed. Judging from the smile he saw reflected in the vanity mirror, Diantha was no exception.

The thick mass flowed under his hands like satin as he carefully worked his way through it. He became aware of a rich rose scent rising from her hair. He inhaled appreciatively. Unlike the cloying floral perfumes worn by so many women, this one did not make him want to throw open the windows for air. To make conversation, he asked about it.

"Attar of rose and cedar. Granny swears by a drop of cedar oil for hair." She shivered a little as his fingertips whispered against the silken skin at the nape of her neck. His body tightened at such sensitivity. His bride would require careful handling, just the kind he excelled at.

Seeing her slightly closed eyes in the mirror, he scooted himself closer to her, so that his thighs lay on either side of her hips. To distract her, he talked of their plans for the day, when they would return to New York harbor for the start of their honeymoon trip to Paris. "Do you know much about the *Columbia*?"

After an initial intake of breath, she stayed still, hands resting in her lap. "Papa's flagship? I've only been on board once, a few days before Mama christened her. It seemed to be quite comfortable, from what I remember." She twisted around to see his face. "The rooms looked cramped at the time, but Papa ordered alterations combining four staterooms into one suite for us."

"I'm sure our quarters will be most comfortable." Without breaking the rhythm of brushstrokes, he maneuvered her hair to one side.

She shrugged. "They should be. From the plans, I think the additional square footage will make the voyage quite tolerable."

He had never heard her speak with such assurance. "Oh? Do you often read building plans, dear wife?" She flushed hotly then and fell silent.

Just as he bent forward to graze the nape of her neck with his lips, the door opened to admit two maids laden with their breakfast trays, and a third bearing coffee and tea.

Either in embarrassment at his teasing or alarmed at his attempted intimacy, she slid off the bed and breathlessly ordered the food to be set down on a table under the window. Mentally cursing prudish brides, Kieran caught himself on his hands to keep from tumbling off after her.

Diantha wanted to sink with humiliation as the maids set down the trays and scurried out of the room. How could she have been so remiss as to sit on the bed with her husband, clad only in her nightgown and robe? The smirks on their faces indicated that the servants' hall would soon buzz with that juicy tidbit. Shutting the door firmly after them, she turned back to Kieran.

She met his glare squarely as he balanced on all fours. The sight affected her strangely. For a moment she could not breathe as his robe loosened to expose an expanse of muscular chest and dark hair. On his hands and knees like that, he reminded her of a painting she had once seen of a panther stalking a jackrabbit. Her knees buckled for a second at the image.

Recovering, she gestured weakly to the trays with their covered dishes. "I fear we shall have to serve ourselves."

The spell broke at her words. Leaving the bed, he padded over to investigate their breakfast, once again the well-mannered aristocrat. Seating themselves, they enjoyed an unexceptional meal.

She found his vivid aqua eyes resting on her frequently as they ate. Alarmed at the way his regard set her heart pounding, she heaved a sigh of relief when he finally tossed down his napkin and excused himself to dress.

She wasted no time summoning her maid to do the same, for their ship left early that afternoon. As she sat in front of Mama's three-sided mirror, she could not help reflect on how much nicer her husband's hands felt in her hair than the servant's.

She grimaced as the woman fastened up the buttons on a coral twill driving dress with old gold trim.

The maid frowned. "I'm sorry, your ladyship. Have I laced you too tightly?"

Diantha wondered if she would ever get used to having a title. "No, my stays are quite comfortable."

In fact, they squeezed tightly, but she ignored the discomfort. "I have never thought this color flattering on me. Why my mother insists that I wear it so often is a mystery." She crammed the matching hat on her head. "I would rather have worn yesterday's dress again."

"But, ma'am, imagine what all those papers would say if you wore the same dress two days running." The servant handed her a pair of kid gloves.

Grumbling, Diantha descended to the drawing room on the first floor. It did not help her mood to see an echo of her dissatisfaction in Kieran's eyes when they met, although he said nothing, doubtless out of good manners.

After the footmen loaded their luggage onto the carriage, they climbed inside for the drive south to the docks on the New Jersey side of the river.

She gazed out the window at small landmarks she and her brothers had picked out years ago: a tree leaning over the road like a giant, an ancient rock fall beside their route. Her throat tightened at the realization that she would not see them again for years, if ever.

"It's difficult to leave home?" His lordship studied

her as he leaned back on the cushions, legs crossed. "I don't blame you; it's beautiful."

Surprised at his perception, she considered how best to express her feelings. "Cliff Heights was never exactly a home. We only stayed there during the summer, or visited for Thanksgiving."

Absently, she watched the dappled sunlight play over his features as they drove through the woods. "Mama would send us here with our governess and tutors when she visited her friends at Newport. We always knew we would experience a degree of freedom here that was never permitted us at other times."

"I think as a peeress, you will find yourself free to do a great many things."

She stared at him, thinking of hours spent memorizing rules of etiquette and precedence for the British nobility. "I fear I have never seen your title as anything but an encumbrance."

He straightened up, brows snapping together. "My family's title predates the union of Great Britain in 1707, and we can trace our line back to the days of Robert the Bruce. Those are hardly burdens."

She arched a brow. "And I suppose your lineage is why you ended up seeking help from my father."

He glared at her as though searching for a rebuttal. "Sarcasm is unbecoming in a lady."

She sniffed. "Snobbery is unattractive in a gentleman." She subsided then, pleased at scoring her point.

They did not speak again until the *Columbia*'s iron hull rose beside them on the dock. Kieran cleared his throat.

"We're going to be in close quarters for the next week. Don't you Americans have a saying about burying the hatchet?" He held out a hand. She took it, marveling at the warmth she felt even through her kidskin gloves.

"I'm not entirely displeased with my choice of bride, you know." She gasped with shock at the blunt words before realizing he was teasing her. Even in jest, however, they hurt.

His eyes filled with remorse, and he moved to the seat beside her. "Forgive me, Diantha. At times I forget that not everyone shares my twisted sense of humor. Truly, my words weren't meant to wound you."

He squeezed her hands gently. "I only meant that despite our difficult situation, I think we can make happy lives for ourselves."

Lives, plural, she thought with a wry smile. She had always secretly hoped to find someone who wanted to make a single life with her. But that dream had died yesterday. As Granny said, this was the only path open to her.

The aristocratic mask had dropped from Kieran's face, and she believed he meant what he said. She nodded.

Leaning forward, he barely swept his lips over hers. "Thank you. I will be sure to guard my tongue in the future."

"Diantha!"

They both jumped as her mother's parasol rapped sharply against the window. Her family had arrived while they conversed. They now stood outside, waiting for a servant in Quinn livery to open the door.

Kieran's whisper caressed her ear as he assisted

her out. "We are quite sure she's not coming with us, correct?"

Aware that her mother would have invited reporters and photographers to observe their departure from a respectful distance, she answered through a fixed smile. "If she is, I'm throwing myself overboard."

His shoulders shook at her hissed reply.

Fortunately, her father soon monopolized the conversation, describing the ship in glowing terms for his son-in-law's benefit. "Five thousand tons, and four-hundred-and-sixty feet long, bow to stern. It might not compare to your *Great Eastern* for size, but my goal is to provide passengers with the most comfortable passage on the seas, not stick a mess of cabins on top of a cargo ship.

"My idiot sons told me I was cracked to take out three perfectly good cabins and make them into a suite. Ha!" He clapped Kieran on the back. "We've sold it for every crossing in the next year, and at a higher price than all four cabins together."

He stopped and faced the younger man, waiting for congratulations. Judging from the revolted look on her husband's face, Diantha gathered that felicitations were not forthcoming. She stepped forward.

"That was exceedingly clever of you, Papa." Placing a hand on her father's arm, she coaxed him into moving toward the foot of the gangway, where the ship's captain and higher ranking crew members waited to be introduced.

After meeting the captain and his first and second mates, her family escorted them to their quarters.

Diantha, remembering the original cramped cabins, walked through the suite of two bedrooms, dressing room, and dining room with relief. Even Kieran could not repress exclamations of admiration at the arrangements.

Even the decoration, in her mother's favored neo-Gothic style, did not lower her spirits. The only difficult moment came when a young steward, after a timid knock on the door, invited Lord and Lady Rossburn to dine with the captain that evening. Her father waved the young man aside. "I didn't have that dining room put in for my daughter to eat with my employees. Bring their dinner here as planned."

"Please inform the captain that my wife and I would be honored to join him this evening." Kieran did not raise his voice, but the words cut across her father's easily.

"How dare you countermand my orders on my own ship!" She flinched as her father bellowed and the steward fled.

Kieran remained absorbed in examining a writing table cleverly built into the wall. "Kindly restrain yourself from answering questions addressed to me." He turned a glacial stare on the older man. Only the glitter of his eyes betrayed his anger.

"By God, you spoiled whelp, I'll take back every penny I promised." Her father's face turned nearly purple with fury. Even her mother watched him nervously, while her brothers seated themselves on the berth to watch the battle.

"Not unless you want a lawsuit. The contract we signed went into effect yesterday." Her husband shrugged as though bored. "By all means, break it. It's your reputation."

Several squeaks and gasps emerged from her parent's throat before he recovered his full volume and gestured to the doorway. "We are leaving! All of you, now!"

Diantha jumped. Her mother and brothers scrambled to follow his pointing finger, and she automatically started to follow. A large hand on her wrist stopped her.

"You're supposed to stay with me." Kieran let go of her and calmly shut the door behind her family.

"Of course. How stupid of me." She laced her fingers together, but to her relief, his anger appeared to have evaporated.

"Old habits?" He gave her a wry grin. "He was rather alarming, wasn't he?"

She regarded him with some awe. "He scared you, too?"

"Not exactly." His lips thinned. "I meant it when I said I'd drag him into court." His hand slid up her arm in a caress. "But he does use that roar of his to get his way, doesn't he."

"Among other methods." She shivered.

His hand dropped from her arm, leaving her oddly bereft. "I think I'll go explore the ship for a bit."

Diantha bit her lip, wondering what she was supposed to do in her cabin by herself. "May I come with you?"

A smile lit up his handsome face. "I would appreciate the company."

"Really?" In answer he held the door open and bowed her into the mahogany-paneled passageway.

* * *

They walked the decks and passages until late afternoon. Diantha told him what she had gleaned about the *Columbia* from listening to her father and brothers talk. Kieran freely confessed that he knew next to nothing about shipbuilding, and listened attentively to her.

When the ship slipped out of its berth, they took their place at the rail to witness its passage down the Hudson. She hoped a few photographers had stayed at the dock. Pictures of the two of them mixing with the rest of the passengers would infuriate her parents.

Although she enjoyed the anonymity of the crowd, she appreciated her tall husband's bulk as he protected her from the inevitable shoving and pushing. They stayed at the rail as the buildings and bustle of Manhattan dwindled behind them, while the sun lowered in the west.

By the time they returned to the suite, a quarrel had erupted between the lady's maid hired by Mrs. Quinn and his lordship's valet as to who should use the single dressing room first.

"Ladies first, of course, Davison." His lordship tossed a loose strand of hair off his forehead impatiently.

"I think it would be best if his lordship dressed first." The dark windblown locks waving about her husband's face riveted Diantha's attention. They looked so soft and thick. Her fingers twitched involuntarily. "Ladies tend to require more time, and we are expected to be late."

And so she washed her face and Florette brushed

out her hair to the accompaniment of her groom's baritone rumbling through the closed door to the dressing room. After a quick knock, he announced that he would await her in the saloon.

As she brought out the gown she had pressed earlier in the day, the Frenchwoman apologized. "I tried to find a suitable gown for this evening, milady, but this is the best I could come up with."

"I'm sure it will do very well, thank you." Diantha sighed at the yards of coral pink taffeta.

It looked better than her traveling dress, she decided as she surveyed her final appearance in the full-length mirror bolted on the dressing room wall. Full evening dress would not suit the confines of a ship, so Florette had selected a dinner dress instead.

Although long-sleeved, it possessed the plunging neckline considered de rigueur for evenings, outlined in bisque-colored lace. A deep flounce of more lace trimmed the pointed bottom of the bodice where it flared over her hips, and formed three wide chevrons down the smooth front of the skirt.

Twisting to see the back, she noticed still more of the pale lace in the softly puffed bustle. "I'm still not sure about the color, but it's so stylish! Thank you, Florette. You chose very well."

"It's difficult to make a poor choice from a wardrobe by Monsieur Worth. Although perhaps milady should avoid warm tones in the future." The maid offered her opinion cautiously, as though expecting a reprimand.

"I suppose." Diantha picked up a silk shawl that matched the trim of her gown. "I've always liked blues myself. Or even red." She sighed wistfully as she left her cabin. Decent women, according to Mama, did not wear any shade of red.

Feeling very self-conscious walking alone, she made her way down the hall to the first-class saloon, which doubled as the dining room. To her irritation, Kieran appeared to be flirting with a stunning brunette in amethyst satin. A number of covert glances from the other passengers indicated that they recognized her, and awaited her reaction.

Refusing to provide fodder for gossip, she focused on the captain, who presented himself almost immediately. "I see Lord Rossburn has met some guests already. Would you be so kind as to introduce me as well?"

She must sound like the stupidest creature in nature, she thought, as the captain presented several people to her. If Kieran had waited for an introduction to that woman, she would eat her fan. Illicit relationships abounded at her family's level of society, and she knew the look of mutual interest when she saw it.

The captain confirmed her suspicions by resolutely steering her away from the dark-haired woman. However, the education in drawing-room warfare she had gained from her mother's social climbing stood her well.

"Please forgive me, but I believe I see my husband." Diantha smiled at the passengers clustered around her. "Newlyweds, you know."

She strolled over to where he stood. Even in her chagrin his sculpted profile robbed her of breath, but she had something to take care of. "Good evening, my dear."

He frowned at her mocking words, but returned her greeting civilly. She placed a possessive hand on his arm and assessed the dark beauty. Up close, the woman's looks did not strike one as out of the ordinary. She appeared to be in her early thirties, although she dressed to the best advantage. The stranger's eyes sparkled with vivacity as she returned Diantha's scrutiny.

Buoyed by a Worth gown, even in the wrong color, she begged her husband to introduce her.

"Indeed, my dear, I should like to do that very thing." He turned to the woman. "May I present—?" He arched his brows with a quizzical expression, and Diantha realized with indignation that he had not even ascertained the creature's name.

"Senhora Henriques, of Brazil, and her husband." Turning, they saw the captain, accompanied by a dapper middle-aged man.

Kieran remained undisturbed by the interruption. "Madam, Senhora Henriques." He inclined his head to Diantha. "Senhora, this is Lady Rossburn."

"I am honored, your ladyship." White teeth flashed in amusement as she curtsied.

"Delighted." Diantha cocked her head. "I do hope you forgive my assumption that you knew my husband. He gave the impression of speaking with an old friend." Anger flashed in the dark eyes as she emphasized the second-to-last word. A few titters sounded nearby. "Of course, I should have remembered that my husband has no permanent acquaintances in the United States."

At that point, the dinner bell sounded. Visibly relieved, the captain escorted the Rossburns to his table. Her warning delivered, she spent the meal discussing the ship's itinerary.

Chapter 4

Kieran made no attempt to avoid Senhora Henriques over the next few days, although to his credit, he did not overtly seek her out. Nevertheless, Diantha's teeth gritted whenever she saw the lovely Brazilian.

Without access to a library, she read every periodical in the saloon at least twice. Mama had included her stitchery in her luggage but she quickly had her fill of needlepoint. Talking with the other passengers provided limited amusement, for they either fawned on her or were intimidated.

She envied her husband his freedom to move about the ship. Convention required her to remain in her cabin unless going to a meal. The rest of the time, her maid or her husband must accompany her. Kieran thoughtfully escorted her about the deck each day, and at least demonstrated the consideration to give her his full attention. Although not comfortable enough with him to speak without constraint, their conversations passed amiably.

They took breakfast in their private dining room

each morning, and usually luncheon or dinner. But whether they dined privately or not, he invariably joined the other gentlemen in the saloon for after-dinner brandies.

When she heard his cabin door close behind him each night, she could not repress a twinge of jealousy. She comforted herself with the knowledge that Senhora Henriques was not permitted to enter the saloon during the after-dinner hours either.

She recorded her impressions of the voyage in a thin composition book she had smuggled into one of her trunks. The first time Kieran had walked in while she wrote at their small dining table, she had tried unsuccessfully to hide it. To her amazement, he neither confiscated it nor insisted she stop. Just to be safe, she secreted it in the lining of her trunk during the day.

He did not approach her bedroom at all, although she became used to the touch of his hand on her arm and at the small of her back as they strolled along the railing. All in all, she thought their marriage off to as good a start as she could expect. Until the day they docked in Halifax.

While the ship took on supplies and mail, she and Florette took a turn around the deck in the chill Canadian air. Returning to her bedroom, Diantha idly thumbed through a packet of congratulatory telegrams delivered with their mail while Florette unpacked a dress for her to wear to dinner that night.

His lordship had received a large packet of mail as well, and had begged off their daily walk to go through it. He had appropriated the dining room table, as he needed room to write replies.

When Kieran did appear in her doorway, she looked up in surprise. In the stuffy suite, he had removed his frock coat and neckcloth.

She could not help noticing how well his vest clung to his torso as it narrowed to his hips. Aware that she had been nearly ogling him, she raised her gaze to his face. "Are you finished already?"

"Not yet. May I have a word with you?" Despite the civil words, his eyes blazed with anger. Curtly ordering Florette to leave their quarters, he grabbed her arm and pulled her through their dressing room to the dining room.

She faced him as soon as he shut the dining room door behind them. "What do you mean by dismissing my maid?"

"What do I mean? What the hell do you think you're about, you conniving little jade?" A vein beat at his temple as he shouted.

She started and moved to place the solid table between them. "Kieran—your lordship—what have I done?" She grasped its edge so he would not see her shaking hands.

His voice dropped to a quiet even more frightening than his raised voice. "What have you done?" He tossed a crumpled piece of paper onto the table's surface. It bounced off a pile of papers to land by her hand. "Why don't you explain to me?"

Afraid to take her eyes off him, she picked it up and unfolded it. Her father had sent him a telegram. As she read, her knees buckled.

Papa not only demanded an apology from Kieran for his insolence the day they left, he wanted to know why he had not consummated the marriage, voiced in terms so blunt that she gasped in shame.

Lifting her gaze to Kieran's, she sought words to assuage his wrath. "I swear to you, I had nothing to do with this. Why are you blaming me?" Her voice shook in spite of her attempt to control it.

Eyes blazing aqua, he leaned in to her across the table. "Of all the brass-faced lies I've heard, that has to be the biggest. You cannot think I am stupid enough to believe you didn't go crying to your father over me."

She stood her ground, her own wrath igniting. "You arrogant stuffed shirt! As if you would be worth my breath to complain about!"

"Don't change the subject!" He snatched the hapless wad of paper and, coming around the table, backed her up to the wall. "He's talking about intimate details that happened *in our bedroom!* My God, and I thought your mother had no shame." He raised the hand clutching the paper.

Diantha instantly collapsed against the panels, arms flying up to protect her head. She braced herself for long seconds, but the blow never fell. Only the sound of her husband's labored breathing filled the room. When she dared to look up, he still stood over her with his hand raised, but the wrath had died out of his eyes. Instead he regarded her with amazement.

"I threw the telegram." He stared at her. "Surely you don't think I would hit you?"

Glancing to one side, she saw where the scrap of paper had fallen.

"Please excuse me—I need to freshen up." Bracing her trembling knees, she straightened her legs. He stepped back, giving her a clear path as she sidled past him.

In the safety of her own room, she made her way blindly to sit on the narrow bed and pressed a hand to her hammering heart. The marriage would never work, not if he flew into rages worse than her father's.

The door to the cabin opened. Kieran entered and pushed it closed behind him. She stood stiffly; her hands clenched as much in fear as in anger.

The latter emotion won out. "Please leave, your lordship."

"Your father hit you." The quiet statement hung between them as she shrugged a shoulder.

"That's his prerogative. All the laws say so." After one glance at his face, she stared at the oriental rug decorating the floor.

"I'm sorry." He did not approach her, but she could not bear the pity in his eyes.

Feeling suffocated, she walked over to gaze out of a porthole. The busy harbor scene outside barely registered on her mind. "Why? I'm sure your father dispensed corporal punishment, too."

"I was on the receiving end of the rod often enough to make me behave, but that's not what I'm talking about." His footsteps sounded on the wooden floor. "I would never strike you."

She froze as she felt his hand on her shoulder. "So you say."

His hand dropped and his frustration showed once more. "You don't believe me?"

"I'd like to, but my parents both have—choleric temperaments." She rounded on him. "And after that display, why should I think you're any different?" Her face stiffened as she fought back tears. "How could you think I would speak of such personal things to anyone, much less my father?"

He ran a hand through his hair. "Who else could have known that we didn't spend the night together?"

She rolled her eyes. "The servants?"

He all but goggled at her. "Are you suggesting that your father set his servants to spy on us?"

"You think not? That's how he runs his companies."

"Diantha, I will not be spied upon! Not by your father or anyone! Is that understood?" His tone sharpened, but not to the proportions of his earlier rage.

"Be sure to tell him that. It's a long stroll back to New York." She smiled sweetly. "But as a member of the aristocracy, you can walk on water, can't you!"

He scowled at her. "You, my girl, are an irreligious termagant. And if you thought the servants sent it, why did you wait till now to say so?"

She stared at his patterned vest of deep blue. "Because you aren't yelling at me now." Her parents would have scolded her now for sounding like a pettish child. Kieran sighed and took her hand, rubbing his thumb over her knuckles.

"I should have kept a tighter rein on my temper. I swear to you I would never raise a hand against a woman." Lacing his fingers with hers, he pressed a kiss onto the taut skin of her knuckle, his gaze never leaving her face. Startled by the unexpected action, she tried to remove it from his grasp, but he did not let go.

Mesmerized by the handsome face so close to hers, she could barely speak. "I cannot entirely blame you for your anger. If I had been in your place, I would very likely have done the same."

A twinkle entered the wide eyes so close to hers. "Truly? Pounding the table and shouting?"

"It's possible." She bit her lip. "I have quite a dreadful temper myself."

He gave her a half smile. "Even after months of being engaged, we don't know each other well at all, do we?"

She supposed she should deny it, but she could not bring herself to do so. "It's not as if we had any chance to. My parents forbade me to speak of my interests, and it would never occur to them to ask about yours."

"Perhaps it's time to remedy that." At his husky whisper, her knees went weak for the second time in half an hour, but for an entirely different reason. He slid his arms around her.

"Perhaps it is." Her heart thudded as she watched his mouth descend to hers. At the touch of his full lips on hers, she inhaled and opened to him, inviting him to explore her mouth as he had before. He complied, bending her back a little to gain better access, tasting her fully.

Her arms twined around his neck. One hand clutched at the broadcloth stretched across his muscular back while the other caressed his nape. She buried her fingers in his thick black locks, reveling in the feel of the soft waves.

His mouth moved from hers to kiss her cheeks and chin, even her eyelids. She became aware of a throbbing sensation in her most secret place, and of a hardened length on Kieran's body that pressed against it, increasing the heat she felt.

"Oh God, Diantha." His breath puffed hot in her ear just before his teeth closed gently on the soft lobe.

She gave a strangled cry at the soft-sharp caress and he lifted his head, panting. "I'm sorry, sweetheart, I didn't mean to hurt you."

"You didn't." She felt giddy, gasping for breath. She feared her tightly corseted lungs would burst. "You just startled me. I liked it."

He straightened, a slow smile spreading across his face. "Did you?"

She followed his movement, not wanting to break contact. At his question, she nodded. "You don't mind?"

He went utterly still before lifting a hand to caress her cheek with his knuckles. "Diantha, listen to me." His manner became serious. "I do not mind in the least that you enjoy my touch. Your pleasure in our physical relations is as important as mine. Do you understand?" She did not entirely, but she nodded anyway. "Conversely, if I do something in bed you dislike, I want you to tell me that too."

She nodded, her brow puckering. "I will, but we're not in bed."

A chuckle shook him. "Not yet. Remember, I only gave you three days' grace."

"But that was for conjugal duties. We're not engaged in those right now." Her eyes widened. "Are we?"

He smiled down at her tenderly. "Let's just say we're engaged in the preliminaries."

"Really?" She blinked. "Eliza was right, they are delightful. Are we going to keep doing this until dinner?"

He struggled to keep a straight face and lost. Laughing, he hugged her closer. "I fear if we did, we would scandalize everyone else on board." He bent to whisper against her lips. "But we could continue a while longer."

She did not know how she could feel so warm and yet shiver as he kissed her again. She sagged against him, lips parted as he licked and nibbled the sensitive skin of her neck. "Kieran, oh yes, that feels very good." Blood pounded in her ears until it resolved into a sharp rapping on the door.

He heard it too and muffled a groan against her throat. Straightening, he held her close as Florette's voice came from the passageway.

"Milady, I cannot wait any longer to press your dinner gown."

Diantha looked up apologetically. "She really does need to start now if I'm going to be ready in time for dinner. It has a great many flounces. And she'll need time to arrange my hair."

Kieran raised his voice. "We shall be dining in our suite this evening. Lady Rossburn can wear what she's got on."

"*Oui*, milord. Shall I inform Davison of the change in plans?" A hint of laughter hid behind the question.

"That would be most thoughtful of you." He grinned as Diantha frowned at his high-handedness. She lightly pushed at his chest.

"I shall require you to do my hair before dinner, Florette."

"*Oui*, milady. I shall return later."

Kieran's mouth covered hers before she could

reply. A few minutes later, however, he lifted his head with a smothered curse.

"The kitchen doesn't know we're dining in here." After a last hard kiss, he rearranged his neckcloth with the help of the mirror over the tiny washstand. "I think it would be best if we occupied ourselves separately before dinner." Seeing her disappointed expression, he arched a wicked eyebrow. "Savor the anticipation."

Diantha wasn't sure if he meant the meal or something else.

After his departure, she tried to write in her journal but could not formulate coherent sentences. Finally, she gave up and dozed in her berth until Florette bustled in.

In the dressing room, the normally placid maid hummed under her breath as she brushed out the rich brown hair and pinned it up again. She took especial care tonight, even taking part of it down and repinning it until she was satisfied. Supposing she enjoyed having extra time to fuss over the hairstyle, Diantha sat patiently under her ministrations.

When the maid finished, she regarded her reflection with some surprise. Instead of following the latest fashion plates, the maid had smoothed her hair back into loose waves that looked as if they would fall out of their own accord. When she quizzed her, Florette just shrugged.

"I thought something different would do for tonight." A small smile played about the older woman's mouth as she turned to gather up unused hairpins.

Hoping the mass would stay in place, she entered the dining room where Kieran waited for her.

His look of admiration as he took in her appearance reassured her, although her confidence faltered when the steward opened a bottle of champagne. She had not touched a drop of alcohol since her miserable wedding day.

As if guessing her thoughts, Kieran poured out a glass and handed it to her. "Don't be afraid to drink it. You won't get a hangover from one or two glasses of wine." She accepted it and took a cautious sip. "Have you ever had champagne before?"

She shook her head and he lifted his glass. "To firsts, then." She took another drink from her glass, enjoying the tickle of bubbles over her tongue.

A knock announced the arrival of the steward with dinner. The ship's kitchen lacked the capacity to serve multicourse meals, but the quality for first-class passengers equaled that of the finest hotels. Starting with barley soup, they worked their way through roast pork, stuffing, and haricots.

The presence of the stewards required their conversation to be general in nature, but Diantha sensed a difference in her husband from their previous dinners in their suite. He focused on her more closely, and his speech lost its formality as he described his travels in Italy. It almost seemed to her that he regarded her as more of a person this evening.

He even teased her about having a sweet tooth when the steward placed dishes of pale custard speckled with nutmeg in front of them. Naturally he would never behave so intimately while dining with others, but she found herself worrying less about his disapproval. When she stood to withdraw to her own room, she repressed a sigh of regret.

Doubtless he would now visit the saloon for his evening brandy.

Florette waited for her, ready to help her out of her dress. When she saw what the maid had laid out, she emitted a small shriek. "Where on earth did that come from?"

The maid lifted up a short-sleeved confection with a bodice consisting largely of lace. "It was in your trunk, milady."

"My mother would never order something like this." She looked over her shoulder, half expecting Mama to enter the room in a blaze of outrage.

"Well, whoever did, it is quite charming. If milady will hold still, I will unbutton your gown." With Florette's assistance, she donned the scanty nightgown. It looked even more shameless on. Her aureoles were visible through the fine lace bodice, and the wide neck nearly bared her shoulders. The only thing keeping it in place was a line of three ribbon ties. It had a matching robe of sorts, made of more nearly transparent lace.

She scurried into bed and pulled the covers up to her chin as soon as Florette bid her good night. Even her berth seemed different tonight. Then she realized why. The maid had pulled out the extension to double its width. She had not noticed earlier thanks to her distraction over her indecent nightwear.

A light tap sounded on the connecting door to Kieran's room. "Diantha? May I enter?"

As her tongue suddenly glued itself to the roof of her mouth, it was fortunate he let himself in. His appearance undid her composure further, for he wore the wine-colored robe and a pair of pyjama trousers, as he had on their wedding night. The corner of his mouth quirked up as she stared at him, clutching the sheets in a death-grip under her chin.

"Surely you're not surprised after our earlier encounter?"

"I suppose I shouldn't be." She licked dry lips. "But you could have been more specific about your intentions at dinner."

"With the stewards in the room? That would have been highly improper." For some reason, he appeared to find her nerves highly amusing. When he seated himself on the edge of the berth, he grinned as she automatically scooted her legs away from his rear end.

"You enjoyed our kisses this afternoon." Kieran placed a light hand on her ankle, rubbing his thumb over the bone. She relaxed marginally at the unthreatening touch, but regarded him warily. "Would you like to start with another?"

The question of what exactly they were starting leaped to the tip of her tongue. As she opened her mouth to ask, he increased the pressure on her leg and ran his palm firmly up her calf to just above her knee. She gasped at the sensation of warmth from his big hand on the lowest part of her thigh, even through the sheets.

"You said if you did something in bed I disliked, I should tell you!"

"Do you dislike this then?" His fingertips gently kneaded her muscles as he slid closer to the head of the bed. An alarming flash of pleasure coursed up to her very core.

She shook her head. "No, but it scares me."

"Because it's new?" His voice dropped to a

husky whisper. She nodded. Mercifully his hand left her thigh, although her skin still burned where it had rested.

He leaned forward. "Then let's try something we know you like." His lips skimmed hers once before fastening greedily onto them. Pleasure jolted through her. Forgetting about the sheets, she wrapped her arms around him to pull him closer.

He cradled her head in one hand as the other slipped around her waist. Eagerly, she opened herself to his searching tongue.

As their mouths mated over and over again, she stroked the side of his face with her fingertips. Timidly at first, but when he showed no objection, she became bolder. She ran her hands over the high cheekbones, fascinated at the strength of his features.

Then his mouth moved to her neck, and coherent thought fled. Panting, her heart pounded wildly as he planted open kisses on the tender column, swirling the tip of his tongue against her sensitive skin. She tried to lean back and offer more to his eager onslaught, but was prevented by her position against the headboard.

Wriggling her hips, she tried to shimmy farther down in the bed. Guessing what she wanted, Kieran's hand slid to the base of her spine to ease her into a prone position. Shivers ran over her at the pressure of his palm at the top of her buttocks.

A soft moan escaped her that might have been his name.

He returned to her mouth, hushing her with another kiss. "Careful, sweetheart, the partitions between berths aren't terribly thick." Trying to catch her breath, she stared, dazed, into his darkened eyes and tried to nod her understanding. Lying stretched out beside and above her, she knew he had full access to her body, but she did not care until she felt the jab of something large and blunt against her thigh.

Fear of the unknown jangled along her nerves and brought her back to herself. She lay next to a strange man in her bed, with only the bedclothes between their bodies. After a glance down, she realized that the sheets had ridden low on her breasts, exposing a great deal of the lacy bodice and the skin it purportedly covered.

Kieran followed her glance and his eyes widened. "This is a great deal more attractive than that tent you wore before."

She tried to inch away as his fingertip traced the neckline, dipping to the first bow.

"I had no idea it had been ordered, and I cannot believe Florette would have selected it. It's indecent!"

"Really?" He raised his eyebrows. "Let's have a look, then."

"Kieran, really!" She struggled to keep a grip on the sheets, but he tugged them down easily. As he gazed down at her clearly visible breasts, she knew she had to be flushing bright pink all the way to her hairline. When he raised his eyes back to her face, they had darkened almost to green.

"Definitely indecent." A muscular thigh draped itself over her legs and he propped his head up on his elbow. "Florette is getting a raise."

"You cannot mean to tell me that I should wear things like this on a daily basis—are you even listening to me?" He seemed absorbed in stroking a lace-covered globe, exploring its fullness before circling her nipple with his palm. It puckered of its own accord, pushing its rosy nub against his hand.

"You have my undivided attention." He rolled the pink flesh between his finger and thumb. "Certainly I would enjoy seeing you in this on a nightly basis, because it would allow me to do this."

Leaning forward, he replaced his hand with his mouth. He lapped at the taut peak with tongue, teasing it through the lace, while his hand moved to her other breast, giving it the same ministrations.

"Kieran!" She whimpered his name and buried her fingers in the almost black waves of hair as he suddenly suckled the hard nub. His lips and teeth gently abraded the sensitized flesh with the wet material. She arched into his mouth, welcoming the weight of his body as he settled over her.

As he suckled her other nipple, her hips bucked against his, encountering that mysterious ridge of flesh once more. But this time, it added to the wild delight she experienced in Kieran's arms. Rubbing against it, the secret place at the apex of her thighs came to life, pulsing with heat.

"Exquisite breasts," he murmured, lifting his head to kiss her mouth again. She shuddered as his hands continued the amorous onslaught for a moment before moving to the top bow on her bodice and pulling. His mouth moved down her neck, raining kisses across the top of the creamy mounds as the bodice loosened.

His hands moved to the second bow. "Skin like

warm silk." He nibbled his way over each full curve, pushing the bodice open wider with his mouth.

The third bow. He pulled the material completely off her shoulders and breasts, helping her free her arms from the tiny sleeves. Blowing on one moist peak until she writhed, he finally covered it with his warm mouth, licking and sucking. "Nipples like steel."

He gave the same treatment to the other one, until Diantha thought she would go up in flames. She grasped at his shoulders, her hands slipping under the embroidered satin to find the thick muscles of his chest.

Her fingers encountered hair as well. Fascinated by the rough texture, she ran her fingertips over it before flattening her palms against the crisp mass. He lifted himself slightly and she pushed the neck of his robe farther apart.

Complying with her unspoken demand, he raised himself up and shrugged out of the garment. Letting it fall to the floor, he stretched out beside her once more, inviting her to touch him as she pleased.

Unsure for a moment, her gaze riveted onto the flat discs of his nipples. She glanced at him for permission before shyly imitating his earlier action, carefully pinching it to hardness with her thumb and fingers. He said nothing, only watched her with glittering eyes. When she leaned forward to swirl her tongue around it, he placed a big hand on the back of her head, pressing her to him, while he whispered his approval. Unfortunately, when she used her teeth, he hissed in pain.

She drew back, stricken. "I am so sorry! I never meant to hurt you."

A smile flashed white in his face. "I know, darling girl, and I'm not angry at all. It's no more than a lack of experience." He stroked her arm. "Do you want to try again?"

She shook her head. "Not if it hurts you."

"Start very gently and increase the pressure little by little, that's all there is to it." He kissed her forehead. "I'll tell you when it feels right." After a little more coaxing, she tried again, attentive to his whispered directions.

"Good girl. Did you like doing that to me?"

She nodded shyly. "Do men like that done to them? I thought it felt wonderful."

He chuckled. "I can't answer for other men, but I find it somewhat stimulating." She dropped her eyes, disappointed that she had not pleased him better. As if reading her thoughts, he lifted her chin. "A woman's nipples are far more sensitive than a man's, which is why you liked it so much. I am thrilled to have a wife who thought to please me."

He eased her down to lay flat on her back and stretched out on his side. His warm hand stroked down her side, following the curve of waist to hip and coming to rest on her leg.

Instinctively she closed her thighs, looking up at him anxiously.

"I want to please you too, remember?" His thumb caressed the fragile skin of her inner thigh in small circles that somehow increased the heat higher up in her core.

His wicked hand moved to her other thigh, fondling and massaging from her knee upward. She thought the fire in her core would scorch her before much longer. Shifting uncertainly she came against the silk-covered protrusion between his legs. Closing his eyes, he sucked in a breath and rubbed it against her.

Instantly, she fidgeted away from him, but he would have none of that.

"Open for me, Diantha." His questing fingers worked at the nest of dark curls, seeking entrance to their hidden seam. One fingertip found its way into the moist folds.

He muffled her exclamation of shock with his mouth as his hand explored places she herself was scarcely aware of. His finger slowly traced her most intimate opening, inside and out, before sliding up to a throbbing nubbin where all her nerve endings seemed to converge.

As soon as he touched it, all thought ceased. Her eyes closed tightly at a series of soft upward strokes on the tender swell of flesh. Her hips rocked voluptuously as he circled and teased, wringing even more moisture from her body.

She shivered as his voice vibrated in her ear, raw with lust. "So wet, darling, so good." One thick digit slowly slid into her channel, withdrew and returned. "So tight." A second one joined it, stretching her deliciously.

Her entire body tightened as though in anticipation of some unknown event. His thumb strummed the sensitive nub while his fingers stroked deep within her, building the tension until she buried her face against Kieran's neck to stifle her moans.

Then she shattered. Her pelvis lifted off the sheets to thrust uncontrollably against his hand as she convulsed with pleasure over and over.

Her universe contracted to their bed and their

bodies. His muscular arm held her together as she clutched at the dark mat of hair covering his chest, nearly sobbing for breath. As the tremors subsided, he pulled her closer, stroking her hair. His voice crooned something in her ear, soothing her.

In spite of his aching cock, Kieran did not move. His untried wife's intense response astonished him. He had never experienced such a sense of power in bed, even with the most skilled of his mistresses. He grinned at the wall in delight as his free hand ran over her body.

A twinge of pain struck his chest. He looked down to see her hand fisted in his curls. Smiling a little, he disengaged it as tenderly as a mother would an infant's.

She looked up at him with hazy eyes. "Are you angry with me?" He shook his head, disbelieving the question, as she swallowed. "I don't think ladies are supposed to behave that way."

"I don't care how ladies are supposed to behave. You were wonderful."

Her radiant smile stole his breath away.

"Thank you." She shyly explored his torso with her fingertips, and he adjusted himself to give her better access. When she reached his waistband, however, she came to an abrupt halt, looking up at him nervously. "I don't know what to do."

He rose from the berth. Keeping his gaze fixed on her, he slowly, deliberately untied the cord of his pyjamas. Her eyes widened as he lowered them, fully exposing his aching erection to her.

"Kieran, please—I can't possibly accommodate

all that." Her blue eyes pleaded with him in the lamplight, but the sight of her near-naked body on the berth only made him harder, if that was possible.

He returned to the berth, grasping at the night-gown still crumpled around her hips. She pushed at his wrists, but failed to stop him from sliding the material down and off her body. The faint scent of her juices reached his nostrils, and he took a deep breath, fighting for self-control.

"Do you trust me?" He could barely choke the words out as he fingered the moisture from her climax along her secret cleft, his desire so acute he feared he would go mad if she said no.

Instead she gave him a small, frightened nod that nearly melted his heart.

"Stay with me, sweet girl." He whispered the words against her ear as he settled over her, parting her thighs to receive him fully. He rubbed his length against her engorged nub until she arched against him, arms locked around his waist.

God, her innocent response to his lovemaking gave him pleasure he had never imagined possible. He could not deny his own need any longer. Reaching between them, he guided himself into her, grimacing with the effort it took not to thrust himself ruthlessly into the tight channel.

Her face contorted. "Kieran, it burns. I don't think I like this part at all." She struggled in his arms, panicking.

He gentled her as best he could. "It will this first time, sweetheart. Shhh, it will hurt less if you relax, I promise. There, now, breathe slowly. Good girl, that's right."

She tried to comply. He felt her relax marginally

and inched in farther, only to feel her tense again. He sighed and lifted his head to look into her eyes.

"I'm afraid the best thing to do is get this bit over with quickly."

Her voice caught. "Anything, please."

He brushed a strand of hair out of her pain-filled eyes. "It's just this once, darling, I swear it."

Then, lifting himself slightly on his elbows, he thrust home, the glorious experience of sheathing himself in her hot moist body mitigated by her cry of agony.

He held her close, whispering to her how brave she was, how good she felt around him, as he waited for her to adjust to him. Kissing each firmly closed eye, he moved experimentally. When she did not cry out again, he asked her if it still hurt.

"The less you move, the less it hurts." She gazed up at him anxiously. "Do you think you could refrain from making any large movements?"

"Yes, I can." Her body clasped him so tightly, he knew it would not be long before he climaxed. Grasping her hips, he made small circular thrusts, rubbing against her mound. She rewarded him by flooding with moisture, allowing him to move more freely.

Within seconds, his pent-up climax burst. He ground against her over and over, burying his face in her shoulder as he exploded inside her.

Much later, after his heart had returned to normal and he had arisen long enough to blow out the lamp, he lay on his back and stared up at the top of the berth. Diantha slept soundly, curled up against his side. He did not know what to make of the intensity of their lovemaking. He did know he would not be seeking out a mistress for the time being.

He frowned in the dark. He had assumed that after he consummated his marriage, he would conduct his life much as he always had, with the exception of having a hostess established in his house who would also produce the next generation of Rossburns. Had he just considered remaining faithful to his merchant-class wife?

No. No matter how she enticed him in bed, the fact remained that she lacked the intelligence and sophistication that he sought in his mistresses. He would enjoy the pleasure she offered until it palled. It always did. He had never so much as spent the night through with a woman and he was not about to start now.

Diantha nestled a little closer to him. Pulling the counterpane up higher on her chilled shoulder, he decided to stay a while longer.

Chapter 5

"Milady?"

Diantha started awake at the sound of Florette's voice through the door. Groggily she wondered why the maid did not enter with her morning tea tray as usual. Then images of the previous night flooded her mind.

"Oh no!" Recalling her unclothed state, she flung the sheets aside, hunting for the flimsy nightdress. She raised her voice. "I'll open the door directly."

Locating the lacy garment at the foot of the berth, she got to her feet and pulled it over her head. Eschewing the nearly transparent wrapper that matched it, she grabbed a silk one instead, hastily shoving her arms into the sleeves.

Just as she grasped the door handle, she looked back at the bed where Kieran had introduced her to so many sensual delights the night before. Her eyes widened in horror at the splotch of blood clearly visible on the bottom sheet.

"Coming!" Darting to the bed, she flipped the

bedclothes up over the telltale sign of last night's activities. Anxiously looking over her shoulder, she scurried back to the door and swung it open, hoping she did not appear as flushed as she felt.

"That smells heavenly. Thank you, Florette."

Diantha thought she noticed a quiver of amusement at the corner of the Frenchwoman's lips, but was too flustered to pay close attention. Where was Kieran? Did gentlemen normally leave after conjugal relations?

"How is your ladyship feeling this morning?" Setting down the tray on a small stand with raised sides, the maid placed a lump of sugar in a porcelain teacup with a pair of tongs. After pouring the steaming liquid into it from a matching pot, she placed a thin slice of lemon into the cup and brought it, balanced on its saucer, to Diantha as she sat on the bed.

"Fine, of course. What else should I be?" Diantha inhaled, relishing the citrus scent. After a sip of the sweetened liquid, she smiled her thanks to Florette.

The middle-aged servant bustled between her room and the dressing room, setting out that day's dress and accessories.

Diantha finished her tea and stood up to return the empty cup to the tray.

"I'm ready to dress now." She turned toward the dressing room and froze.

Florette had pulled the sheets off the bed in order to replace them with clean ones. The bloodied muslin lay heaped on the floor.

Diantha stared at it while her suddenly numb mind tried to think of something to say.

Shaking out fresh sheets over the mattress, the maid smiled kindly over her shoulder. "I asked the cook to heat some water for a warm bath this morning, if you would care for one."

The nightgown, the doubled berth, and knocking before entering this morning. Diantha wanted to curl up into a humiliated ball on the floor. "How did you know?"

"An educated guess, *ma mie*. His lordship's 'change of plans' were quite obvious. And he appears to be *un homme d'action*, not at all the kind to wait once he makes up his mind." She peered at her closely. "Did he treat you well?"

Apparently taking Diantha's speechlessness as a "yes," the servant put the finishing touches on the berth and ordered her into the dressing room.

"I will wash these myself, very discretely, and inform his lordship that you will enjoy a late breakfast. Meanwhile, the stewards will bring the hip bath and hot water." She let herself out.

Diantha, somewhat reassured by the woman's matter-of-fact manner, slipped into the dressing room so that no one would see her *en déshabillé*. A bath did sound wonderful. Last night's pain had subsided even before sleep overtook her. Only a few twinges remained and a good soak in warm water would eliminate those.

She supposed she should feel guilty for not replacing her nightgown after they finished last night. But Kieran's attentions had left her too sated to move, and his solid body felt so good to curl up next to. She could not recall the last time she had slept so well.

* * *

She discovered that she had quite a hearty appetite that morning. Settling herself at the table in their suite, she smiled at the steward and unfolded her napkin as he brought her a plate.

When the door to Kieran's room opened, she looked up hopefully. Her heart sank a little at the entrance of his valet, but she greeted the man courteously.

"Forgive the intrusion, my lady!" The servant stopped short and bowed, his Scottish accent deepened by surprise. "I merely wished to use the passage from this room. I will go around from Lord Rossburn's instead."

She gestured to the passage door. "Please, proceed. Normally the room is empty at this time of day; you had no way of knowing otherwise."

She addressed him again, fascinated by his speech. Kieran's voice, trained by years at English boarding schools, usually held only a trace of a burr. "How does the voyage suit you so far, Davison?"

"Verra well, your ladyship." His polite expression changed and he gave her a genuine smile. "And I hope your ladyship is feeling well this morning?"

She shot him a sharp look, but his face betrayed nothing more than benign civility.

"I am very well myself, thank you." She nodded her dismissal and turned to her breakfast.

The steward had cleared the table when Kieran finally made his appearance. Judging from his windblown hair and overcoat, he came from a walk on the deck. Greeting her formally, he removed his coat and gloves, while the steward piled the tableware on a large tray and left. She stood up, planning to visit the saloon.

"You weren't at breakfast." To her shock and delight, he kissed her full on the lips. Softly, he added, "How are you feeling this morning?"

She pulled back in annoyance. "Why is everyone asking me that? I am fine."

"Truly?" He scanned her face as if trying to see into her mind. "When Florette informed me you would eat later, I feared that I had offended you last night." He took her hand. "Or worse."

"Offended me? How on earth can you ask that?" Without thinking, she linked her fingers with his.

He cleared his throat. "I understand that some ladies don't care for lovemaking."

She stared at him. "Really? How odd."

She had no idea why this should make him burst out laughing, and said so in no uncertain terms.

"I believe they object to some of the more improper aspects of it." A twinkle lit his eyes.

She considered his words. "I suspect their husbands are doing it wrong."

"Oh, you've become an expert after one night?" His grin robbed the words of any ill intent.

"You seemed to think I did well enough!" He bowed, acknowledging the hit. She paused, choosing her next words carefully. "Even the most carefully chaperoned girls hear conversations they should not. I've overheard more than one of my mother's friends whisper about their husbands causing discomfort."

"That should never happen again." His emphatic words startled her. As though to lighten the conversation, he changed the subject.

"I came down to ascertain your well-being first, and then to ask if I might escort you around the deck."

Relief flooded through her that he still wanted to spend time in her company. "That sounds much more pleasant than reading. Wait here, I shall get my hat and mantelet."

She hastened to put on her outdoor clothes and return. Kieran crooked his arm for her. "I'm delighted to take priority over the saloon."

She chuckled. "Only because I have no access to a library, mind you."

"We shall visit a bookstore when we stop in London. What kind of reading do you enjoy?" With that, they set off down the corridor.

By mutual consent, Kieran did not come to her bed that night, but their concord lasted only until the following afternoon.

Diantha stormed into her cabin, all but slamming the door behind her.

Florette, seated near the porthole to mend a flounce, looked up in surprise, then rose to help Diantha out of her mantelet.

"Milady, what has happened to disturb you? The walk with Mrs. Haddon did not go well?"

Diantha furiously ripped her hat from her head, partially ruining the fashionable curls the maid had pinned up earlier that day. "The promenade went well enough. Until I found my husband."

"Oh?" Florette retrieved the elegant creation from its landing place on the floor.

Diantha freed herself from her wrap. "Mrs. Haddon

and I came across him as he admired a pendant of Senhora Henriques."

"That does not sound particularly terrible." The maid smoothed the hat's ribbons prior to putting it away.

"He was tracing the filigree work with his finger." She paced the room, skirts rustling. "While she was wearing it!"

"Ah!" The older woman's face cleared as enlightenment dawned. "Tsk, on a small boat like this, milord should have known he would get caught."

Diantha took another turn around the room, fuming. "Smiling up at him and batting her eyelashes like something out of a penny dreadful—"

Florette made a sympathetic noise. "I am so sorry, milady. How humiliating for you."

"—at my husband, which he would do well to remember." The lacy nightgown of two nights before caught her attention as it lay on top of a pile of neatly folded clothes. "You can put that thing away. If he thinks he's coming back to my bed anytime soon, he had better think again."

"Milady, please calm yourself. This back-and-forth is making my head spin and you have ceased to make sense." At the servant's blunt words, she stopped.

Florette coughed slightly. "Men behave like that. And your husband is known for enjoying the company of women."

"I'm a woman." She looked at her reflection in the mirror. "Why can't he enjoy my company?"

The Frenchwoman tutted. "You must make him enjoy your presence. Don't make scenes over his little indiscretions. Charm him, captivate him. Make him feel welcome. As a wife, that is your best hope."

A bitter laugh escaped her at the maid's earnest words. "Yes, I know. Hide my real feelings, tolerate his indiscretions. That is a wife's path in life."

"*Oui*, milady." The maid rolled up her sewing and prepared to leave. "I am sorry."

"I want another path." Diantha whispered the words, then stopped the other woman. "Florette, could you find something in my wardrobe in which I might look remotely attractive at dinner this evening?"

A slow smile broke across the Frenchwoman's face. "I am sure I can, milady."

True to her word, the maid found a few dresses which did not rob her skin of color and make her brown hair dull. "I think my mother expected me to wait until after the honeymoon to wear this."

"Most of your wardrobe looks like it was chosen for someone else, milady." Florette carefully coaxed a curl to lie over Diantha's shoulder. "There isn't a great deal to choose from."

"My mother invariably selects colors that suit her." Diantha turned her head slightly, admiring the effect of the rich brown curl against her fair skin. "That looks very well! Thank you."

"I found a length of ribbon for a choker as well. If you will allow me." The maid tied a length of black velvet around the younger woman's neck.

Diantha stood up. "I just hope I can find the courage to leave our rooms in this gown." The only ensemble suitable for dinner was an evening gown of aqua satin that exposed her shoulders and the very tops of her breasts. Although acceptably low for a married woman of her station, she had never exposed so much skin before. Florette smiled and settled a silk shawl over her shoulders.

Kieran waited outside her door, impeccably dressed in a frock coat, embroidered vest, and dark ascot tie. A glint of admiration sparked in his eyes before he raised an eyebrow at her more formal dress. She stared back at him coldly before taking his proffered arm, and they walked to the saloon in silence.

She expected the other passengers to look askance at her as well, but several of the matrons present greeted her with obvious sympathy. Evidently gossip about her husband and Senhora Henriques had spread. Seething, she nevertheless put on a pleasant demeanor during the meal and exerted herself to converse amiably with the other diners, including her husband.

The *senhora* kept her distance until after the meal, when she approached them. "Lord Rossburn, how nice to see you again. And your very young wife." She nodded to Diantha.

"What a lovely ensemble." The older woman cocked her head to one side. "I quite understand why one would not wait for an appropriate occasion to wear it." Turning to Kieran, she tapped him playfully on the arm with her fan. "I beg you not to scold her, my lord. I recall how confusing society was when I emerged from the schoolroom."

Diantha's temper kindled at the woman's mocking smile. She placed a hand on Kieran's arm. "You must have an excellent memory to recall events that far back, madam. I can only hope mine works as well when I attain advanced years."

A few smothered laughs could be heard throughout the room. Kieran's eyes turned to aqua ice. "You must excuse us, Senhora. Lady Rossburn is feeling tired this evening, and I must escort her to her room."

She resisted him when he started out the door. Another ripple of amusement spread through the room. At this, he simply put his hand over hers where it rested on his arm and pulled her after him.

"You made a fool of yourself in there." He tossed the words over his shoulder as he towed her along the narrow passage.

"Why not? You had already done so with that horrid female." She struggled to keep up with him, her tightly laced corset preventing her from catching her breath.

"And if you had just ignored her, it would have blown over easily enough." He opened the door to her room and thrust her inside. "She's the one who would have looked like a fool."

Diantha refused to be treated like a naughty child. "And I suppose you would overlook a man who offered you an insult."

"That is entirely different." He twisted the door handle and escorted her inside. "Good evening, madam." With a bow, he left again, shutting the door firmly behind him.

Florette silently helped her out of the satin gown and into her nightclothes. Diantha lay awake long after the maid had left the room. In the early hours of the morning, she heard Kieran return to his room. Imagining him in the *senhora*'s arms, she pounded the pillow several times in frustration, then buried her face in it to stifle her weeping.

Kieran's feet thudded along the passageway as he paced back to the saloon. The wretched girl had attended a finishing school near Paris. Surely she had developed some grasp of basic social behavior among the worldly French.

A wife never publicly acknowledged her husband's flirtations with another woman. It simply was not done. Besides, he only intended to amuse himself, not seduce. The *senhora*, while a delightful shipboard diversion, would play no part in his life after the voyage. Nor did he harbor any illusions that she regarded him as anything more than a pleasant episode.

Females had thrown themselves at him since his school days and he delighted in the physical pleasures so many of them offered. Nearly every married man he knew strayed eventually. Once he and Diantha lost interest in one another, he expected he would too.

Without an overcoat, the brisk night air penetrated his evening wear as soon as he stepped onto the promenade deck. Surely she knew that as his wife, her position in society was unassailable. She would have the protection of his name and title for the rest of her life. In return, he expected her to behave in a manner suitable to her position in society.

A memory nudged him, of a day several years after illness had twisted his mother's joints into painful lumps. He recollected no words, only images. His father excusing himself for a ride. The misery on her face as she watched her husband leave, and his own shock when he realized she knew who his father was visiting.

He slowed down, nodding at a couple as they strolled past. His father had exercised the utmost discretion about his affair. Certainly the previous Lord Rossburn had never thrown his inamorata into his wife's face. That had appeared to provide little comfort to his mother, though.

What clawed at him wasn't Diantha, but the marriage itself. He resented being confined to a relationship he had not sought. Perhaps he was like his father after all.

He rejected that notion. By all accounts, his parents had married for love. He and Diantha had not. With no emotional attachment on either side, was infidelity that much of a betrayal?

He grasped the handle of the saloon door and paused. What kind of man caused a woman to suffer for something that wasn't her fault?

As he entered the room, Kieran noticed several glances in his direction. Most of the women and a few men regarded him with expressions of disapproval, while the *senhora*'s smug smile only irritated him further.

He ignored her blatant lure and joined a convivial group of men gathered at the opposite end of the room. When one of them suggested repairing to the card room, he accepted with a sense of relief.

* * *

The next morning, Florette took one look at Diantha's swollen eyes and sent for a cold compress. She neither asked questions nor gave any indication that she had heard about last night's confrontation, although Diantha was sure the entire ship must know about it.

However, as the maid brushed out her hair, she did remark that Lord Rossburn spent several hours playing cards in the first-class saloon the previous evening.

As she watched their reflections in the dressing room mirror, Diantha considered the woman's words. "That sounds rather like spying on my husband."

"I would not dream of doing anything so disrespectful, milady." The servant sniffed as she wound her hair into a chignon and secured it. "I merely happened to overhear it in passing and thought you might be interested."

Her reflected gaze caught the servant's in the glass. "Indeed. In that case, it would not be in the least offensive to mention what you might overhear— in passing."

Florette nodded. "I understand perfectly." They exchanged mischievous smiles.

"Would milady care to take a stroll around the deck?" She shook out Diantha's mantelet.

"Thank you. I think the fresh air would do me good." Her presence outside her cabin would also stop any talk that she had gone into hiding after last night's debacle. A thought struck her. "Odd."

"I beg milady's pardon?" Florette, buttoning her own mantle, raised an eyebrow in question.

"At least my husband doesn't keep me under lock and key."

Encountering Kieran during their stroll caused her some anxiety, but he greeted her courteously and even joined them. She expected he also wished to avoid gossip, but he proved pleasant enough company.

The rest of the day passed unexceptionally, and as the *senhora* pleaded a headache and excused herself from dinner, Diantha quite enjoyed the meal. In the Brazilian beauty's absence, her husband exerted himself to amuse her, along with the rest of the company. She discovered he was a gifted storyteller as he described his childhood in the Highlands.

The reason for all this attention became clear after they had both retired. A soft tap on their connecting door heralded his entrance. Diantha sat up in her berth. "What are you doing here?"

She had blown out the hanging lamp and could not see his face in the dark, but his baritone caressed her. "I should think that would be obvious. I thought we could continue your introduction to sensual pleasures."

Her heart leaped at the idea of repeating their activities of two nights ago. Until a shrewd voice in the back of her mind asked if he was trying to procure her complaisance with physical delights.

"Buying people off," as her father called it, often did not involve the direct payment of money. He got what he wanted by providing much desired goods or services to the other parties. Certainly she would not deny she wanted Kieran to make her fall to pieces again.

But she also recalled the contempt with which Papa regarded those who gave into him easily. Much as he hated being balked, he respected those who stood up to him far more than those who didn't.

"I'm still feeling a little pain from before." While technically she still felt slight tenderness, her excuse sounded flimsy even in her own ears. She bit her lip. If he insisted on exercising his rights as a husband, she could do nothing about it.

His sigh sounded loudly through the dark. "I understand your fears, but I assure you that the pain will be less than before."

"You told me that I would not have to do anything in bed that made me uncomfortable, and I fear it would this evening."

He growled in his throat. "Something I am beginning to regret. Diantha, I thought you trusted me."

"I do." *In bed, anyway.* Just now she wanted to be left alone. "But I still wish to wait until I am more recovered."

"Very well." He bit the words out and closed her door a great deal more loudly than he had opened it.

The next day he spent a lot of time conversing with the *senhora*. When Diantha demanded an explanation, he retorted that he only inquired after her headache.

She decided her health should take a corresponding downturn. By the time they disembarked at Le Havre, she had barred him from her bed for the remainder of their voyage. The train ride to Paris, in a private car arranged for by Quinn Shipping Line's French office, took place in an atmosphere of frigid civility. Even the knowledge that the Henriques had remained on board to travel to Lisbon failed to cheer her up.

They stayed in a town house in a fashionable street of the eighth arrondisement. After the dark-panelled suite aboard the *Columbia*, Diantha settled into the airy rooms with pleàsure.

Her elation crumbled when she discovered that Kieran had already gone out for the evening. Finding that she could not face the dining room alone, she ordered a tray in her boudoir.

She tried reading after she finished the solitary meal, but rejected the French fashion periodicals after discovering several articles about her own trousseau in them.

Even Monsieur Jules Verne's latest work, found after she wandered down to the library, failed to keep her interest. After the first chapter, she glanced at the gilded Louis Quinze clock on the library's immense marble mantelpiece. Not even midnight. She sighed, shelved the book, and returned to her room.

Florette appeared several moments after she rang for her, chattering happily about returning to her native land. Diantha let the words flow past her as she prepared for bed. Her mood sank further when the maid revealed that his lordship told his valet not to wait up for him. She also hinted that Diantha should consider admitting him to her bed. Diantha set her jaw and dismissed the older woman.

* * *

Hours later, Kieran cracked the door of her bedroom. He absently pulled off his gloves as he peered inside, aware of a pang of disappointment. Delightful as it had been to look in on his acquaintances at the Grand Café, he intended his absence to teach his wife a lesson. This jealous fit of hers had to end.

He had chosen not to pick a quarrel with her under the curious eyes of their fellow passengers during their voyage. In the privacy of a town house, however, he planned to put his foot down. Much as her response to his lovemaking fascinated him, a man did not allow his wife to dictate those he did or did not speak to.

As his eyes adjusted to the darkened room, he could make out the pale blur of her face and the hand flung palm up on the pillow. Drawn by the memory of her soft skin, he entered the room. A fold of his cloak caught the edge of a small table, and knocked a figurine onto the carpeted floor. The thump awakened Diantha.

"Who's there?" She started awake, staring wildly in his direction. He realized she could not see his face.

"It's only me." He approached slowly. "I'm sorry if I frightened you."

She fumbled around the surface of her bedside table. The rasp of a match sounded, followed by a small flame that resolved into a larger one as she lit a candle. "What are you doing in here?"

He frowned, taken aback by her hostile question. "I'm your husband, Diantha. I belong here."

"That is a matter of opinion." She stifled a yawn

and sat up a little straighter. "I have had a long day and I wish to sleep, sir." The sheets fell to her waist.

Kieran swallowed. Her lawn nightgown covered her to the chin, but the rosy tips of her breasts remained visible through the thin material. "I have had a long week of your missish behavior, madam. Most husbands would not show such patience to a wife who banned them from her bed."

"Most husbands would not have spent their honeymoons flirting with another woman under their wife's nose." For someone who had just woken up, she struck him as remarkably quarrelsome.

"You have got to stop carrying on like a jealous shrew every time I engage in a little harmless flirtation!" He crossed his arms. "For heaven's sake, I only talked to her."

"Where everyone on the ship could see you!" Her eyes flashed in the candlelight. "And for your information, I was not remotely jealous. The embarrassment was bad enough."

"I am not the one who caused a scene in the middle of the saloon." He slapped his gloves against his thigh. "May I remind you that you are now expected to act like a lady, not a vulgar merchant's daughter?"

"For your information, the two are not mutually exclusive. Although I would probably find better manners in a tugboat captain." Shooting him a single glare, she blew out the candle. "Good night, your high and mighty lordship!"

The sheets rustled as she rolled herself up in them. As his eyes readjusted, Kieran saw her curled up in a ball, her braid trailing down her back outside the bedclothes. Its heavy length tempted his fingers to stroke it.

He brought himself up short. If he caressed her, it might lead her to think she was getting the better of him.

"Good night." On those curt words, he stalked out of the room.

Chapter 6

By clever management, Diantha did not meet her husband the following day until luncheon. She took a tray of croissants and chocolate in her room, and spent much of the morning composing notes to acquaintances living in Paris.

Only when Florette brought word that his lordship had left the house did she emerge. Dispatching her correspondence to its intended recipients, she sent word for the chef and majordomo to meet with her in the morning room. Although she had never been permitted to speak up during her mother's consultations with staff, she had learned a great deal by observing them.

The meetings with both servants passed more easily than she expected. After they ended, a footman appeared with several invitations and notes that had arrived that morning. This did not surprise Diantha; news of their arrival had appeared in *Le Monde* and other newspapers. She divided the mail from people she knew into three piles. As a bride on her honeymoon, she decided to answer them in the order she pleased.

The smallest and most important notes contained greetings from her friends. The second consisted of notes and name cards from friends of her parents, and the third, of friends of her parents that she liked.

The second pile she placed on the back of her writing table for moments of extreme boredom. She regarded it with a smile of triumph. Until today, Mama had supervised the order in which she responded to letters and notes.

A number of envelopes bore names and addresses she did not recognize. She identified a few of the unknown writers as opportunists trying to pretend an acquaintance on the strength of the newspaper articles. Those she tossed into the wastepaper basket. The rest she set aside to ask Kieran about.

While exploring the town house, she found a copy of *Le Monde* in the library, doubtless abandoned by her husband. Closing the door to the room, she spent a pleasurable hour catching up on Parisian news until a footman summoned her for lunch.

She looked about the dining room with pleasure as she permitted herself to be seated. Like the rest of the house, it created an atmosphere of airiness. Instead of the carved wooden panels her mother favored, silk moiré covered the walls of this room in a cheery shade of pale yellow. The damask tablecloth almost gleamed in the sunlight entering through two large windows opposite the door. It formed a simple background for the low bouquet of fragrant spring flowers arranged in a porcelain epergne on its top.

Her heart jumped nervously when her husband's big frame filled the doorway. Nor did he appear pleased, stopping short on the threshold at the sight of her.

Mindful of the servants waiting on them, she gave him a civil greeting. He returned one equally unenthusiastic. Except for that exchange, only the clink of silverware on porcelain or quiet requests to the servants filled the silence between them.

To Diantha's irritation, he did not look in the least like he had lain awake much of the night, as she had after he left her room. He must have pomaded his hair just before joining her, for no wave marred the smooth dark strands combed back from his forehead.

Without the necessity of conversing with him, her awareness of his appearance increased. She tried to focus on her plate, but could not resist a glance in his direction. His hands, although large, handled his knife precisely as he spread foie gras on a slice of bread. Memories of their caresses sent shivers over her skin.

Out of the corner of her eye, she watched him lift the tidbit to his mouth and heard the delicate crunch as his teeth bit into the thick crush. His tongue flicked out to lick a crumb off his upper lip. She swallowed, unable to look away.

She had noticed the firm mouth from their first introduction. Now, knowing the touch and taste of his lips, she found herself wondering if she would ever experience them again. No, she admitted as heat coiled deep within her. She wanted to feel them again, to kiss that full lower lip with its miniscule cleft echoing the one in his chin.

A soft chuckle interrupted her reverie. To her utter mortification, she realized she was staring at him. His eyes darkened and a smug smile played across the mouth she had just admired.

Furious at her weakness, she dropped her gaze to her own plate. Only when the footmen presented the fruit course did she recall the matter of the morning's correspondence.

She broached the subject as she neatly quartered a fig with her knife and fork. "Some letters arrived this morning from persons I am unfamiliar with, your lordship. If you would be so kind as to go through them and tell me if you recognize them, I could then dispose of those trying to encroach."

"How would anyone know our direction?" His brows furrowed in confusion.

"Did you not read the newspaper articles announcing our presence at this house?" She cleared her throat. "I fear my mother provides information on my family's whereabouts on a regular basis."

"Good God! I trust I am not going to spend the rest of my life reading accounts of my comings and goings in the newspapers." He gave her an accusatory glare. She clenched her hands around the silverware, reminding herself to keep her temper.

"Indeed, I share your hope. Such intrusions are monstrous!" The words came out more vehemently than she expected. She took a breath to calm herself. "However, the immediate task is to be sure we do not inadvertently snub your friends."

"Very well." He snapped out the words before finishing an apricot. She took a breath. One more unpleasant subject remained for her to bring up.

"Will you be dining at home this evening?" She kept her gaze on the table.

"I shouldn't think so." He answered carelessly. "I've been invited to dine at the Jockey Club by an old acquaintance, and then we shall probably go look in on the Opera."

Her fingers spasmed in her lap. The ornate new home of the Paris Opéra had been under construction since 1862. Interrupted by France's ill-considered war with Prussia in 1870 and the resulting uprising in Paris, it had only opened this year. Having gawked in fascination at the construction site during her previous stay in the city, it vexed Diantha to no end that her husband would see the finished building first. Very likely he would pay attention only to the dancers in the *corps de ballet*, while she sat at home alone.

Her teeth gritted in an effort not to turn into a screaming virago. "If you are finished, perhaps we might adjourn to the morning room now."

There, they quickly dealt with the last of the correspondence. To her surprise, he did not leave immediately. Idly, he plucked a note out of the desk.

She tensed, hating the way he picked up her letters. "That is from a friend of mine."

Her anger must have shown on her face, for he put it back with an embarrassed cough. "Forgive me."

"I plan to answer my own friends first." Still fuming, Diantha tucked the letter farther back inside the desk. She raised the drop-leaf front and challenged him with a look to open it.

He merely lifted an eyebrow. "As you wish, my dear." With a mocking bow, he turned to go.

"Kieran." He paused at the door. "I would appreciate it if you would apprise me of your evening plans earlier in the day. I have already ordered dinner for two, which I shall now have to cancel."

He turned on his heel, brows drawn together. "Trying to keep tabs on me? As I said before, I will not be spied on."

She struggled for words. "I have never heard anything so ridiculous in my life! I only desire to make our stay in this house as easy as possible. Surely you could announce your plans before you disappear for the morning." She disregarded the fact that she had spent the morning hiding from him.

"No, madam, I cannot tell you my plans in the morning, because I am not accustomed to deciding where or how—or with whom—I am spending my evening until much later in the day." He drew near to her during his speech, but she stood her ground.

"You weren't married before." As soon as the words left her mouth, Kieran stiffened. She braced herself for whatever he might say next.

"True, I wasn't." He considered her speculatively. "I could send my excuses to my friends, under one condition."

"Which is?" She could smell the faint scent of sandalwood soap emanating from his body, he was so close.

"I will dine with you this evening if you in turn will resume our physical relationship."

She drew back as though slapped. "Certainly not! I will not be coerced!"

"Why do you insist on refusing me?" He ran a hand through his hair as his voice tightened in frustration. "As your husband I would be within my rights to insist on your cooperation."

She paced a few steps away from him to quell her own agitation. "Why should I admit you to my bed? However nice it was, you still ran off to that dreadful *senhora* the next day, humiliating me in front of the entire ship! You didn't even have the decency to apologize."

"I shall not apologize for actions that did not harm anyone!" He hissed the words as he followed her.

At his steady approach, she slipped behind an overstuffed chair, not taking her eyes off him. He sighed.

"Diantha, I shall not strike you." He ground the words out through clenched teeth, but at least he stopped following her. "No matter how thoroughly you provoke me."

She mastered her trembling knees. "I appreciate that, my lord. But I do not appreciate being told that my company is so very dull that it is only acceptable with the promise of—"

She broke off, floundering for an acceptable expression.

"Conjugal relations. Sex. Making love." He listed the terms as he came around the chair. She edged back a step but did not retreat farther. He placed his hands gently on her shoulders. "Come, now. Let us begin again."

His fingers worked sensuously at the joining of her neck and shoulders, and she closed her eyes in enjoyment. She opened them again to see a flash of triumph in his eyes. "Making love" indeed. He only caressed her to manipulate her.

"No." It cost her not to give in, but better to have him staring at her as he did now, infuriated, than smirking in contempt. His hands dropped to his sides.

"As you wish then. I shall see you tomorrow." Just as he bowed, a small cough interrupted them.

In the doorway, the majordomo presented a sterling salver containing a small white rectangle. "Forgive me, but the lady was quite insistent."

Kieran strode over to pick up the calling card. "The Dowager Comtesse de Pontrevault. A distant connection through my grandmother's family." Before she could speak, he ordered the majordomo to admit their visitor.

As soon as the door snicked shut behind the little man, he addressed her. "We'll finish this discussion later. The dowager is prominent in Parisian society. It might not be a bad thing if we could persuade her to take you under her wing."

Diantha opened her mouth to speak, closed it again, and simply nodded her agreement.

"How is your French? It's important that you make a good impression on her."

She arched a brow. "May I remind you that I attended finishing school just outside Paris? I am quite sure my command of the language is adequate to greet the comtesse." She could not repress a smile as she strolled over to a gilt-edge mirror over the mantelpiece. "And I am certain she speaks English."

"How typically American!" He frowned at her. "For your information, the rest of the world is not going to learn English for your convenience."

Straightening her lace collar, she shrugged. "Something you had best mention to some of your compatriots, then. I've never met as many snobs as I did in England."

"I happen to be a Scot, thank you." He crossed his arms and observed her actions with a cold stare.

"One in need of a comb." She beckoned him over. "Here, let me fix your hair." He approached, still radiating hostility.

"I never said you were a snob." She spoke softly. "Just disheveled."

Somewhat mollified, a smile twisted his lips as he caught sight of his reflection. Most of his hair remained in perfect order, but the side he had run his hand over hung in loosened waves.

"Let me fix that." She plunged her fingers into the silky strands before he could move.

"What are you doing?" He pulled his head back, out of her grasp, but it was too late.

"I don't have a comb with me." She chuckled in spite of the scowl on his face. "At least now you don't look uneven."

Dark waves framed his face, brushing the edge of his firm jaw, enhancing the wide-set eyes inches from hers. She found it hard to breathe. "Much better."

"Is it?" Her lips tingled as his gaze settled on them. "I suppose I'll have to take your word for it then." Her hands dropped to his shoulders and he bent closer to her.

The door opened.

Kieran closed his eyes and sighed before wheeling around to greet their guest.

"The Dowager Comtesse de Pontrevault." Undoubtedly the majordomo had seen them, for he addressed the announcement to an invisible spot in the middle of the room. He bowed an elderly woman into the room and left after Diantha requested him to send up suitable refreshments.

They found themselves under the observation of a pair of twinkling eyes the color of a summer sky. "Ah, newlyweds. I recall my own days as a young bride." The comtesse halted just inside the room, straight as a pillar in her fashionable ensemble. Although past sixty, her only concession to age was the walking stick she rested her joined hands on.

Kieran recovered first. "Madame, how kind of you." He kissed the fine-boned hand held out to him and addressed her in slightly accented French. "It is an unexpected and welcome honor."

"It is entirely my pleasure, Lord Rossburn. I trust your family is well?" The lines around her eyes and mouth crinkled as she smiled at him.

"So far as I know, madame. Much as I enjoy your lovely country, I look forward to returning home." He gestured to Diantha. "May I present my wife?"

Her wide grin at the noblewoman earned a glare from her husband, which she ignored. "Madame, it is so very good to see you!" Her schooling served her well as she greeted the woman with flawless French.

"Dianthe, ma fille!" The comtesse rustled toward

her in a cloud of organdy and bergamot perfume. "Why so formal, my dear?"

As they kissed one another's cheeks and embraced, she could not resist smirking at her husband over the other woman's shoulder. His dumbfounded expression gratified her excessively.

Their guest chatted on. "You cannot conceive my delight, Lord Rossburn, to hear that my granddaughter's dear friend was engaged to marry so distinguished a man." She patted Diantha's cheek. "Roch will be devastated."

"As your grandson is a dreadful flirt, madame, I imagine he will recover the next time he sees a pretty girl." She gave Kieran a saccharine smile. "Wouldn't you agree, my dear?"

His cheeks darkened at her tone, though whether with chagrin or embarrassment, she could not tell. Before he could reply, she begged the older woman to take a chair and sat down on a sofa nearby. As they exchanged news of their families and gossip, Kieran took the seat next to her, crossing his legs and laying his arm across its back. Diantha sat up a bit straighter. The long fingers, near enough to just graze the fabric of her sleeve, distracted her from the other woman's conversation.

A footman appeared bearing petits fours and small fruit tartlets on a round tray, along with glasses and a bottle of sherry. After everyone had been served, Kieran leaned forward.

"How long have you and Lady Rossburn known each other, madame?"

Diantha glanced at him, but his face betrayed only curiosity.

The comtesse beamed. "She and my only granddaughter became friends when they attended the same school four years ago. When Sabine begged me to include her new friend in an invitation to visit me, I agreed."

She reached over and patted Diantha's knee. "I had no idea what to expect, but I have a soft spot for Sabine and braced myself for a wild American."

"I think she expected me to show up dressed in animal skins." Diantha chuckled.

"Instead a charming young lady got out of the carriage, with impeccable manners. Except for her penchant for swinging from trees." She shook her head, tsking.

Kieran sat bolt upright, an unholy grin lighting his features. "What? Madame, you must tell me!"

Next to him, Diantha could not keep from laughing even as she protested. "No, I beg you! Not that story again!"

"Again? You mean all Paris knows about this—proclivity of my wife's?" Kieran looked at her, trying to imagine his shy, slightly stodgy wife engaging in such outrageous behavior. She glanced over, merriment brimming in her face.

As their eyes met, something passed between them, almost like affection. Startled, he realized she had never completely relaxed in his company, even during their one night together. He wondered what would have happened between them if they had met like this, instead of in the stifling atmosphere surrounding her parents. Then the comtesse spoke and the moment slipped away.

"My son, the current comte, and I were strolling

at the far end of our garden one afternoon—it is designed as a wilderness and abuts the Loire, I must invite you both to visit someday—and out of the blue we see Miss Quinn swinging out from a tree overhanging the river! I was never so stunned in my life." She thumped her stick on the floor for emphasis.

"She had removed her jacket and looped it over a branch above her head, then used it to launch herself from one side of the trunk around to the other." Wagging a bony finger, she regarded the younger woman with mock severity. "I wanted to give you the scold of your life!"

"And so you did," Diantha replied drily. A second later, she giggled. "But you had to stop laughing first."

"Wicked girl, you nearly gave me a fatal spasm! What if you had fallen in?" The comtesse shook her head even as another chuckle escaped her.

"Pooh! I was entirely safe." Kieran watched in near amazement as she bantered with one of the bastions of Paris society. "I learned how to pick out sturdy branches when I was a girl."

He could not resist joining in with a bit of raillery. "Come now, you don't expect us to believe that. Even in America, I doubt that governesses routinely teach young ladies the varying strength of different trees."

"Certainly not." She sniffed disdainfully. "My brothers taught me at Cliff Heights. One tree hanging out over the Hudson was especially fun."

He gaped at her. "Do you mean to tell me that you did that hanging a hundred feet above the river?" She nodded. "Good God, it's a wonder you weren't killed."

"My sentiments exactly, your lordship." The comtesse shuddered, and changed the subject.

After twenty minutes of general conversation, she sighed. "I must take my leave before long, but I should like to invite the two of you to dine with me this evening, if you are free. I would enjoy a longer talk with dear Dianthe."

Before he could open his mouth to accept such a singular honor, Diantha spoke. "I fear his lordship is engaged to dine with friends this evening." Although her voice sounded properly regretful, when she looked at him a spark of anger replaced the laughter that had danced in her eyes.

"I am sure they would understand if I sent them a note, my dear." He fixed his gaze firmly upon hers, willing her to be silent. She raised one eyebrow and turned her back to him.

"As you can see, his lordship is everything that is obliging, but I am under the impression that these are very dear friends, since he is meeting them while on his honeymoon." He did not miss the emphasis on the last three words. "Under the circumstances, madame, I could not possibly ask him to beg off."

The old woman regarded the two of them through narrowed eyes. Kieran immediately stood to assist her as she heaved herself to her feet with the help of her stick. "By all means dine with your friends, Lord Rossburn. I entertain often and you shall come another evening." She faced his wife. "My dear, before I take my leave, I insist you show me over this delightful little house."

Regally, she extended her hand for Kieran to kiss, and swept Diantha before her out of the room.

He stared after them. Something had just happened, but he had no idea what.

The comtesse wasted no time in demanding that Diantha show her the boudoir. As soon as she settled into a cushioned chair, she fixed her bright eyes on the younger woman. "Now, tell me at once what is wrong between you and that delicious young man."

Diantha gulped once. Then the entire story burst out of her about their awkward engagement, the *senhora*, Kieran's flirtation, and his refusal to accept the realities of married life.

"Ah." Uttering the one syllable, her friend closed her eyes and sat quite still.

"Madame?"

Only an upraised finger answered her. Interpreting the gesture as a sign to remain mute, Diantha waited. At last the comtesse opened her eyes.

"*Ma fille,* it is my experience that a husband is like a new pair of shoes. They are not going to change into another kind, and they are never comfortable." She bestowed a smug smile on the younger woman. "But you can break them in."

"That's all very well as far as it goes, madame, but I don't think my husband will take well to 'breaking in.'" Diantha pleated and unpleated a fold of her twill skirt.

"Child, you don't tell them what you're doing!" Slender fingers detached Diantha's hand from her skirt and squeezed it affectionately. "Stop that. You'll cause a permanent crease."

The comtesse sat back and scrutinized her from head to toe. "In truth, I must ask why you're wearing so unflattering an ensemble. The fit is impeccable, but the only yellow you should ever contemplate wearing is pale lemon. And even that would require great caution."

"Thanks to my mother, I have exactly three becoming gowns in my trousseau, and one of those is unsuitable for daytime." Diantha did not hide her bitterness. The comtesse had met Mrs. Quinn.

The older woman cleared her throat. "I am sorry to say it, but your wardrobe might account for the *senhora*. Although from what I have seen, Lord Rossburn's charm has doubtless helped him conquer any number of female hearts."

"Doubtless." Diantha echoed the word, staring at the patterned rug under her feet. She lifted her gaze to find the comtesse regarding her with half-closed eyes.

After a sharp nod, as though confirming something to herself, the older woman rose from her chair and paced the room. "What we need is a plan of attack. Starting with your wardrobe."

"I agree, but I can't very well burst in on Monsieur Worth and tell him his clothes look dreadful on me." The master couturier's ego matched his genius.

"You shall not burst in at all. You shall write him and ask if he might see you for fittings tomorrow—I am certain he will not refuse the former Mademoiselle Quinn. I presume you have a generous allowance?"

Diantha calculated mentally. "Not enough for an entire new wardrobe at his prices. Perhaps I could purchase a few items from a less expensive modiste."

The comtesse blanched. "After the journals have puffed off your dresses from Worth? Fatal, *cherie!*" She considered. "No, we shall just have to select essential pieces, starting with a ball gown. You should receive your invitations tomorrow for the one I am holding in Sabine's honor."

The two made a few more plans before she escorted her guest downstairs and bid her good-bye with a warm embrace. Through the open library door, she noticed Kieran's dark head as he sat reading, but she did not go to him.

With a lighter heart than she had known in months, she hurried up the stairs. According to the Comtesse de Pontrevault, she had some things to do.

Chapter 7

In the ensuing days, Diantha could not help but give thanks for the comtesse's plans. They kept her occupied enough to avoid brooding over Kieran's frequent absences. Although he treated her with punctilious courtesy, he spent much of his time away from the town house near Avenue Montaigne.

Having heard back from several school friends, she arranged to meet them for shopping or luncheon or walks in the city's famous parks, but that left many hours open to take umbrage at his defections. On one particularly bad afternoon in the Luxembourg Gardens, she witnessed the galling sight of her own husband strolling along in company with a beautiful woman of noble ancestry and rather less elevated morals.

Fortunately Diantha was accompanied by the comtesse and her granddaughter. Both set out to assuage her feelings. The older woman pointed out that Lord Rossburn was one of several men attending the creature in question, while Sabine tried to divert her with an anecdote about the journey to Paris from her husband's estate.

Dejected, Diantha begged to be taken home.

The comtesse sighed. "*Ma fille,* you will look like a goose if you flee the field. He is with the Marquise de Tourelle, one meets her everywhere. We cannot have her preening herself for routing you. Come along, one more time around the boat pond."

For Diantha, the sunlight shining down on the green grass and the gravel promenade dimmed. Even the lively shouts of children trying to prod their toy vessels across the shallow basin failed to cheer her.

Upon taking leave of her in the town house's drawing room, the comtesse reminded her of a fitting she had the next morning.

Charles Worth had not only welcomed Diantha to his establishment on the rue de la Paix, he oversaw the creation of her new wardrobe himself. Thanks to her money, her family name, and the sheer number of seamstresses the couturier employed, the first of her carefully selected gowns arrived within a week.

By the night of the de Pontrevault ball, her new ensembles hung in her wardrobe. The comtesse had strictly forbidden her to wear any of them before this evening, despite her heated protests.

"You must strike him like a bolt from the blue." Gravel spurted as the ever present walking stick had pounded into it several days earlier. The comtesse had invited her for luncheon and they took a promenade afterward in the garden of her Paris house. Just at that moment, she scolded Diantha for wearing a new carriage dress in a shade of cornflower that turned her eyes to sapphire. "You're stealing your own thunder!"

"I did not put it on until his lordship left the house." Her meek reply earned only a disapproving sniff. Regretfully, after returning home and avoiding Kieran's eyes, she had complied with her friend's dictate. She hoped it would work.

After the hairdresser finished the tedious process of curling her hair and pinning it to her head, Diantha rose to her feet and stretched her back. Across the room, the maid sighed in disapproval as she finished laying out the ball gown. "Madame la comtesse would tell you to hurry and get dressed."

"I am quite ready to continue, now that the blood is once again flowing in my lower half." She thanked the hairdresser, a slender man with pointed black mustachios, and turned to her servant as soon as he took his leave. As Florette helped her into the voluminous underskirt, Diantha asked anxiously if she had been wise to allow him to cut her hair into the fashionable but daring bangs.

"*Alors,* milady, they are most becoming. One notices your eyes more." She buttoned up the bodice and turned to pick up the overskirt from the bed. Diantha held out her arms to allow the other woman to fasten it over the bodice and skirt.

She recalled her disappointment the first time Monsieur Worth had presented the gown to her. A mannequin had worn a dress of creamy satin unadorned with any contrasting color, ornamented only with three poufs down the back and a deeply flounced hem which fanned out into a train. Then he had snapped his fingers and an assistant had fastened the overskirt into place.

In minutes the plain gown disappeared under a web of crimson lace which fitted the line of the bodice exactly before flaring to cover the skirt to the tops of its flounces. It had been cut to fall on either side of the bustle, held together below each pouf of satin by crimson velvet tabs sparkling with diamante buttons. More diamante glittered here and there on the overskirt, giving an impression of both severity and opulence. And it was red. She smirked as she imagined her mother's expression of horror at the idea.

A crimson velvet choker came along with the gown, but Florette placed a leather-covered box on the dressing table. "From milord." Diantha opened it.

"How lovely!" A necklace of rubies and diamonds in the shape of graduated bows nestled against the velvet interior along with a matching pair of earrings and an aigrette. She lifted each piece out to admire its painstaking workmanship.

A quarter of an hour later, Diantha placed her gloved hand on the polished banister of the stairway and descended to the foyer. A sharp sense of disappointment overcame her when she discovered that instead of awaiting her at the bottom of the stairs, Kieran had prosaically disappeared into the library.

Glaring at the closed door to that room, she sent for her opera cloak. Only after she wrapped its encompassing folds around her did she enter the library. Kieran sat reading a newspaper, a half empty snifter of brandy at his elbow.

In his black and white formal evening attire, he looked downright stunning, an effect that only increased when he lifted his aqua eyes to smile at her.

"You're not even late. I was expecting to have another twenty minutes to read at least." He finished off his brandy and stood to retrieve his black evening cloak from where it lay tossed over a chair.

"Papa could never abide tardiness." She watched him swirl the black cloak around his shoulders in one fluid motion. "Thank you for the jewels. They are lovely."

"I don't suppose they're very impressive next to some of those I saw your mother wearing." He held out an arm to escort her through the foyer. "It's an eighteenth-century set that came up for sale unexpectedly, and the comtesse informed me at dinner last week that I should look for rubies for you."

He spoke diffidently as they stepped outside into the dusk. A footman snapped to attention and opened the carriage door. "Presumably they go with your rig this evening?"

Thinking of the elegant gown under her cloak, Diantha smiled at last. "Very nicely."

"I hope you don't mind the lack of a tiara. There is a diamond one left among the family jewels, but it's in Scotland."

The play of shadows and light from the vehicle's lamp obscured the expression on his face, but she fancied he sounded almost shy about his offering. "Nonsense. The aigrette is perfect for my hair this evening." She twisted her head to show him the glittering spray of diamonds holding a deep red rose in place next to the knot of hair at her crown. Long ringlets fell artfully from its back.

"The earrings flatter you as well." The timbre of his voice deepened as he lifted one of the baubles for closer inspection. "Delicate and unique."

She shivered as his fingertips stroked the delicate lobe. If she turned her head, she could plant a kiss on his palm. "We should go." Barely able to whisper the words, she stepped toward the carriage. Kieran assisted her inside and waited while she arranged her flowing skirts before climbing in.

During the short drive to the Hôtel Pontrevault, she had to resist caressing her ear where it still tingled from his touch. He had made no other attempts to wheedle his way into her bed, but she suddenly wondered if he intended the ruby set as a bribe. No, she thought, it would appear odd if he had not given her something out of the sizable dowry she brought him.

As they approached their hostess' home, the carriage slowed and joined a line of others waiting to pass under the gray stone arch into the courtyard. Her husband asked if she had visited the great house during her school days.

"Yes, Sabine is dreadfully spoiled." She chuckled. "Her family would come and fetch her to visit periodically, and she always begged them to let me come too."

"You were very close?"

"Are." She paused. "My parents would not allow me to correspond with her after she married, but on seeing her again, it was as if we had only been separated for a month. I suppose that sounds foolish, but it is so."

"Not at all. I was an only child." His voice came out of the shadows wistfully. "I have a number of friends I feel the same way about."

Kieran looked out of the window at the slow-moving line ahead of them. "Whatever is taking them so long?"

"It's hard to maneuver several carriages in the courtyard." Opposite from him, she peered out too. "The house was built in the seventeenth century on an odd-shaped piece of property, so it's not an exact square. I don't know why the designer didn't put the garden on this side of the house and the court- yard on the other. I gather at the time this street was more prestigious than the one bordering the garden, but it would have been a more practical arrangement." Catching herself, she subsided and changed the subject to a more conventional one.

Although laid out off-kilter, the courtyard still presented an air of dignity as the carriage inched its way to the covered portico. Wrought-iron lamps blazed off of the glossy varnish of each vehicle, and illuminated a row of boxed shrubs set around its perimeter. Fairy lights glowing in the greenery added to the festive air as they descended from the carriage and mounted the steps up to the immense main door, now thrown open wide to admit guests.

Strains of music greeted them before they en- tered, for the comtesse had engaged a quartet to play near the entrance. She herself chose to greet her guests at the arched doorway to an antecham- ber to one side of the vestibule, out of the drafts of the cool night air. To one side of her stood the current Comte de Pontrevault and his wife, to the other Sabine and her husband, Baron Serreux, in whose honor she gave the ball.

Footmen glided forward to take their wraps as soon as they stepped inside. Allowing her wrap to fall gracefully from her shoulders, Diantha smoothed the lace of her overskirt and dared a glance at Kieran.

Her husband stood frozen in the act of handing his cloak to an attendant, his gaze riveted on her. Triumph bubbled inside, but she took care only to lay her furled ostrich feather fan on his arm. "Shall we proceed?"

He continued to stare at her.

"Kieran?"

He collected himself and offered her his arm.

Several minutes later the comtesse, resplendent in deep blue watered silk and black pearls, kissed her cheeks in greeting. "It would appear to be going well. He looks stunned."

Diantha glanced over to see the comte and her husband conversing. "I believe the word is 'pole-axed.'"

"What a dreadful sounding phrase." Sabine inclined her strawberry blond curls toward them as she giggled. The gold embroidery on her gown and the diamonds at her throat glittered in the candle-light.

"I suspect it is one of your grandmother's trench-ant phrases." The lines around the comtesse's eyes wrinkled in amusement. "I shall have to tax her with it next time I write to her."

"Do! Mama strongly disapproves of it." Diantha gurgled with laughter as she moved away from them.

Kieran's ears pricked up at the sound of his wife's amusement. She paused to speak with another acquaintance as he bowed over the hands of his hostesses and shook hands with the baron. Placing his fingers under Diantha's elbow, he appraised her appearance out of the corner of his eye while they continued to greet other guests.

He had come to think of Diantha as somewhat plain except for her excellent figure. Tonight, she looked like an exotic bird as she moved among the crowd. The rich color of the lace flattered her dark blue eyes, and the material itself frothed about her shoulders and low neckline in a way that made a man want to tug it down farther.

As she strolled through the room ahead of him, the whisper of her train along the parquet floor enticed him to follow. He ran an appreciative eye over the way the pale satin material of her bustle flowed as she walked, until he looked about and saw several other men examining her covertly.

When she halted in the doorway to the next anteroom, he took his place beside her, placing a possessive hand on the small of her back. She looked over her shoulder at him and raised an eyebrow at the gesture but said nothing. Then, with a disinterested shrug, she stepped away from him. For the second time in the space of an hour, he stood dumbfounded.

Then his brows snapped together. He did not know what she was up to but he had no intention of stepping aside.

Diantha, it seemed, had other ideas.

He caught up with her as the ballroom opened out before them. She smiled up at him impishly. "I believe I see your marquise, my dear." She gestured to the lovely widow who had thrown countless lures out to him since he had arrived in Paris.

Without another word, Diantha extended her hand to a lanky young cavalier who hurried over with a flowery compliment. Laughing, she slipped away into the crowd without a backward glance.

A light touch on Kieran's arm claimed his attention. Beside him, Solange de Tourelle cocked her head and observed his wife's departure. "She's much prettier than I expected." Her low voice purred into his ear. "But as you said, a trifle wet behind the ears. Come dance with me, *mon cher.*"

Watching out of the corner of his eye, he did not think Diantha looked remotely wet behind the ears as she tapped the fan against her boyish escort's shoulder. With her cheeks flushed she looked prettier than he had ever seen her before.

"My dear Lord Rossburn." His would-be inamorata tapped her foot as she waited for him. Without another word, he swung her out among the waltzing couples, but not without a last glower over his shoulder. The stripling bowed and left his wife when she held out both hands and bestowed a dazzling smile on a craggy-faced man who looked vaguely familiar.

The marquise pursed her lips in distaste when she observed the encounter. "*Mon Dieu*, tell me that decrepit old woman did not invite Sir Harry Emerson."

Kieran stiffened. "If you refer to the Comtesse de Pontrevault, I should point out that she is a connection of mine."

Somewhat sulkily, his partner begged his pardon. They reached the end of the ballroom, where a small orchestra played in an arched alcove. Negotiating the turn to dance back up the room, a flash of jeweled buttons and white satin caught his attention. The unmistakable back of Diantha's gown flared out gently as she whirled in the arms of the man he had come to dislike already.

He broke in on Solange's flow of inconsequential gossip. "Who is this Emerson?"

A look of annoyance crossed her face. "A compatriot of yours, although assuredly not of our class. He owns a factory of some kind and is nearly as wealthy as your new father-in-law. I believe he bought his title a few years ago." She shrugged, clearly tired of the conversation, and they finished the waltz.

After obtaining champagne for the marquise and himself, he turned her over to her next dance partner with a sense of relief and went in search of Diantha. He found her engaged in an animated conversation with the factory owner and tamped down an unexpected flash of anger.

Forcing a smile to his lips, he strolled forward and begged to be introduced. As she made the two men known to each other, he sized up the other man.

Only a few inches shorter than he, Emerson possessed the rangy quality of a lean wolf. Kieran put his age somewhere in his late thirties, judging by the sandy hair going to gray and the faintly lined forehead. Although dressed in an impeccably tailored evening suit, the other man betrayed his background as soon as he opened his mouth, for he spoke with an unapologetic Yorkshire accent.

"Harry Emerson, North Riding Shipyards." He held out his hand. Despite Kieran's hostility, he admired the man's lack of pretentiousness and held out his own. As they shook hands, he realized Emerson was assessing him closely, too. "I've built a few steamers for Quinn over the years, known Diantha since she was a girl." He turned his head to watch the marquise dance past before regarding Kieran with cool green eyes. "I'm sure your lordship knows what a lucky man you are to have married her."

His temper flared again but he replied smoothly. "Indeed I do, Sir Harry. In fact, I came over to ask her ladyship if she cared to dance." He did not exactly lie, for he had expected to dance at least once with her. In the first place it was only proper, and also he had noticed during their engagement that while she was a graceful dancer, men often overlooked her.

This did not appear to be the case this evening. In the friendliest manner possible, she smiled and informed him that while one waltz remained open for him, the rest of her dance card was filled.

"In fact, here comes my partner now." Handing her champagne glass to Kieran, she held out her fingers to the comtesse's grandson. "Roch, your timing is perfect. The introduction is just starting." As the first strains of the next tune played, she strolled onto the floor.

He could not take his gaze off her satin-covered derriere for several seconds. Looking around, his lips pressed together. Several other men in the room eyed her backside just as appreciatively.

While he did not precisely spend the rest of the evening dancing attendance on his wife, he did stay in her vicinity as best he could. By the time he claimed his waltz he had experienced a considerable sense of ill-usage.

"Why didn't you save me the supper dance?" He frowned down at her as soon as the music started.

"You had apparently already asked the Marquise de Tourelle. Why are you in such a pet?" The diamonds in her aigrette flashed as she tipped her head back to look at him.

Like a burr under his skin, the justice of her reply only served to irritate him further. He had spent the supper interval watching her dining with Sir Harry, who had, in his opinion, hovered unnecessarily close when not waiting on her.

When he taxed her with this, she sighed. "You are exaggerating the case. While he is undeniably charming, and enjoys female company, his heart is unattainable." Her face saddened. "He buried it when his wife died years ago."

"You have treated him with particular favor all evening." Even to his own ears, the accusation sounded petty, for Diantha had not passed the bounds of propriety.

She raised her eyebrows. "Why not? There was a plan afoot to marry me to him at one time. That's why we came to London in the first place last year."

The sprightly music of the orchestra filled the silence between them as he grappled with this bombshell. It had never occurred to him that she might have had another suitor.

As they twirled in silence, he noticed the fragrance from the rose in her hair and the fine texture of her skin in the light from the chandeliers.

Remembering the night before their wedding when he had discovered her in her father's library, he wondered if she had only given him an excuse for her drunkenness. When the music came to an end, he could only think to bow.

Not until the carriage drove them back to the Avenue Montaigne in the small hours of the morning did he dare to ask her the question that weighed on his heart.

"Do you regret not marrying Sir Harry?" He stared straight ahead.

She paused before replying. "It wasn't really a matter of regret. It was much the same as our own engagement. Mama and Papa simply informed me I would be married, and to whom." No trace of self-pity entered her voice. "You came along before anything had been decided for certain between Papa and Sir Harry."

"That must have been difficult for you, being passed around like a refreshment tray." He reached over to take her hand.

A breath of laughter sounded beside him. "An apt, if lowering, description." She rallied a little. "But as I said, his heart would never be mine."

"Is that important?" He blurted out the question before he realized what he had said. Of course, she would consider it important; all young girls had romantic notions.

"I thought so when I was a girl, but that's not very practical, is it?" She withdrew her hand. "A woman must make her marriage satisfactory, I suppose."

Kieran took a deep breath. "Would you have preferred Emerson over me?" He did not understand why he attached so much importance to her answer, but his shoulders tensed as though waiting for a physical blow.

"All things considered, no." In the wave of inexplicable relief that washed over him, he did not ask her to elaborate.

Diantha hurried upstairs as soon as they entered the house. What had possessed her to speak so freely on the drive back? She must have drunk one glass of champagne too many. Living with Papa and her brothers had taught her that gentlemen did not enter into the sentiments of females.

She awoke Florette where she slept on a cot in the dressing room and returned to the bedroom. Sinking onto the slipper chair in front of the vanity, she removed the earrings and necklace herself before the maid came yawning out to take down her hair.

"You can brush it out in a moment. If I'm laced up much longer, I fear I shall burst." She turned about as Florette unfastened hooks and buttons, and stepped out of the rustling pile of satin with her help. When the corset came unlaced at last, Diantha took in a great breath, relishing the freedom of her chemise and drawers.

She removed her own shoes and stockings as the maid gathered up the discarded gown and petticoats for cleaning and pressing. The soft creak of an opening door barely registered with either woman.

"You're dismissed, Florette."

Diantha sat up with a jerk, dropping a stocking. Kieran leaned against the frame of the doorway. Her body tightened under his heavy-lidded stare. "She hasn't brushed my hair yet." Her voice came out in a breathy squeak.

"I can do that." He advanced into the room. "Good night, Florette."

"Good night, milord." The maid placidly curtsied and disappeared, leaving Diantha to face her husband with a pounding heart. The confidence that had buoyed her all evening dissipated. She clasped her hands together on the surface of the vanity, much like a schoolgirl sitting at a desk.

Kieran picked up the brush and slowly ran the bristles through her hair. "Are you afraid I'll hurt you again?"

"No." Some of her tension fell away at each stroke. "I don't think you wanted to last time."

The brush whispered down each strand in a gentle rhythm, followed by his hand. "What then?"

She shook her head. The turmoil in her heart did not rise from physical fear, but from something deep in her own soul. "I feared you might think my conversation earlier was foolish."

"I won't deny it took me by surprise." He pulled Diantha to her feet, settling his hands on the curve of her hips. Heat grew low in her midriff as his thumbs made small circles at her waist. "You seemed very happy to see your former suitor this evening."

"I have always been very fond of him." Her eyes widened as a suspicion struck her. "Surely you aren't jealous of him! I told you I prefer you to him."

Kieran stiffened. "When I see my wife holding hands with a man I've never set eyes on before in my life, I am not jealous. I am concerned that she is not behaving in a manner befitting her position."

"It was only a harmless flirtation." She enjoyed the look on his face when she threw his words regarding the *senhora* back at him. "After all, I only talked with him."

"You danced with him twice, and went down to supper with him." He growled the words as he picked her up and carried her to the bed. "You are my wife, if you'll recall."

She glared up at him from atop the neatly turned down coverlet and sheet. "Perhaps you should have remembered that fact before you started gallivanting all over Paris with the Marquise de Tourelle. You don't even want me!"

"On the contrary, I want you very much." He untied his sash and slipped off his robe.

She sucked in her breath at the sight of his bare chest and the burgeoning arousal pushing against the silk pyjamas.

In the candlelit room Diantha could see him far better than in the shadows of the ship's cabin. His chiseled features, the muscular shoulders and chest tapering to a slim waist and long legs, all combined to weaken her. He was so very beautiful, and he stood looking down at her as his own eyes darkened with desire. She could not resist the potent combination.

As if he read her mind, he seated himself on the edge of the bed. Balancing with a hand on either side of her head, he bent forward to place a gentle kiss on her lips. She opened to him and within seconds, he wrapped her in his embrace as their tongues mated over and over. The jut of flesh between his thighs hardened rapidly, but when he drew back, it was only to stroke his fingertips down her throat.

Catching sight of the ostrich feather fan on the

table beside her bed, he picked it up and lazily stroked the inside of her bare arm with it.

She inhaled in surprise when goose bumps rose over her entire body from the gossamer touch. Watching her intently, he trailed the plumes across her exposed breastbone and down the other arm. Her nipples peaked against the thin linen chemise and a tingle came to life in the flesh between her legs.

He teased her neck with the end of the feathers, playing the cloud softness over her sensitive skin till she squirmed and giggled. "Stop, you're tickling me!"

He desisted at once, setting the fan aside before returning to unbutton the chemise. She closed her eyes as he settled over her, his weight unfamiliar and yet welcome. Air cooled her breasts as the cloth fell away, followed by Kieran's warm hands caressing them. She hoped he would suckle, but instead he slid a palm under her back to lift her slightly.

Opening her eyes, she saw that he wanted to remove the chemise completely. Sitting up a little she assisted him in freeing her. Then he eased her back down to the bed, running his fingertips over the soft globes with their puckered tips. She arched against his touch, silently begging for more.

"Not yet." He murmured the words as he sat back on his heels. The sight of the hardened erection between his silk-covered thighs made her breath come faster. The idea of being impaled on his member without pain excited her. Following the direction of her gaze, his lips curved in a sensual smile. "Soon, my bonny wife."

His hands dropped to her waist and he pulled at the silk tie holding her drawers up. Sliding the loosened garment over her hips and down her legs, he discarded it and impulsively dropped a kiss onto her navel. As his tongue swirled around the tiny indentation, she shivered in anticipation.

He lifted his head, his own breath coming in quick puffs. As if reading her mind, he touched himself through the straining silk. "You want this, don't you?"

Heat rose in her face. She would rather die than admit something so wanton out loud. "No!"

"Oh?" One thick eyebrow arched. "We'll have to do something about that then." Standing up, he made short work of freeing himself from the pyjama trousers, letting the silk pool around his feet before crawling back onto the bed.

His eyes lit with a wicked twinkle, he stretched out over her and kissed her deeply.

She responded fully. Her hand buried itself in the curls at the back of his neck. Sighing happily into his mouth, she twined her tongue around his.

"You taste like brandy." She whispered the words against his lips.

He lifted his head, eyes gleaming. "I had some while I waited to come in." Their light softened as his knuckles grazed the side of her face.

She snorted. "That was waiting? I didn't even have my nightgown on!"

Rolling onto his side, he laughed down at her. "I saved myself the trouble of removing it." Before she could reply, he pulled her to him and nuzzled the soft curve under her jaw.

Diantha moaned softly as his mouth drove coherent thought from her mind. Vaguely aware that he reached past her for something, she could only cling to his shoulders under the onslaught from his lips and tongue.

She jumped as something soft stroked up the back of her leg and lingered on a bare buttock. She broke the kiss to discover he had reclaimed the fan.

"Kieran!" The word tore out of her with a gasp as he traced the contours of her behind with the cloud-soft feathers. "That's disgraceful!"

"I suppose I'll just have to stop then." As soon as the ticklish fronds left her skin, she scooted onto her back. Undeterred, he merely switched his attention to her front, running the fan along the side of her face onto her neck. She twitched and instinctively raised her hands to push it away.

He easily trapped them and held her hands above her head under his forearm. "Leave them there, darling. Just lay back and feel." He whispered the words against her ear as he slid one leg over both of hers, effectively holding Diantha in place.

After a moment of panic, she realized she could easily slide her hands out from under his arm. He slowly drew the fan down the center of her body to the nest of curls at the apex of her thighs. She could only clutch at him, panting, as jolts of pleasure snaked over her skin.

"No more." He growled the words and tossed the fan aside. His mouth fastened over one aching peak, greedily suckling and nibbling. His free hand wandered to the damp cleft between her thighs. Mindless with desire, she opened to admit him.

"Let me go, Kieran, I want to touch you." The ragged whisper tore from her throat as his circling fingers found slick flesh and teased her most sensitive spot.

"Yes." He took her hand and placed it on his engorged manhood. "Here." She tried to draw back, but he held her firmly. As she cautiously stroked him, his eyes fluttered shut and he groaned.

Amazed, she realized she had the power to affect him the same way he did her. A sense of power unlike anything she had ever known overcame her as she watched his response to her touch.

When he opened his eyes and pushed her onto her back, she accepted him without hesitation, spreading her legs to accommodate his body. She did tense when he carefully pushed into her, but he had not lied. Instead of pain, she felt only an exquisite sensation of being filled that increased with each thrust.

Her heart pounded as she felt her entire body tightening as it had before. At last Kieran ground into her with a guttural cry. His explosion set off her own, waves of pleasure washing over her until she could only lie, spent and sweating, beneath him while he rained kisses on her face.

Wordlessly, he eased off her onto his side. Pulling her close, he tucked the bedclothes around Diantha and stroked her hair. She fell asleep with her cheek pressed into the crisp hair on his chest, listening to the steady beat of his heart.

Diantha hoped she had not made a mistake in giving in to him.

Chapter 8

She woke up alone. Scrambling into a nightgown and summoning Florette, Diantha's heart twisted curiously as she looked about the room. Only the indentation he had left in the mattress showed that Kieran had come to her last night.

Sabine had confided that the baron spent the night with her after they made love, but perhaps he differed from most men. She shied away from asking Kieran directly. It seemed indelicate, and in the back of her mind she feared he would abandon her bed again if she made too many demands on him.

"Damn." She didn't dare say the vulgar word too loudly. "I want him too much."

As his lordship insisted on what he referred to as "a braw proper breakfast," the servants set up a table for two in the back salon each day. Normally, Diantha avoided the room until she knew he had finished eating. But this morning her appetite demanded something more filling than her usual cup of chocolate and buttered croissant.

As soon as the maid arrived, Diantha dressed

and ordered her hair done in a simple chignon. Soon she stood in front of the closed door to the salon, her fist lifted to knock.

She caught herself. As the lady of the house, temporary or not, she did not need anyone's permission to enter. She opened the door. "Good morning."

Kieran lifted his eyes from a copy of the *Times* thoughtfully provided by the house's owner. He stood up as soon as he saw Diantha and greeted her with a kiss on the cheek. "Good morning. May I fill a plate for you?"

An assortment of warming dishes sat on a credenza nearby, each holding a different kind of food. She regarded his plate. It held ham, smoked herring, brioche, and what appeared to be the remains of poached egg and toast.

"No, thank you for offering. By all means go on with your breakfast; I shall serve myself." A few minutes later, she sat down with what she considered a suitable meal.

As he pushed in her chair, Kieran observed her selections with a frown. "You'll never last the day with a single egg and a dab of stewed fruit! Allow me to bring you a slice of ham."

"I don't care for any meat, thank you!" His brows snapped together and she realized she had spoken more forcefully than he deserved.

"Please forgive me for speaking so sharply. I appreciate your concern, but I do know what I wish to eat." She watched his face, hoping he would not scold her too severely.

"Of course you do. I shouldn't have treated you like a child." He sat down at his place and she waited for the recriminations to start. Instead, he cut off a bite of herring.

Relieved, she took a fresh brioche from the napkin-covered bowl between them and availed herself of the butter and marmalade. When asked about her plans for the day, she replied that she intended to call at the Hôtel Pontrevault that afternoon, but had no other decided plans.

"Would you care to come for a drive in the Bois de Boulogne before that? We could wait on the comtesse together afterward."

Her pulse leaped. He had escorted her to balls, teas, and concerts since their engagement was first announced, but her mother had orchestrated those outings. He had never before invited her anywhere of his own accord.

"I should like that very much!" She tried to control her delight. He would think her a great fool if he knew how much this meant to her.

He finished the last of his tea. "I beg you to excuse me until luncheon. I have some instructions to send to my steward that will take some time." He nodded to her and left the room.

Seeing that he had abandoned his newspaper, she picked it up and opened it with a delicious thrill. Her father never permitted his womenfolk to read any newspapers but those aimed at ladies. Filled with gossip and fashion news, Mama and Granny devoured them, but the inane content bored her to tears. A glance at the clock told her she had twenty minutes before the servants entered to clear away the breakfast items. Sipping a cup of *café au lait*, she settled down to read.

The sound of the door opening ten minutes

later to admit her husband again startled her into nearly dropping her cup. Thrusting the newspaper under the table, she prayed he had not noticed it.

"We forgot to settle on a time for our drive. Would two o'clock suit you?" A bemused smile curved his lips. "Whatever are you doing?"

"I fear I am also slow this morning." She paused in scrubbing a spot from her gown with a napkin, relieved that she had not chosen one of her new ones to wear. "I wasn't paying attention to my surroundings and my coffee when you entered."

The corners of his eyes crinkled in amusement. "The article you were absorbed in reading must be interesting."

Her heart plummeted. Stooping to retrieve the hapless newspaper from under the table, she held it out to him.

He stared at her and shook his head, perplexed. "I'm finished with it."

"You don't mind that I read it?" She folded it nervously.

"Good God, no!" He waved her back to her chair. "I've never seen the point of forbidding a woman to read about anything but fripperies. I should be thankful to have a wife who can discuss something besides her embroidery and her neighbors."

Instead of returning to her seat, she threw her arms around his neck. "Thank you! I shall try not to sound like a bluestocking in front of your friends." His strong arms tightened around her and he laughed in her ear.

"Here I was going to step out to Cartier, and I

find I only needed to offer you a newspaper to get on your good side."

The embrace loosened as she stepped back to look up into his face. "I shall be proud to wear the rubies you gave me. Besides, I gather that you have pressing needs on your estate to spend money on."

His hands rested at her waist. "I do, but I think I could spare something for a few baubles." A wry smile twisted the lips so near her own. "I'm afraid my father sold most of our family treasures to provide for our tenants."

"That must have been difficult for all of you." She lifted a hand from his shoulder to touch his jaw. His smooth skin warmed her fingertips.

He shrugged. "It was, but it had to be done."

Catching her neatly manicured fingers, he brought them to his mouth for a kiss. "Perhaps I might find some sapphires to match your eyes."

She gulped as shivers ran down her arm. She hoped the novelty of his touch would wear off soon, for it undeniably impaired her thought process. "There's no need for sarcasm, my lord. My eyes are quite ordinary."

"I am beginning to think, my lady, that there is a great deal about you that is far from ordinary." Before she could ask him his meaning, he bowed and took his leave of her for the second time that morning.

The drive that afternoon proved more entertaining than Kieran expected. The realization that Diantha at least took an interest in events beyond society drawing rooms heartened him, and as they tooled along the rue du Bois, he introduced subjects of discussion he found interesting. Although she did not pretend to follow everything he said about agriculture and horses, she listened attentively and even asked a few timid questions.

"I am terribly sorry to keep pestering you, but my education is unremarkable, except that I was allowed to listen to my brothers' mathematics lessons." She colored a little as they drove through the dappled shade cast by the leafy canopy above. "It seems that I have inherited Papa's gifts in that area, and it tickled him to encourage it. Mama was appalled."

"Of course she was!" He burst out laughing, and after biting her lip, she joined in.

Over the next several days, while they did not spend every moment together, they did seek each other out more often. She encouraged him to tell her more about his estate than he had intended. He suspected her attentiveness to be based in the duties that came along with her title, but he appreciated the effort.

He even mellowed enough to tolerate the presence of Sir Harry Emerson at a small party his wife put together for dinner and the Opera on one of their last nights in Paris. At close quarters, the factory owner turned out to have a self-deprecating wit, which Kieran enjoyed; and a keen enthusiasm for music, which startled him.

His own interest in the arts extended little further than admiring a pretty opera dancer, and he listened to the spirited discussion of the evening's performance with increasing boredom. He did bolt to attention when Diantha stood up at the start of the second interval and requested the older man to escort her to inspect the grand staircase.

Only the request from the Comtesse de Pontrevault to accompany her to visit a friend in a distant box prevented him from trying to follow the pair. After gritting his teeth through ten minutes of gossip, he forced himself to slow to her pace on the return to their box.

Diantha and Sir Harry came up the stone and gilt staircase, their heads close together. Kieran hung on to the shreds of his temper as passing strangers smiled at the handsome couple. Emerson carried himself with a natural dignity, and his wife looked quite elegant in a low-cut gown of deep rose with touches of black sarcenet ribbon. The diamond aigrette glittered in the light of the chandeliers overhead. He had indeed paid a visit to Cartier, and more diamonds flashed at her neck and her wrists.

As they neared, he strained to hear their words through the chattering throng.

"Do you think you could do that?" His wife looked up at Emerson with puckered brows.

"I'll have to put the word out to my contacts." Emerson caught sight of them and patted her black-gloved hand where it lay on his arm. "Lord Rossburn. Madame, did you enjoy speaking with your friend?"

As they strolled down the crimson carpeted hallway after the performance, he asked her about the conversation with the older man. A slight flush rose to her cheek but her expression remained tranquil. "Sir Harry is merely executing some commissions for me, since we leave Paris shortly."

He narrowed his eyes. "Something you do not entrust to me."

"As you characterized a visit to the Louvre as being dragged to a musty museum filled with pictures of the dead, no, I do not trust you to find paintings I might like." Giving him a nervous smile, she changed the subject quickly, leaving him to wonder what she hid.

She did not refuse his advances that night, and as always, her wholehearted response to him touched him deeply. They stayed awake for a while afterward, and he found himself speaking of his home, Duncarie.

She stroked a hand over his chest. "You're anxious to get back."

"Yes." He thought her loveliest like this, lips swollen and dark blue eyes dreamy, with her silken skin pressed against his as he held her. "Going away to school was always a wrench."

She sighed. "I always envied my brothers because they were allowed to leave. My year at finishing school was the most wonderful of my life, except for being away from my grandmother."

"Would it be excessively uncivil to say I like you a lot better now that you're away from your mother?" He grinned down at her, expecting her to make a sharp retort.

Instead, some of the light died out of her eyes. "Yes it would." She dropped her gaze to the linen pillowcase. "But then I like me better now, too." She rolled onto her side, facing away from him. An invisible barrier rose between them that did not dissipate when he ran his fingers down her back.

"I should like to go to sleep now, Kieran. There's a great deal to oversee before we leave."

As had become his habit, he stayed with her until she fell asleep, even dozing himself.

When he roused, the candles had guttered out. The temptation to stay the night next to her warm body teased at him, but he resisted it. He did not wish to face the recriminations when he eventually lost interest in her. Careful not to wake her, he slipped out of bed and shrugged into his robe. Picking the pyjamas off the floor, he felt his way in the dark to his door.

He feared he resembled his father too strongly to be good husband material. Better not to hurt her any more than was necessary.

Lord and Lady Rossburn left Paris a few days later. They stopped in London to allow Diantha to meet some of Kieran's friends and relatives who had gathered for the Season. At first, she enjoyed attending dinners and balls free from her mother's domination, but she resented condescending remarks about her family's mercantile background.

She particularly dreaded the final dinner party of their stay. A "family party" hosted by the excruciatingly correct Duke and Duchess of Folkestone, connections of Kieran's mother, it promised to be deadly dull. To bolster her morale, she and Florette selected her toilette for the evening ahead of time, going over every detail in the days previous.

Now she stood in the center of her room while Florette scrutinized her appearance. They had decided on a gown of rose-colored velvet that enhanced her complexion and eyes. The Rossburn parure had arrived from Scotland and diamonds glittered attractively against her brown hair. The matching pieces adorned her neck, ears, and wrists. After a last twitch of her hem, the servant stepped back. "Milady will do great credit to us this evening."

Diantha prayed for patience. The maid's determination to present her to London in the best light possible verged on the rabid. "How gratifying."

As she descended to the landing above the entry hall, Kieran's voice floated up. "Dammit, Diantha, we should have left ten minutes ago!"

"I'm terribly sorry for the delay, but we should still arrive in plenty of time." She offered the apology a little breathlessly, for Kieran stopped shouting as soon as she appeared. Now his appreciative gaze lingered on the swell of her breasts, exposed by the gown's low neckline. She rubbed her thighs together under skirts, embarrassed at a rush of moisture under the aqua heat of his appraisal.

He cleared his throat. "You do look very well this evening, but we are late." Signaling to a waiting footman, he took her wrap and settled it around her shoulders.

The cool aristocrat of their betrothal had returned and Diantha could have ground her teeth in frustration. The instant his hands left her, she stepped away. "Stop fidgeting. We shall arrive in plenty of time."

He said nothing to this retort, but his eyes turned to ice and remained that way until they entered the drawing room at Folkestone House.

"Try to refrain from outrageous remarks," he murmured beneath the butler's announcement of their presence. Diantha sucked in a furious breath. Just then one of his more obnoxious relatives, an earl, greeted them. "I say, here's our wild Scotsman and his merchant bride!"

Diantha nearly burst out laughing as Kieran's jaw clenched. She patted her husband's rigid forearm. "I will when they do."

Despite her threat, she reigned in her disdain until after the meal. When the ladies returned to the drawing room, the duchess turned to her with a smile. "My dear, you have enchanting manners. No one would believe you grew up among wild Indians. You must tell us what it was like."

A blistering reply rose to Diantha's lips, but she realized the elderly woman spoke in complete sincerity. "Has Your Grace never read any factual account of life in America?"

One of Kieran's second cousins by marriage sniffed. "Excessive reading is highly undesirable in a lady of quality." From the nods of approval, the rest of the company agreed with her.

Diantha had had enough. She settled herself on a divan and accepted a cup of tea. "Naturally, the greatest challenge is that everything is made of birch bark," she began.

When Kieran and the rest of the gentlemen entered after their port, they discovered her explaining, with a straight face, that promenades along Fifth Avenue took the form of covered wagon trains in order to fend off hostile natives.

Before her outraged spouse could speak, the Earl of Goring harrumphed. "I have traveled to New York myself, never saw any such thing. You owe the company an apology, madam."

Diantha gave him a cool stare. "If you bothered to educate females or allowed them to read a newspaper on occasion, they might stop asking me how many Indian attacks I've survived."

"The female mind is unsuited to the rigors of disciplined study, Lady Rossburn." The earl delivered his opinion as he flipped his coattails up to seat himself a few chairs away from her. "At least the mind of a *true* lady is."

A thrill ran through the room at the insult. Diantha merely raised an eyebrow and regarded him in silence for a full five seconds, while Kieran took a place behind her chair.

"Rot." Turning her back to the spluttering peer, she asked the woman on her right to recommend a good milliner.

"Looks like Rossburn saddled himself with quite the oddity." The loud whisper could have come from anyone in the room. Titters broke out from several places.

Eyes blazing, her husband raked the company with a ferocious glare. "I prefer to think of Lady Rossburn as extraordinary."

They excused themselves shortly afterward. Despite his public support, he gave her a resounding scold on the way home for daring to turn her back on an earl.

She did not back down. "I don't care if he's the Prince of Wales! If that man ever sets foot under our roof, I am instituting divorce proceedings." Fuming, she gathered her evening cloak closer around her in the chilly coach. "And if you're so upset with me, why did you defend me in there?"

"What kind of man lets someone insult his wife?" Still angry, he sat stiffly beside her. "A fine opinion you must have of me!"

"I think more highly of you than you realize." Diantha snapped the words out. "I only wish you felt the same. 'Extraordinary'!" She snorted. "It makes me sound like a suspension bridge."

Unsurprisingly, he did not come to her bed that night, a circumstance that both relieved her and irritated her further.

They continued in the same stilted manner for the following day. Neither apologized, and the impasse had not broken when they boarded their train north.

Diantha dreaded the journey, for they would first travel overnight to Aberdeen and then by coach to Kieran's estate. Even in a comfortably fitted out private railcar and a well-sprung coach, traveling while cooped up with a surly husband would try the patience of a saint.

To her relief, Kieran became more affable as the car hummed north. The second morning of their journey, he assisted her onto the railway platform himself, and led her through the crowd to their coach. Already out of sorts from a day and night spent in the confines of the railcar, she regarded the out-of-date vehicle with a jaundiced eye. A second, even older one stood behind it to carry Florette, Davison, and the luggage. She gave the maid a sympathetic look.

Kieran exchanged greetings with the coachmen, both of whom treated him with a familiarity she did not think a peer would have tolerated.

"Come, Diantha. It's time to go home." He extended a hand to her with the expression on his face of one close to attaining a long-anticipated treat. Expecting a long day jolting through vast empty tracts of land, she suppressed a sigh and permitted him to hand her up.

Inside, she discovered that the vehicle remained in good condition. A faint smell of new varnish clung to the interior, and she ran her fingers over thick cushions covered with new upholstery before settling back against the squabs.

It rolled over the busy streets of Aberdeen with scarcely a bounce. In her relief, she resolved not to fall into a foul temper over rough country roads.

As it turned out, she forgot about bumps as they moved out into the countryside. Outside her window, immense vistas of long narrow valleys stretched into the distance, some with forested sides, some carpeted with grass. She gazed, fascinated, as they passed small farms and herds of sheep and shaggy red cows. Each mile brought the peaks of the Grampians closer.

Kieran looked out with as much pleasure as she did. "You're lucky we have a sunny day. In damp weather you can hardly see beyond the side of the road."

Shortly before noon they stopped at a small inn bearing a brightly painted sign depicting a trout caught on a fishing line. Only a few other stone houses straggled down the road on either side of it.

Diantha guessed the grooms had made arrangements on the way to Aberdeen, for no sooner did they descend from the coach than the landlady bustled out, double chins quivering, to announce that a private room awaited them upstairs, luncheon would be served directly, and she would show my lady to the best bedroom herself.

Kieran dammed the flow of words with a warm greeting. "Mrs. Teagle! You haven't aged a day since I last visited the Trout. How many hearts have you broken since then?"

"Flummery, ye wee devil!" She simpered in spite of her protest. "Get inside and wash up before your chicken gets cold." Davison, standing nearby, winced at her overfamiliarity, and the grooms stared woodenly ahead. Kieran, however, roared with laughter and introduced her to Diantha.

Diverted by anyone who could refer to her six-foot-two-inch husband as "wee," Diantha controlled her quivering lips and accepted the woman's curtsey graciously. She and Florette followed her into the whitewashed hallway and up a dark wooden staircase to a compact bedroom. Taking advantage of the waiting cans of hot and cold water, she washed her face.

Kieran stood at the window when Mrs. Teagle showed her to the dining room. Curious to see what interested him, she crossed to his side. The view did not differ from what she had seen beyond her coach window all morning, but the wild beauty called to a corner of her heart she had never known existed.

He absently placed an arm around her shoulders and drew her to him. She rested against him, contented, until the entrance of the bustling landlady interrupted them. After heaving a sentimental sigh at their loverlike attitude, she briskly directed two maidservants in setting out their lunch. With a last curtsey she left them, shutting the door behind her.

"The fare is simple enough, but I assure you there's no better cook between Duncarie and Aberdeen." His earlier ease lessened as he challenged her to criticize the meal.

"I wouldn't dream of dismissing someone's hard work." She replied with more asperity than she had intended, for she recognized the stout landlady's efforts to provide a satisfactory meal.

Not one wrinkle marred the immaculate cotton tablecloth, and the cutlery gleamed from recent polishing. Flowers in a Staffordshire vase decorated the table in a cheery splash of color. They dined heartily on a tender hen accompanied by vegetables and oaten cakes that she learned were called bannocks. Rich scones with clotted cream and strawberry preserves provided a finish.

Back in the coach, the afternoon passed agreeably, if more slowly than the morning. She and Kieran read and conversed about various points of interest that he pointed out. After a few hours, her eyelids drooped closed and she thought to rest them for a moment.

She opened them some time later with her head pillowed on his shoulder. Stifling a yawn, she hastily sat up. "How long did I sleep?"

"Only about an hour." He stretched his arm and rotated his shoulder.

"You should have awakened me." She rubbed her eyes with her fingertips. Looking out the window, she noticed the road curved toward a stone bridge spanning a stream that crossed their route. To cover her embarrassment, she asked about it.

"Oh, those." His face took on an expression of

scorn. "They're new. The English built them after Culloden, along with the road."

"That was almost a hundred and thirty years ago!" Diantha shook her head in bemusement. "How old does something have to be before you consider it old?"

"There were Rossburns on our land when Robert the Bruce came to the throne in 1306." His chin lifted. "I suppose that gives us a different perspective."

Although the vital man sitting beside her seemed a far cry from the chillingly polite aristocrat she had married in New York, she wondered if they would ever overcome the differences in their backgrounds. That lowering thought occupied her mind for the next few miles, until Kieran touched her wrist.

"We're nearly there. Look."

The road dipped into a wide glen and turned to follow the course of a lively stream flowing between two stony banks. Where the stream widened to form a pool, a terraced garden marched down to meet it. A graceful Georgian mansion rose at the opposite end of the garden. It should have looked out of place under the beetling slopes of the hills behind it. Instead, its gray stone invited the travelers nearer, as though offering an oasis of civilization in the untamed vale.

Kieran proudly pointed out several smaller houses scattered on the floor of the glen. "Crofts. We managed to avoid completely enclosing our land when we were stripped of our power. Some tenant families have been here as long as we have."

"Good heavens! It sounds like I've stepped back

into the feudal era." She clapped her hand over her mouth, but not before he fixed her with an icy stare.

"Hardly, as you'll find out."

"Yes, I'm sure I will. I do apologize." He growled in his throat but said nothing more.

The house grew larger as they drew closer, revealing graceful proportions and tasteful embellishment. Diantha blinked twice as she noticed one more attribute.

"Kieran? Is the house, well, glittering?" Her question seemed to restore his good humor, for he chuckled before replying.

"It's built of granite from a quarry near Aberdeen. The stone contains a large amount of mica." Still grinning, he shrugged. "So, it glitters in the sun."

"How charming!" Relieved to see him smile again, she focused her attention on the house. "I look forward to meeting your family."

"It's just my mother and Aunt Iona anymore." She detected a wistful note in his voice, which disappeared with his next words. "And it looks like you won't have to wait long. I think Iona must have dragged out every last member of the staff to meet us."

Diantha gulped. Ahead of what appeared to be at least a regiment, if not a small army of servants, an imposing woman in gray stood waiting on the steps of the courtyard as the coach swept in.

Their two days of traveling fell onto her shoulders like a heavy weight. Surreptitiously, she straightened her hat and moistened her lips as Kieran stepped down from the carriage and turned to assist her. As she placed her hand in his, he squeezed it gently.

"You can do this." His soft murmur barely reached her ears. She straightened her back and stepped out.

"How lovely!" She forgot her nerves as soon as she looked around her.

They stood in a courtyard bordered by the house on three sides. The silvery granite rose smoothly from the ground to the roof three stories above, ornamented by pilasters carved of the same stone and pediments above each window. A carved balustrade interspersed with statuary ran along the roofline, giving the house an elegant finish.

"The other sides of the house have more interesting features." Despite his deprecation, Kieran looked about with glowing eyes and a tender smile. Giving her his arm, he led her forward.

"Allow me to present my aunt, Lady William Upton. On the death of her husband, she was good enough to return to her childhood home and look after us." He bowed over the older woman's hand. "Aunt Iona, my wife."

"Lady Rossburn." Kieran's aunt possessed a strong family resemblance in her nearly black hair and wide-set eyes. She did not have her nephew's easy smile, though, as she sketched a curtsey. "I am pleased to welcome you to Duncarie."

Her voice warmed slightly as she turned to him. "I'm sure you're relieved to be back, Kieran, especially under these circumstances."

Diantha's teeth set. The cool tone suggested that he deserved pity for his marriage, as did the contemptuous glance in her direction. It would serve no purpose to start a quarrel with one of Kieran's close relatives, however. She acknowledged the curtsey with one of her own.

"Thank you, Lady William. You are most kind and it is a pleasure to meet you. I look forward to exploring my new home." She gave a small smile as the dark eyes narrowed slightly. "And please, you must call me Diantha."

"You should not curtsey to one of lesser rank. And that gown is far too showy for the country." Turning to her nephew, she took his arm. "I shall see that she understands proper etiquette before we present her to company."

After an apologetic look over his shoulder, Kieran merely asked his aunt how the estate had fared in his absence. Taking a deep breath and resisting the urge to throw her reticule at the back of his head, she trailed along behind them, feeling more out of place than she had since her marriage.

Chapter 9

Meeting the servants did not tax her ingenuity, although she chose to ignore Lady William's gimlet stare as she strolled down the line. The woman's pursed mouth radiated disapproval as Diantha paused to exchange a few words not just with the butler and housekeeper, but with each member of the staff. She had no doubt whatsoever that the woman longed to give her a set down, except that ahead of her Kieran had a smile or greeting for everyone.

At last they finished speaking to the last two servant girls, a pair of scullery maids.

Lady William dismissed everyone, and the line disintegrated into knots of people returning to their duties. "We shall take tea in the drawing room." Her tone of voice might have offered Diantha a bowl of hemlock.

Taking her place beside her husband, she followed his aunt through the wide doorway into the entry hall. A fanlight above the door allowed the westering sun to shine on the sky blue-tinted walls and whitewashed paneling. Columns separated the front third of the hall from the rest and alcoves on either side held handsome porcelain urns.

She wished she could explore the room closely, but they immediately headed toward a stairway on the right, their footsteps echoing on the pale gray flagstone floor. Passing a round table and several upholstered chairs along the wall, she followed the Rossburns up to a long hallway paneled and floored with oak. Although floor to ceiling windows admitted natural light at one end, compared to the airy entry hall, it struck her as closed-in and dark.

"The gallery. When dining privately, the family gathers here before going down to dinner." Continuing to the far end of the narrow room, Lady William opened a door. "We serve tea in the drawing room, and naturally when entertaining for dinner, we meet beforehand in here."

"Naturally." Diantha all but rolled her eyes, earning her a stern look from her husband. Entering the drawing room, though, she exclaimed in delight. Situated on a corner of the house, light poured in through windows on two sides to illuminate a large room of graceful proportions. The pale blue of the entry hall repeated itself here in the wall coverings, drapes, and carpet, accented with touches of gilt and cream. Even Kieran's aunt thawed slightly at her unfeigned admiration.

Chippendale and Georgian furniture blended harmoniously in several arrangements suitable for intimate conversation. A low table in the center of one such grouping already held tiered plates of delicacies, and a footman brought in the silver tea service before Lady William had time to tug on the tapestry bellpull.

"Allow me to serve this afternoon, Lady Rossburn." Seating herself on a sofa, she invited Kieran to sit on a chair at her right hand and Diantha to take one on her left. "I'm sure you will grasp the intricacies of properly serving tea in no time. Do you know how you wish me to prepare it?"

Familiar with formal teas since childhood, she bit her tongue. Irked nearly beyond measure by the woman's condescension, she concentrated on removing her gloves until she could speak with a civil tone of voice.

Kieran spoke up opposite her. "Diantha takes her tea with lemon and sugar." She supposed she should be thankful to him for stepping into the breach, but his slowness only added to her annoyance.

"No milk?" Her aunt by marriage conveyed the impression that she had committed some grave solecism.

"No, thank you." Forcing a friendly note into her voice, she accepted the cup and saucer the older woman handed her. "It is odd in that I do enjoy cream in my coffee, but I prefer tea without it."

As soon as Kieran received his cup, he changed the subject. "I didn't want to ask in front of the servants, but how is my mother?" His eyes betrayed grave concern.

"No worse, but no better. Dear Doctor Andrews consults with her weekly, but she continues in great pain."

He sighed. "I suppose she is resting? I had hoped to introduce Diantha to her this evening."

"My dear boy, your sentiments do you great

credit, but she does need to be cushioned against shocks."

Diantha nearly choked on a bite of watercress sandwich.

Kieran chuckled. "My wife may not be conventional, but she is hardly a shock to the system, Aunt." His eyes twinkled over the top of his cup as he sipped. "At least not a bad one."

In no mood for his teasing, she nearly blurted out a few words that would have shocked him as well as his aunt. Only the opening door saved her from such shrewish behavior.

"Kieran!" In the doorway stood a man nearly as tall as her husband, similar enough in features and coloring that they could have been brothers.

"Barclay!" Her husband set his cup down and rose to his feet. Striding over, he greeted the man with a backslapping embrace. Diantha watched, amazed. She had never seen men do more than shake hands in greeting. On her right, Iona winced.

"Nephew, do sit down and allow your cousin to have his tea." His mother poured milk into a teacup, following it with the clear brown liquid.

"Damme, I swore to Mother that you wouldn't arrive before six at the earliest." The newcomer crossed the room with Kieran. "I hope you forgive me for not being here to greet you and your lovely bride." He sketched a bow in Diantha's direction. Thankful that someone seemed to notice her, she smiled back.

"Barclay, your language." Uttering the remonstration in the fondest of tones, his mother handed him his teacup. He accepted it, but stayed on his feet.

Kieran laughed. "Since it's a surprise to me that you're here, of course I do! It was good of you to stay for us."

His cousin opened his eyes wide. Darker than Kieran's, they sparkled bottle green instead of aqua. "My dear boy, what else is family for? Now, do I actually get to meet my charming new relative or not?"

"Only if you promise not to steal her away." Kieran strolled over to her. "Diantha, I'd like to present my cousin, Barclay Upton. Barclay, the new Lady Rossburn."

"Delighted to meet you, your ladyship." Underneath his charming manner, she detected a sharp look of appraisal in his eyes that disquieted her. It disappeared so quickly she wondered if she imagined it. And she must expect some curiosity from her husband's family.

"I owe you an apology." Mr. Upton's soft-spoken words surprised her as he kissed her hand. "Forgive me, Lady Rossburn, for ever thinking my cousin married you only for your fortune. I'm sure he kept your loveliness a secret out of a wish not to make his male relatives jealous."

Kieran had informed them that she was rich and had not even bothered to describe her appearance? That knowledge hurt, though knowing herself to be merely pretty at best, she did not know why it should. "Please, call me Diantha."

"And you must call me Cousin Barclay." With a warm smile, he took a seat opposite his mother. "And my mother shall be your aunt Iona."

Following a look of malevolence at her offspring, that lady collected herself and tittered. "My dear,

I'm sure my nephew felt no need to send us a description of any detail of Lady Rossburn's appearance, or her wardrobe. The newspapers did not spare us a single detail!" She left the word "vulgar" unsaid, but they all understood her meaning.

The newspaper stories her mother had given to the American papers must have been published in Britain as well. A wave of hot shame rolled over her as both men looked at the older woman.

That combined with Iona's rudeness, Kieran's indifference, and two long days of travel to overwhelm her. Close to tears, she set her cup and saucer down with a rattle.

"Please excuse me. I must dress for dinner." With that, she stood and nearly bolted out of the room.

As soon as she shut the door behind her, she realized what a fool she had made of herself. She could not very well go back into the drawing room and she had no idea how to find her bedchamber. Fortunately, a footman arrived to light the chandeliers then. Hearing her request, he bowed and asked her to follow him.

By the time she reached her chamber, through a confusing maze of hallways and stairs, she learned that Charles had grown up on the estate and his parents lived on the far side of the glen, and that his lordship's people were chuffed that he brought home a bonny young wife with a fouth of siller. Grasping that he intended the last part as a compliment to her person and fortune, she thanked him and slipped inside.

Despite her anger at the woman, she had to admit that Kieran's aunt possessed exquisite taste. A high four-poster bed of carved cherry wood sat against one wall. The embroidered hangings harmonized with the pale dove gray walls in a restful palette and matched the drapes and upholstery. She could see where the sun had faded the fabric in places, and guessed that refurbishing the house had taken second place to helping the estate prosper. An alcove held a carved antique dressing table and mirror, while in a corner bay, a cherry wood writing table with a blue and white porcelain inkstand and quill-holder invited her to sit down and write.

Her trunks lay open in the middle of the room. Peering into the armoire, she discovered that Florette had already put away several of her gowns. Locating the bellpull, she rang for the maid.

Then, unable to hold back her tears, she sat down at the vanity and buried her face in her hands.

When Florette entered, she placed a comforting hand on Diantha's heaving back and turned to the under housemaid accompanying her. "Milady is homesick. Fetch ice and a cold cloth at once, and send up cans of hot water for the hip bath."

As soon as the door closed, she bustled over to close the armoire door. "Now, tell me what has really upset you, *ma mie.*"

After a gulp, Diantha blotted her eyes with her handkerchief. "Lady William is ghastly! She has taken an instant dislike to me, and the feeling is entirely mutual."

The Frenchwoman made a disparaging noise in the back of her throat. "I have already heard much below the stairs about this aunt. She is the sister of milord's father, and has ruled here for nearly fifteen years, even before milord's father died."

She winked. "It is only to be expected that she should detest you on sight. You are now the lady of the house, and she must either go back to her dead husband's family, who do not like her either, or stay on as a poor relation."

Moving to the trunk, she lifted out another paper-wrapped gown. After placing it on the bed, she gave Diantha a conspiratorial smile. "Do not despair, milady. All the servants are asking Davison what you are like, and he has been most complimentary."

"I realize it is a difficult situation for Lady William." Diantha sighed. "I shall see if conciliation works to sweeten her."

The maid's first words came back to her mind. She straightened and swiveled to face the maid in disbelief. "I have to use a hip bath?"

Florette coughed. "It seems the house does not have running water."

"It will when I'm done with it." Diantha muttered the words as she stood to allow the maid to help her out of her traveling dress.

Her mood did not improve when Kieran knocked on her door a few minutes before the dinner hour. After a perfunctory enquiry about the comfort of her room, he gave her a sharp scold about her earlier behavior.

"What do you mean by haring out of the drawing room like that?" He paced the rug before the fireplace. "She went to a great deal of trouble to prepare a suitable welcome for you."

"You mean she made sure to make me feel like a guest in what is supposed to be my home!" Her indignation boiled over as she sat in front of her dressing table. "And you did nothing to prevent it!"

"Perhaps you would prefer that I order her bags packed and throw her bodily out the door?"

As her mind had dwelt on an image of him doing exactly that several times while she bathed and dressed, she pressed her lips together for fear of saying something truly intemperate.

They had not fully resolved their differences by the time he escorted her to join his aunt and cousin, and they entered the drawing room with an air of decided coolness between them. Aunt Iona smirked over her sherry, although Barclay hastened forward with a compliment which soothed Diantha's ruffled feathers.

During dinner itself, his aunt rejected all Diantha's attempts to win her over. Not compliments about the tasteful decoration of Duncarie or an enthusiastic question about the house's history improved her temper.

In only one area could Diantha have redeemed herself in the older woman's eyes. No sooner had the two of them entered the drawing room after dinner, leaving Kieran and Barclay to cigars and brandy in the dining room, than the woman looked pointedly at her abdomen.

"Are you increasing yet?" Iona seated herself behind the tea table.

"I beg your pardon?" Diantha sank onto a cushioned bench, unable to believe what she had just heard.

"You have been married over a month. I would think my nephew is enough of a man to have gotten a child on you by now." Iona poured tea for both of them and held a cup out.

Trained by years of etiquette lessons, Diantha

reached forward to take it. "I hope that I have a chance to get to know Kieran's family and household first." Collecting herself, she fidgeted with the cup.

Iona looked down her aquiline nose. "The family expects an heir. Your first duty is to provide one."

Wishing to bring this appalling conversation to a close, Diantha straightened further in her seat. "Possibly my husband might disagree with your assessment. After all, he does have more resources at his command than prior to his marriage."

The older woman set her own cup down with a clatter. "Trust a member of the merchant class to bring up money! You should be thankful for the privilege of providing the next link in such a long lineage."

Diantha took a deep breath and prayed that Kieran and Barclay joined them before she attempted to strangle Iona with a drapery tie.

"Should we be blessed with a child, madam, you will doubtless be devastated to learn that he—or she—will be treated as a child and not some inanimate object."

Before the other woman could retort, the drawing room door did open to admit the gentlemen. Her narrow face immediately smoothed into a tranquil expression and she blandly asked if either of them cared for tea.

Needing to distance herself from the wretched woman, Diantha wandered over to the piano in a corner while the other three busied themselves around the tea table. She pretended to leaf through the sheet music on its top while she struggled to quell the rancor raging through her. Only Kieran's earlier criticism kept her from tearing into his aunt or leaving the room.

"My mother can be a sore trial at times."

She started at the soft comment dropped in her ear. Lifting her gaze from the music, she saw Barclay holding out her refilled cup with an apologetic smile. She really did not wish for any more, but could not refuse the kind gesture.

Nor could she abuse the woman to her own son. Taking the cup from him, she forced a smile to her lips. "I'm sure I don't know what you mean."

He gave a crack of laughter that caused his mother and cousin to look up from their murmured conversation with lowered brows. "She takes a great deal of pride in her family. Did she lecture you dreadfully on your duties to the Rossburn name?"

His sympathetic tone comforted her and she gave him a warmer smile than she first intended. "She and my husband both did. I suppose I shall have to get used to it." Then she realized how her words sounded. "Forgive me, I spoke out of turn! Certainly I meant no disrespect to your family."

"As my family name is Upton, I have no reason to feel resentment." His lips quirked into a lopsided smile. "For that reason, I have always been a bit of an outsider myself when visiting Duncarie. Not that Kieran has not always been everything that is gracious. Most of the time, at any rate."

"Were you a frequent visitor in your childhood?" She cocked her head to one side, enjoying his undivided attention.

"No, only once a year or so until I reached the age of seventeen. That's when my mother moved back." Diantha nodded at the explanation.

"I've always thought the estate remarkable, although my uncle nearly ran it into the ground." He lowered his voice tactfully. "It could be much more profitable with proper management. I, at least, am thankful that he married into a family possessing some business acumen."

Diantha smiled her appreciation. It made a pleasant change to hear her family complimented for its fortune instead of denigrated. Still, this conversation had veered into dangerous waters.

As if realizing the same thing, her companion turned his attention to the music. "Do you play, Cousin Diantha?"

"Hardly, Cousin Barclay." She held up her left hand, fingers outstretched. "As you can see, my reach does not even cover an octave and a half. My music master gave up trying to teach me to play when I was fourteen. He convinced my mother that I should be considered equally accomplished if I was taught to sing instead."

With a teasing glint in his green eyes, he held his hand up, palm facing hers. Nearly as large as Kieran's, elegantly shaped with long fingers, his hand could have engulfed hers easily.

"I do play, although indifferently. We should try a duet for voice and piano sometime."

"Admiring my wife's wedding ring?" Somehow her tall husband had crossed the room without her notice and stood right behind her. He did not look angry, but a sharp glance at their nearly touching hands caused hers to drop to her side.

Barclay raised an eyebrow but spoke mildly. "How nice of you to join us, Cousin. While her ring is quite handsome, I find many other admirable qualities in my new relative." Unnoticed by either man at that moment, Diantha saw the speculative flash in his eyes before he covered it up with urbane teasing.

"I was telling her I should be delighted to accompany her any time she wishes. On the piano, of course."

"Ah, is that it?" Her husband's face looked friendly enough, except for a faint chill in his eyes.

"Surely you don't think I'd behave badly with your wife, cuz!" Barclay chuckled.

"Ah, but I've seen you charm so many females with that particular look on your face."

Kieran smiled down at her. "I didn't know you could sing. Would you and my cousin favor us with a song?"

After a brief search, Barclay handed her a piece by Mssrs. Gilbert and German Reed. She choked back a laugh at the title, and launched into "With Rage Infuriate I Burn!" with gusto.

As her parents had spared no expense in her vocal training, she delivered a creditable performance of the witty lyrics. Barclay's description of his skill on the piano matched his uninspired playing, but she thanked him anyway. He had certainly demonstrated more kindness than his mother.

By the song's end, Kieran's good humor returned, although Iona regarded her with suspicion. As well she might, Diantha thought to herself. She refused to allow the woman to set her aside in her own house.

Pleading a long day of travel, she escaped from the drawing room shortly afterward. Another footman conducted her to her chamber door, where she entered and gladly submitted to Florette's ministrations. By the time the maid blew out all but one candle and slipped out the door, she drowsed against the pillows, warm under an eiderdown quilt.

Wriggling her toes luxuriously, she sighed contentedly, staring up at the canopy. Iona Upton or not, it felt heavenly to stretch out on a comfortable bed without her corset.

She closed her eyes and frowned. By rights, running Duncarie should now be her responsibility, but Florette had pointed out the woman's precarious position.

The door opened again. Doubtless the Frenchwoman had forgotten something. Wanting to consider possible courses of action to claim her rightful place here, she did not open her eyes or speak. Cloth rustled nearby; the maid must have remembered something she wanted to clean.

Without warning, the sheets and coverlet shifted. Her eyes popped open as the mattress sagged under the heavy weight of a body sliding into bed next to her. Two muscular arms wrapped around her and warm lips nuzzled her nape, causing her to shiver and gasp involuntarily.

"Kieran, I'm tired." She tried to scoot out of his arms only to have them tighten around her.

His bold hands came up to cup her breasts through her cambric nightgown, his thumbs circling their peaks to stiffness. "I came to apologize for scolding you before dinner. That was thoughtless on your first night here."

She became fully alert as his breath against her skin sent shivers down her spine. "Is that what this is called?"

His body shook with suppressed laughter even as

his fingers joined his thumbs, rolling her nipples until they ached. In between planting kisses over the back of her neck and shoulders, he spoke again. "I noticed your overtures to my aunt at dinner. She was at her worst this evening for some reason."

And this afternoon. She didn't voice the thought aloud, for he moved closer to her at that moment, and she realized with a shock that he was naked. All thoughts of Aunt Iona flew out of her head as the head of his heated shaft rubbed her backside through her nightgown.

A dark pulse stirred between her thighs as one hand left her breast to slide down her waist to her hip. She tried to turn onto her back, to open toward him. Gently, he squeezed her hip, stopping her.

She tilted her head back, trying to see him. Only his shoulder and the side of his face filled her vision. "You don't want me to—"

His lips brushed the sensitive skin behind her ear. "I want you like this."

"Why?" A sense of disappointment filled her. She wondered if he had tired of her plain face already. Then the tip of his tongue replaced his lips on her tender flesh, licking in slow circles down the side of her neck.

Instantly her back arched as pleasure crinkled down her spine. The motion ground her hips against the hard ridge of his erection and thrust her hardened nipple into his waiting palm.

His other hand left her hip and delved into the cleft between her parted legs. "Better access." He gasped the words as she rocked against his questing fingers.

He held her to him as he stroked her slit, feeling the thin cloth rapidly dampen under his fingers. Intermittently he toyed with the secret nub that controlled her passion, teasing it until her night-gown was wet and she moaned in his arms.

He had not planned to come to her tonight. Able to sleep in his own bed for the first time in months, he had expected to drop off immediately. Instead he had tossed restlessly on the smooth sheets. For the first time since he had moved into the laird's bedchamber, someone occupied the bedroom connected to it.

Images of Barclay's hand so close to Diantha's as they stood by the piano had run through his mind. He could not imagine that his cousin would make improper advances to his wife. Still, Barclay's considerable charm might turn her head.

And what male in his right mind would reject her unfeigned response to carnal pleasures?

Marriage of convenience or not, the idea of his wife in bed with another man stirred a primitive urge to somehow claim her, to mark her as his alone.

Now he held her, his cock throbbing in time to her hoarse breaths. One of her hands clutched the arm that held her, and the other gripped his butt as he thrust against hers. As he continued to fondle her most intimate flesh, the scent of her musk rose to his nostrils, nearly driving him mad with lust.

"Please, Kieran!" She writhed in his arms, seeking her release. Not yet, he decided. He wanted to experience more of her first.

His hands left her. Instantly she turned to him, wrapping her arms around his neck and kissing him fervently. One slim leg hiked itself a little over his hip as if inviting him to enter her.

He smiled against her eager mouth. "Slow down, my bonny wife. We have all night."

She lifted her head away from him, and in the dim glow of the candle by her bed, he saw surprise in her eyes. "Bonny? That means pretty, doesn't it?"

Unexpected tenderness welled up in his heart. "Yes, it does." Caressing her face with a hand, he leaned into her. Her eyelids fluttered closed as he slipped his tongue between her lips. Then he tasted her, circling his tongue around hers in a leisurely dance.

She followed his lead, slowly curling the tip of her tongue against his, then pulling back to run it over his lower lip. "You have a bonny mouth." She paused, looking at him as though expecting a rebuke.

"Thank you." He kissed her again, slanting his mouth over hers, taking his time as he rolled her onto her back and straddled her. He tilted his pelvis slightly to bring the sac between his legs into pleasurable contact with the soft cloth of her nightgown.

The garment fastened with a row of buttons down the front. Her breath caught as he unbuttoned them and parted the two sides. She arched her back in blatant invitation, but only after he had freed her arms from the gown's long sleeves did he stretch out over her.

Starting with her gloriously sensitive neck, he kissed and nibbled his way down to her breasts. Gathering their bounty in his hands, he took turns laving and gently nipping each pink bud until Diantha groaned with desire.

He trailed more kisses down her body as he pushed the flimsy nightgown down her legs and off. Crouching over her, he licked around her navel as his hands slid beneath her thighs.

Her legs twitched at the unexpected caress, but she opened for him without protest. Her hands buried themselves in his hair, running through the loose waves.

His mouth moved lower and she tensed. Glancing up, he saw the shock in her face. He held her gaze as he deliberately scooted lower on the bed. He lowered his head, but before he could taste her, she tried to slide out from under him.

Expecting such a reaction, he easily caught her hands with his. Pinning her legs open with his shoulders, he planted a soft kiss on the sweet curls protecting her most intimate flesh and looked up at her alarmed eyes. "Don't be shy with me, sweetheart. I'm your husband."

"It can't be normal to kiss me—*down there.*" She regarded him anxiously.

He knew better than to force her to submit to his desire. "I said you should tell me if you didn't like something I did in bed, and if you don't like this, I promise I'll stop." She relaxed immediately.

His thumbs rubbed her imprisoned hands, wanting to reassure her. "But it's only fair to try something before you condemn it. Count to thirty before you tell me to quit. Fair enough?"

She nodded hesitantly, and he gave her a smile. "Good. Start counting, then."

"One—"

Still holding her hands, he swept his tongue into the silken folds. He groaned as her salty taste filled his mouth. Starting at her tight opening he explored her thoroughly, dipping inside her, licking along each nether lip and up to the proud nubbin above. Her legs opened to offer more of herself to him and her hands now held his in a death grip.

All power of coherent speech left Diantha's mind at the first touch of his tongue on the most secret place of her body. Her breath hitched and she bit her lip to keep from crying out at the intense pleasure. She watched his dark head between her thighs, unable to believe what she was permitting him to do. As though he felt her gaze, he lifted his head to meet it with his own.

Her heart pounded. The impeccable aristocrat had disappeared, replaced by this feral man who awakened shameful, wonderful, primitive desires in her body.

"Scream for me, darling." He whispered the words before suckling on the bud where her body's pleasure centered. She tried to resist, but then the explosion hit. Losing all control, she cried his name as wave after wave of ecstasy thundered through her body.

No sooner had she caught her breath than he levered himself over her. Grasping her hips, he sheathed himself inside her with one deep thrust. Groaning, he repeated the motion again and again, in an ever-increasing tempo. Not wanting to lose him, she wrapped her legs around his waist.

That small move sent him over the edge. Bracing

himself on stiffened arms, he drove his thick staff into her repeatedly as his back arched and he threw his head to the rear. She joined his wordless moans at the glorious sensation and reveled in the release of his hot seed deep inside her.

Panting, he collapsed on top of her. As he pressed kisses onto her neck, her collarbone, her face, she stroked his sweat-slicked back until her own breath returned. "Will you stay with me tonight?"

Without a word, he moved onto his side and gathered her close. Her eyes drooped and she drifted off to sleep in his arms.

Chapter 10

At some point during the night, Diantha roused, vaguely aware of a sweet kiss and a tender whisper before Kieran left her bed. By the time Florette's entrance woke her up fully the next morning, the rumpled sheets on his side of the bed had grown cold.

"Good morning, milady. I trust you slept well."

As the maid opened the drapes to admit the morning light, the younger woman stretched her feet toward the bottom of the bed, seeking her nightgown. Brushing her foot against some lace, she grasped with her toes and stealthily bent her leg to bring it within reach of her hand.

"Very well indeed, thank you." Gripping the bed-clothes firmly around her naked body, she grabbed the cambric and pondered how to pull it over her head before she had to leave the bed. The mussed sheets proclaimed her husband's presence in her room last night as surely as if she shouted it from the rooftops, but protocol demanded that even married women maintain the polite fiction that they never indulged in conjugal romps.

The ever-tactful maid solved her dilemma. "I shall personally oversee the heating of milady's bathwater." A twinkle in her gray eyes belied the stiff formality of the words.

Lips quivering, Diantha nodded her head graciously. "Thank you, that would be most appreciated."

After their playacting, the maid pulled out a muslin bed jacket and placed it on the bed. Curtseying, she disclosed the information that the family ate breakfast in the north back parlor. "Chef says that the aunt orders that only milord's mother is permitted to take breakfast in her room, but that he awaits your directions."

She raised her eyebrows. "Convey my thanks to—?"

"MacAdam, milady." Florette grimaced. "A Scot, of all things. At least he studied in France."

When she finally located the north back parlor, she discovered both Uptons ensconced at the breakfast table. Barclay instantly rose and begged her to allow him to prepare a plate for her, while his mother delivered a look which conveyed a poor opinion of females who slept until the shocking hour of nine o'clock.

Diantha had given some thought to dealing with Kieran's aunt as she sat in her hip bath earlier. It would not do to divide the household into armed camps, but she had settled on a few small steps to start with.

"Good morning, Cousin. Good morning, Aunt." She ignored the indignant muttering from Iona's end of the breakfast table. Declining Barclay's offer of assistance, she strolled over to inspect the dishes on the sideboard.

Seeing the offerings, she understood the reason behind the family's choice of chef. Certainly the temperamental individuals who ruled her mother's kitchens would have resigned before preparing porridge with cream, bannocks, or venison pasty.

Her cousin by marriage pulled out a chair for her. "I heartily recommend the fried trout; it's fresh from our own loch. The venison is ours as well."

Odd that one who claimed to feel like a stranger here referred to each thing as *ours*. Making her selections, she moved to the table and smiled her thanks.

Kieran breezed into the room just then. Dressed in a riding habit, hair blown into waves, he exuded vitality. Watching his muscles bunch under the tight breeches, she swallowed.

Aunt Iona frowned. "I am quite sure we have sufficient servants to ring for a bath before coming to breakfast in all your dirt, Nephew."

He waved her objections aside. "I've eaten already, Aunt. I shall only have a cup of tea." Helping himself to tea, two rolls, and marmalade, he bent to kiss Diantha's cheek before seating himself. Barclay's eyebrows shot up to his hairline and Iona looked ill.

As he sipped his tea, his eyes twinkled at her over the rim of the cup. "What a delightful dress, my dear. You look every inch the lady of the manor—this morning." He lowered his voice on the last two words, conjuring a memory of just how unladylike she had appeared and sounded last night.

She darted a glare at him, then bent to her meal until the heat faded from her face and neck.

In a faintly disapproving tone, Barclay asked her unrepentant spouse where he had ridden. They fell into a discussion about estate problems, relieving her of the necessity of speaking.

When they concluded, Kieran turned to her. "Diantha, have you formulated any plans for the day yet?"

Her blushes under control, she placed her knife and fork on her plate. "I hoped you might be able to take me over the house today. I would enjoy a closer look at it."

His face clouded. "I'm so sorry; I have months of paperwork to catch up on in my study." A sharp sense of disappointment filled her. "I'd offer Barclay's services, but he's going to be working with me. However, I'm sure Aunt Iona will be able to answer any questions you have."

Her heart plummeted. The company of a woman who despised her would ruin any pleasure in examining her new home.

Iona dabbed at the corner of her mouth with her napkin. "I very much regret that my duties preclude jauntering all over the house. If you will excuse me, I must consult with the housekeeper and chef."

Diantha inhaled sharply. Iona had just confirmed that she had no intention of giving up her hold on Duncarie. By doing so in front of Kieran, her adversary had made it impossible for her to protest without looking like a petty child. However, the woman had left an opening, which she seized on.

"Then would you be so good as to inform the housekeeper to come to me at her convenience? I should at least like to know how to find my way around." Iona opened her mouth and shut it. Diantha gave her a smug smile; she had turned the tables on the older woman.

Kieran smiled and rose from the table. "An excellent notion. Send her to my mother's rooms, Aunt. I wish Diantha to meet her and I'm sure we shall still be there when you're finished."

Iona left the room in obvious disapproval.

As soon as the door closed behind them, Diantha swung to face her husband, eyes wide. "I'm not prepared—that is, I wasn't expecting to meet your mother so soon." She winced as his eyes chilled. "Forgive me, I do wish to meet her. I just didn't know it would be this morning. I gather she is feeling better?"

"She said she was when I sent a message this morning." He unexpectedly looked older than his twenty-nine years. "We shall see."

Barclay placed his napkin on the table beside his plate. "Kier, I know you're anxious to see her, but do be careful not to tire Aunt Alicia." He bowed slightly to Diantha. "If you wish, I could show you a little of the house while my cousin changes."

Disarmed by his diffident manner, she accepted. While not particularly knowledgeable about architecture, Barclay proved informative about the history of Duncarie House.

"This house was built after the son of the Rossburn killed at Culloden in 1746 got himself into King George II's good graces and got our land back. The old castle was razed as part of the English retributions, you know."

He slanted a glance at her. "A good many of the Highland families at the time called us traitors, but he was entitled to his position. And he proved a good landlord to his people, I suppose. He was popular at any rate."

They stood in the library, a room of warm oak paneling filled with light from floor to ceiling windows. Diantha all but salivated at the rows of books lining the walls, their spines adding a note of muted color to the atmosphere. In the distance, the glen of Duncarie stretched away beyond the glass panes.

Barclay beckoned her to the window. "Cariford is north. That's the one seaside village on our lands." He pointed over her shoulder. "This house was built with the earnings from kelp ash. During the wars with France, it sold for as much as twenty-two pounds a ton."

Diantha nodded as she looked over the expanse of ridges leading away from the house. She knew about the fishing ships her father was supplying in exchange for her marriage.

"The gallery is out here, you two."

They turned, Barclay dropping his arm to his side. Kieran stood holding the door open. He had combed his hair neatly into place, but a few damp strands still curled along the line of his collar. In a tailored black suit and his cravat knotted into an ascot, he looked every inch the handsome aristocrat.

Then his eyes met hers, brilliant aqua darkening as a wicked smile curved his lips. More like a wolf in lord's clothing, she thought, with an answering smile.

Remembering the kisses she had received the night before from that sensual mouth, she thought she just might have gotten the best of the bargain her father had struck.

"I shall wait for you in the office, then." They both started when Barclay spoke.

Her husband nodded, approaching Diantha as Barclay closed the door behind him. "What were you looking at?"

She spread her hands with a rueful smile. "I don't know. I see the estate, of course, but I haven't really *seen* it."

Staring out at the glen, he linked his fingers with hers. "Do you like it?"

Nonplussed, she cocked her head. "That's an awkward question. The estate comes with the marriage, just like—" She broke off before she went too far.

"Like me." Kieran finished the sentence in a flat voice. The truth behind their marriage hung between them.

Diantha's heart pounded, but she nodded. "I'm sorry. Doubtless you wanted a different answer."

A glint entered Kieran's eyes. "Perhaps I expected you to respond to me as enthusiastically as you did last night."

For the second time that morning, embarrassment scorched her face and neck. She stared at the hem of her gown until he lifted her chin with his fingers. His expression revealed nothing.

If she told him how her attachment to him grew with every passing day, he would ridicule her. She summoned up her most composed manner. "I fail to see why our duty to produce an heir cannot be pleasant for both of us."

He drew himself up and sucked in a breath. "Duty? Is that what made you cry my name out last night?"

Something snapped within her. He asked her to expose her emotions while he guarded his.

"My feelings have no place in this marriage and we both know it." She remained dry-eyed, but her voice shook with pent-up anger.

His fingertips brushed her jawline. "And yet you still respond to me—ardently." His voice vibrated along her nerves and her heart pounded.

"Yes." As mesmerized as a bird by a serpent, she raised herself on her tiptoes and touched the tiny cleft in his lower lip with her tongue.

Instantly Kieran gathered her close, a growl leaving his throat as he opened her mouth with his and kissed her deeply.

She shuddered at the contact. She should protest, but could not stop kissing him long enough to speak. When at last they paused, she could only close her eyes and mutter, "Why must you taste so good?"

At her words, he backed her against the side of a bookcase bordering the window. She gripped the tendrils at the back of his neck as his arms tightened around her. The edge of his teeth pulled gently at the skin at her jaw and her head tipped back to give him better access. Kieran wanted her too, and she reveled in the knowledge.

Their mouths gentled after a few moments and they broke the kiss. Diantha's pulse raced as he rested his forehead against hers. Beneath her hand, his chest rose and fell as he panted.

His breath warmed her ear. "I'm sorry. I didn't come here to pick a quarrel with you."

"Compared to my parents, this was barely a spat." Try as she might, she could not keep the bitterness out of her voice. She gave him a wry smile. "And it did end rather well."

He chuckled, but sobered the next instant. "I know we did not marry under auspicious circumstances." He paused and cleared his throat. "But you should not think your happiness is immaterial. This will be your home now, and I hope you like it."

Diantha could not seem to stay angry at the blasted man. "What I've seen of Duncarie is beautiful. I've never seen such wide stretches of land without buildings and roads. It's almost frightening to see that much emptiness." Her voice softened. "And yet it calls to me."

Wrapping his arms around her, he pulled her in front of him as they both stared out the window. "Aye, it does that." He rubbed his cheek against her hair as she leaned into the warmth of his body. "We'll ride the estate together, you and I, and you'll find it's anything but empty."

She chuckled. "You'll find that tedious, I fear. I can just about stay on a horse."

He stepped away and looked down at her. "You don't ride?" He gave a small laugh of surprise.

She shook her head. "One doesn't, really, in New York or Newport. Or in France."

He hugged her closer. "I'll have our head groom give you lessons. He taught me when I was a wee laddie. We can find a suitable horse for you in the stables. You're not afraid of them, are you?"

Her brow puckered. "No, but riding them is uncharted territory for me."

He had the impudence to wink at her. "Well, we found out last night how much you like doing new things."

A cough echoed in the high-ceilinged room. They broke apart to find a gray-haired man in a frock coat trying hard to repress a laugh as he watched them. Diantha wondered if she was doomed to spend the rest of her life in a state of acute embarrassment. At least this time a deep blush covered her husband's face as well.

"Your mother was wondering where you were, my lad. I said I'd hunt you down." His shoulders shook with a gust of laughter before he regained control of himself. "I shall go and tell her you were delayed."

Crimson-cheeked, Kieran thanked the man. "We shall be along directly." He turned to her. "My dear, this is Doctor Andrews, who treats my mother. Doctor, Lady Rossburn."

She cleared her throat. "How do you do, Doctor. I am so terribly sorry you had to witness, er, us."

The medical man bowed, lips quivering. "An excellent prognosis for a happy marriage, your ladyship." He nodded to her husband. "I shall inform your mother that you shall be with her in a few minutes." His chuckle hung in the air after he left them.

Having straightened their hair and adjusted their clothing, she and Kieran followed a hallway from the gallery to one outthrust wing of the house. She learned from him that the dowager baroness lived in a suite of rooms and almost never left them. "She suffers a great deal of pain from inflammation of the joints, as you'll see."

She touched his arm in sympathy, wishing she could do more to ease the sadness in his eyes. "I am so sorry."

They entered a sitting room swathed with shadows. Heavy draperies permitted only a few chinks of light in, and thick rugs muffled the sound of their footsteps. Several paintings hung on the walls, most depicting the sky-filled landscapes of Dutch painters.

A white-haired woman lay propped up on a chaise longue, her legs covered by a blanket. Pain had etched lines around her mouth, but she welcomed them with her son's smile. Next to the chaise, two empty chairs stood, angled so their occupants would face her.

She held out a misshapen hand to them. "Kier, my love! Can you forgive me for not coming downstairs yesterday?"

He stepped away from Diantha to cradle the gnarled fingers in his palms. "Of course I can, Mama. Aunt Iona told me you were having quite a difficult day." He seated himself on one of the chairs. "And I hope you aren't going to cause yourself more pain by seeing us today."

The Dowager Lady Rossburn smiled at his half-teasing, half-serious tone. "And since when am I dictated to by my own son, pray tell?" She turned to Diantha. "Now, introduce me to my new daughter."

Diantha suppressed a wince at the sight of the inflamed knuckles and nearly immobilized fingers. Having seen how her grandmother suffered from rheumatism in winter's cold and damp, Diantha could not imagine the pain this woman endured on a daily basis.

Nevertheless, his mother gave her a warm smile and bade her take the second chair. Summoning her maid, she ordered the curtains opened slightly to admit more light. "Much better. Now I can see both of you."

As they conversed, Diantha discovered that her mother-in-law showed no trace of Iona's hauteur. Relieved, she readily answered the questions put to her about her family, New York, and their wedding trip.

At one point, Lady Rossburn lay back against the pillows and sighed. "The thing I hate most about my wretched condition, after the pain, is being confined to these rooms." Seeing her son's stricken expression, she smiled. "I could not ask for better treatment, my love. But even the most comfortable cage is still a cage."

Eventually she showed signs of tiredness. They rose to their feet and Kieran bent forward to kiss her cheek.

She gestured to Diantha. "You as well, my dear. I am delighted that my laddie married such a charming young lady."

Taken aback, she sought for an answer to that comment. "You're very kind, I'm sure."

"Now that my son is back, I want to see both of you as often as possible." Lady Rossburn rubbed her elbow absently. Diantha guessed that joint pained her as well. "Together or apart."

She smiled down at the invalid. "I should like to visit you as often as you wish, your ladyship."

Her husband spoke at the same time. "I'm back

now, and shall come and see you every day if you like."

Looking from one to the other, she nodded. "I shall welcome your company." Her breath caught as she finished speaking, and Kieran instantly summoned her maid.

Leaving her to the ministrations of her servant, they stepped back out into the hallway. He paused, closing his eyes and breathing deeply.

Diantha looked at him in concern. When he opened his eyes again, they glittered with unshed tears. Instinctively she moved to embrace him, but he stepped away. She dropped her arms, hurt rising in her own throat.

He swallowed. "She wasn't always like that. When I was a boy she loved to ride and dance. She and my father would visit tenants together, and host house parties every fall." He shrugged. "Then she started complaining of aches here and there. It only got worse."

"She's very brave." Diantha did not know what else to say.

He nodded, a smile of infinite sadness flitting across his face. "I wish to God she didn't have to be. You will go see her, as she asked?"

"Indeed I will!" Afraid he would reject her again, she curled her fingers into fists to resist touching him. "I liked her very much."

Before he could say anything, the housekeeper sailed into the hall, albeit with thinned lips and snapping eyes. "I am Mrs. Menzies. Her ladyship will allow me to show Lady Rossburn the house."

Ignoring her, Kieran lifted one of Diantha's hands to his lips. "Thank you."

* * *

The next weeks settled into a regular pattern as she adjusted to her new home. She woke up alone each morning, whether Kieran had visited her bed the night before or not.

Breakfasts usually involved veiled sparring with Aunt Iona, although she slowly gained ground within the household. The butler, Jarrard, most of the footmen, and the lower housemaids gave her little difficulty when she issued orders.

Mrs. Menzies, however, invariably replied with, "I would like to consult Lady William." The upper maids, as resistant as she to any change, followed her lead.

MacAdam, exercising the tyranny accorded a skilled chef, simply informed Kieran's aunt that he would consult with young Lady Rossburn about the menus. Even Iona did not dare risk losing him.

She fell into the habit of taking tea with her mother-in-law on the days when the older woman enjoyed sufficient health to see visitors. Even when pain prevented the old woman from rising from her bed, Diantha would stop and sit by her.

Her maid, Poole, welcomed these visits. "You do cheer her up, my lady. The dowager baroness calls you a ray of sunshine." She set a tea service down so that Diantha could pour.

She turned to her mother-in-law, aghast. "You do not refer to me by such a namby-pamby term, ma'am!"

Quiet chuckles shook the fragile frame. "I could promise not to do so in the future!" Kieran's impish smile broke out across her face at Diantha's disgust, and the two women burst out laughing.

A quick knock came on the door, followed by her husband's voice. "What mischief are you two up to now?" Poole opened the door at once.

His teasing glance took in his mother and the teacup that Diantha helped her to hold. "Allow me."

As he assisted his mother to drink her tea, Diantha watched him. The same hands that could control a hunter eager to gallop out of the stable yard now delicately helped an old woman ease a porcelain cup to her lips. And she knew only too well the pleasure they could wring from her body.

The three of them enjoyed nearly an hour of conversation before Lady Rossburn's pain required her to rest.

They walked back to their rooms to change for dinner in silence. Only then did he take her hand to brush his lips along her knuckles. "Doctor Andrews tells me my mother is in better spirits these days. Thank you."

With those words he disappeared into his room. Diantha stared after him until Florette hurried her inside to change.

One evening, Kieran announced that her riding lessons would start the following morning.

Torn between pleasure at his attentiveness and dismay, Diantha raised her one solid objection. "I don't have a riding habit."

"Really, Nephew! You cannot expect a female to drop everything on one of your whims. We shall have to alter one of mine." Thanks trembled on

Diantha's lips until Iona sniffed. "Of course, if you'd married a female of your own class, none of this would be necessary."

She subsided under Kieran's scowl, but even Barclay looked concerned at this gap in her education. Guessing that Iona would have more barbs to deliver after they withdrew, Diantha signaled a footman. "I believe I shall have a second glass of wine this evening, thank you."

Nevertheless, two days later she emerged from her room attired in an out-of-date riding habit hastily cut down by Florette. Trying to manage the trailing skirt without dropping her riding crop, she walked right into her waiting husband.

"Oof! For a little thing you have a great deal of force." He stooped to pick up the crop from the floor where she'd dropped it. He was dressed for riding as well.

Diantha beamed at him. "You're going to come with me? I am so relieved!"

Kieran cleared his throat, looking slightly uncomfortable. "I thought I would at least see you out to the stables."

She took his arm. "Please promise me you won't laugh."

"I promise."

In the stable yard, he led her up to a burly middle-aged man engaged in chewing out a young groom. She suspected it was just as well the man's thick burr and Scots dialect precluded her from understanding most of his words.

Kieran let the man rant until he paused for breath. "Archie! I have your new pupil here. Diantha, allow me to present Archie Green, one of our mainstays at Duncarie."

She observed the leathery Scot as he was introduced. Grizzled waves of red hair stood in disarray above a pair of blue eyes that looked innocent until he scrutinized her for several moments in complete silence.

"Gie me your hands, then."

Taken aback, Diantha glanced at her husband, then back at the servant. "I beg your pardon?"

He blew an exasperated breath. "Your hands, woman. Let me see them!"

Another glance at Kieran revealed him biting his lip and looking straight ahead. Hesitantly she extended her gloved hands. His callused palms enveloped them in a disconcerting tactile inspection.

Snatching them away, she glared at both men before addressing Green. "What are you doing?"

"How else am I supposed to know how light or heavy your hand is?" He indicated a saddled dapple-gray horse tethered to the stable wall. "You dinna think I'm going to risk that poor animal's mouth with a daftie who canna ride?"

She turned to her husband. "What did he say?"

He struggled to keep his face straight. "He doesn't want you to hurt the horse." A grin broke out despite his efforts. "So, Archie. What's the verdict?"

The middle-aged man shrugged. "No' bad. She'll do well enough for Dancer."

Her husband choked back a laugh as she whirled to face him. Her heart lurched. He had never looked so handsome as he did this instant, giving her a lopsided grin in the middle of a stable yard.

"Well enough, then. I'll leave you to your lessons, wife."

In her dismay, she actually clutched his arm before she realized how childish the action was. She released him. "I shall be sorry not to have your company."

Kieran caught her fingers and gently squeezed them. "I am sorry, but I have some business to tend to on the other side of the estate."

His face softened and he lifted her hand to brush a kiss across her knuckles. Diantha's toes curled in her boots. "No need to worry. Archie will keep you safe till I collect you."

With that, he strolled over to where his chestnut stallion attempted to escape from a harassed groom. Gathering the reins, he easily mounted the horse and cantered out of the yard.

Diantha watched him with a sinking heart. He had no trouble leaving her behind.

"Well? Are ye comin' or no'?" The impatient question interrupted her musing. She nodded to Archie and followed him toward the dapple-gray.

Given the man's horse-centered view of the world, she approached her lesson with trepidation, but her fears soon evaporated. Once he finished tsking over the shame of a mistress of Duncarie who couldn't ride, he set about showing her the basics with great patience.

He did immediately correct her when she asked how long he had worked as a groom. "I am a *ghillie*, your ladyship. Grooms only work in the stable, but I am responsible for goings-on all over Rossburn lands." She cocked her head and he grinned up at her as he led the horse toward a paddock. "Tha' means I let his lordship know if we need to do a burn on the moor so grouse can feed, or if there's poachers about. Or when Mr. Barclay is tryin' to do somethin' daft."

"So you answer directly to Lord Rossburn? How is it you're teaching me to ride, then?"

"A ghillie is the laird's to command. If he says to carry him across a wee bog so his soles dinna get damp, the ghillie does it."

"How revolting! Surely Lord Rossburn would never demean someone so."

Archie chuckled. "Weel, if it came to tha', I might tell Master Kieran to walk on his own legs."

He lifted his chin. "I taught him to ride when he was a laddie, for the old laird said no one on the estate had my touch wi' the beasties." He stroked Dancer's wither with an affectionate smile. "So o' course the young laird willna trust anyone but me to teach you. Now sit up straight. You're a lady, no' a sack o' tatties."

As soon as they reached the open road, Kieran gave the horse its head. Mefisto broke into a gallop. Only a few clouds scudded across the sky and the passing air carried the scent of sun-warmed juniper. Kieran tried to savor the pleasure of riding his lands after months away.

Unfortunately the hurt expression on Diantha's face kept rising in his mind's eye. He admitted to himself that part of the reason for abandoning her to Archie's brusque, if thorough, tutelage stemmed from her earlier words in the library.

They still stung. Diantha accepted him in her bed out of mere *duty*?

He had always attracted women easily. Even the most censorious dowagers simpered and preened under his coaxing. Matrons and maidens alike batted their eyelashes or attempted their wittiest sallies when he danced with them.

In return for the pleasure his lovers gave him, he was generous—in bed, at any rate. His deepest emotions he kept off limits to outsiders, of course.

Diantha presented a conundrum. Unlike a mistress, he could not dispense with her presence when his interest in her waned. And he refused to countenance his wife giving herself to another man. The image of her supple curves stretched out on another man's bed arose.

Mefisto broke stride unexpectedly. He realized he had gripped the reins so tightly that the horse tossed his head in annoyance.

It dawned on him that he had no wish for another woman yet, either. In view of his father's habits, the knowledge relieved him, but that did not solve his dilemma.

The one woman he could not charm was his own wife.

Scowling, he turned the horse onto a trail leading to an upland moor. His steward, Johnston, and Archie had both suggested it for the estate's sheep. The herd's normal pasture remained a quagmire after heavy spring rains. In an effort to preserve the animals and their valuable wool, Barclay had ordered them into the nearest tenant's field. Understandably, the cottar resented the loss of his only arable land, and the sheep had to be moved again.

Kieran slowed Mefisto to a walk and examined the moor as he neared it. The sheep could not stray far, for the only access was across a wooden bridge that spanned a narrow ravine. Heavy growth covered the pasture and an outcrop of rock at the far end might provide a sheltered spot for a shepherd's hut.

He urged his mount forward. No sooner did Mefisto's front hooves strike the planks than the animal shied back. Kieran pressed his knees into the rigid sides, but save for breathing, the animal might have been stone.

"What's gotten into you?" He dismounted and gathered the reins. After a firm tug, the horse followed on stiff legs, apparently satisfied to let the human go first.

The weathered timbers creaked under Kieran's feet, but that did not surprise him. It took some cajoling before Mefisto placed one hoof gingerly on the span, then another.

A sharp crack vibrated up through Kieran's boots, and then the entire framework tipped down toward the bottom many feet below. Had he not grasped the horse's reins, he would have followed. Fortunately, Mefisto danced back again and Kieran suffered nothing more than a few scrapes as the beast inadvertently dragged him to safety.

He struggled to a sitting position and remained there for several moments to catch his breath. He had released the horse, who now regarded him from several paces away. "Yes, I know, you told me so." The horse snorted and pulled up a mouthful of coarse grass from the side of the road.

As soon as his heartbeat slowed to something resembling normal, Kieran stood and peered down at the wreckage. He guessed the fall would have been no more than twenty-five feet. It might not have killed him.

But it probably would have. His knees did wobble slightly as he turned back to the horse.

Mefisto lifted his head. Foam still dripped from his mouth, streaked with pink. Kieran's weight must have cut the tender flesh. Worse, the beast held a hind hoof delicately off the ground as though afraid to step on it.

Running a hand over the back of the leg, Kieran found a hot, swollen area that he feared might be a severe tear. The animal flinched away with a whinny.

"Poor boy, you didn't deserve that, did you." He sighed as he led the limping horse back the way they had come. "Come on, then. It's a long walk home."

Archie assisted Diantha down from the saddle. "I've seen worse. Be back here in the morn, ten sharp." He tugged his forelock and winked. "Wi' some work, ye'll make a grand horsewoman."

As he led Dancer away, Diantha chuckled. She lingered in the stable yard, hoping Kieran would return as he had said. He might enjoy the ghillie's assessment of her skills. She inhaled air redolent of horse, and found she rather liked it. Her mother would be horrified if she ever found out, of course.

Imagining her maternal parent's disapproval, Diantha smiled broadly and inhaled again. She decided to ride as often as she could.

However, she could not loiter about the stables all morning. Conscious of a disconcerting pang that her husband had not returned, she slipped back into the house to change.

After a virtuous, if dull, hour in her boudoir reviewing the linen count, Diantha discovered that Kieran had not shown up for luncheon. Knowing he planned to meet with the steward, she finally remarked on his absence over the fruit course.

"A husband need not account for his whereabouts to his wife." Iona helped herself to a few sections of orange with a pair of tiny tongs.

Barclay's eyebrows drew together as he peeled a peach. "That's odd, he seldom misses an appointment. I expect he's quite safe, Cousin, but I might send out a few men on his route if he doesn't return in the next hour or two."

Diantha told herself to be satisfied with that. She distracted herself after the meal by hunting for the plans to Duncarie House in the library. However, even the discovery of a portfolio of original drawings and notes failed to hold her attention for long. Tucking it under her arm, she returned to her room.

As she placed the sheets on her writing desk, the soft sound of footsteps on carpet came from Kieran's bedchamber. With a sense of relief, she approached the door leading to it.

She took a breath before turning the handle, for she had never before set foot in what she considered his domain. Nonsense, she told herself. She was Kieran's wife, for heaven's sake! To her disappointment, she found only his valet.

Davison bowed, then placed a pile of perfectly folded shirts into a wardrobe. "Good day, my lady. I fear his lordship has not returned yet."

"I thought I heard him, forgive my mistake."

"I'm sure he will be back shortly." With another bow, he departed, shutting the door behind him.

Diantha circled the room. The predominant color was deep green, relieved from becoming oppressive by warm wood paneling and plenty of light. Simple damask panels, not ornate fringed swags, hung in front of the floor to ceiling windows.

She paused before Kieran's dressing table. A shaving mug and brush stand occupied a tray on one corner, with a razor half-open beside it. She guessed a wooden box held the few pieces of jewelry he habitually wore.

A silver-framed daguerreotype caught her attention. It showed Kieran's mother sitting next to a handsome man whose arm stretched behind her shoulders. She recognized Kieran's father from a portrait in the gallery. Diantha raised her eyebrows. Her parents had never taken so casual a pose, even for private family portraits.

A small child with dark curls and his father's eyes sat between them, gazing solemnly at the camera. She couldn't help but smile. Even at that age, Kieran possessed a piercing stare. The heads tilted toward one another and the hands joined as the parents held their son told of a loving family.

The Rossburns must have always demonstrated a great deal of physical affection. Diantha traced the protective circle their arms made around Kieran. Only Granny had hugged her with any regularity.

Her taffeta skirts rustled softly as she picked up the frame and moved toward the windows to examine it more closely.

She paused before the foot of the bed, an enormous four-poster covered with a small ocean of deep

green damask, and tilted the picture into the light.
She guessed Kieran must have been around five or
six. Even then, the dimple in his chin showed clearly.
He had not developed his father's patrician profile
yet, and black curls surrounded his young face.

The image of cuddling a baby with those same
dark curls arose and her heart squeezed. One of
the few aspects of marriage she had looked forward
to was a child of her own to cherish. Distressingly,
her courses continued to appear each month without fail.

"What the devil are you doing here?"

She started and gripped a bedpost for support.
Her full-grown, very bedraggled husband stood on
the threshold, one hand on the door handle. And
he did not look pleased to see her.

Kieran's arms ached from being hauled up the
old bridge by his horse. Various body parts twinged
and throbbed. He still grappled with the fact that
he had damn near died earlier. And he had missed
luncheon. He wanted nothing more than to retreat to the privacy of his chamber with food, a hot
bath, and a change of clothing.

At the sight of his wife framed by the bedposts,
looking rather delectable in a gown of rich blue, it
did occur to him that the food might wait. Then his
gaze fell on the object in her hand.

"Kieran, what happened to you?"

He swung the door closed behind him and advanced. She cringed away, ending up nearly draped
across his coverlet.

He ignored the tempting sight to snatch the

frame out of her hand. "How dare you sneak among my belongings? I'm not your brothers to steal volumes of Shakespeare from!"

She sat up, her eyes narrowed. "I was doing nothing of the sort. You're acting as if I went through your private papers." She emitted a small gasp. "And how do you know about the books?"

Kieran realized she must not remember their conversation the night before their wedding, but he was in no mood for amusement. "You were still in my bedchamber, handling my things." He held up the daguerreotype.

By now Diantha had found her feet. His normally timid wife approached him until her nose nearly touched his chest. "I'll thank you to remember that I've already touched some exceedingly private *things* of yours." She tipped her head back, two bright pink flags of anger on her cheeks. "And you liked it. A great deal!"

Her finger jabbed his solar plexus. "You certainly don't have the least qualm about coming into my room whenever you please."

Her wrath startled him enough that he backed up a step in his turn. "That is entirely different!" He floundered for a reason to uphold a statement even he found ridiculous. "I don't go rummaging through your possessions," he said with a sense of triumph.

She sniffed. "No, you just avail yourself of my body whenever you feel like it." Her pretty face settled into a scowl. "And I was not rummaging. I thought I heard you, and came in because I foolishly thought you might be interested in hearing about my riding lesson."

She indicated the daguerreotype he still held.

"I committed the cardinal sin of admiring your family."

The scrolled silver edges bit into his palm. "Your approbation is noted." He did not quite eliminate the anger from his voice. "Appearance does not always match reality, however." *Why in God's name had he said that? The morning's events must have rattled him more than he thought.*

Diantha still regarded him, hurt in her eyes, for the second time that day. He wished he could confide in her, but his wife was the last person in the world he should explain his feelings to.

"If you will excuse me, I have some things to attend to." Even to his ears, the words sounded priggish.

She stiffened. "Indeed, I haven't the remotest desire to disturb you further." She marched to the door separating their rooms. "Rest assured, I will never disturb the sacred precincts of your bed-chamber again without an invitation."

Opening it wide, she looked at him over her shoulder. "I suppose it's too much to expect you to offer me the same courtesy." She strode through the doorway, slamming the door hard enough to rattle the pictures on either side of it.

Kieran stared after her for several heartbeats. Finally, he returned the portrait to its resting place. He touched the glass cover. Had his father started his chronic womanizing when it had been taken? His mother looked cheerful, as she usually had before pain became a part of her every breath. Perhaps in those days, she had not known about his father's secret life, either.

Kieran discovered at tea that he had worse problems than painful memories. Diantha did prepare a cup for him, but responded to his request for additional lemon by spearing several slices with her fork and depositing them with a loud clink into the porcelain shell. He responded with his best outraged glare, but was forced to direct it at the back of her head as she conversed with Barclay and Iona.

The situation did not improve by dinner. She addressed him when spoken to, although in tones of arctic civility. Thoroughly irritated by the time he retired, he slid into his robe and marched into her room, determined to settle the quarrel. As he hoped, she was still awake, sitting up in bed to read.

At his entrance, she straightened up and squared her shoulders. Laying the book aside, her gaze swept over him. "To what do I owe the honor of this visit?"

Used to lovers who resorted to tears and shouting when angry, Diantha's glacial demeanor gave him several ideas on how to proceed. He took several steps into the room, prepared to charm her. "I believe we should try to kiss and make up, my dear."

Her gaze turned to blue steel. "You're certainly strong enough to force me, but I shall not accept your attentions willingly."

Fury almost choked him. "I have never forced a woman in my life. And I am not about to start now." He turned on his heel and left. As he shut the door behind him he realized his wife had the power to wound him.

* * *

Diantha hugged her knees, heart pounding. She'd never successfully stood up to anyone before. She stared at the door connecting their chambers for some time, gnawing her lower lip and wondering what she should do next. She should apologize for implying he would attack her. He always treated her with tenderness, even affection, in bed. In truth, she loved the way he made her feel.

She brought herself up short. She already found herself far too attracted to Kieran. If she gave him her heart, he'd smash it into smithereens.

No, he could not toss her out of his room while expecting to enter hers anytime he wanted. She refused to apologize before tomorrow.

The following morning, however, Kieran shut himself into his office with the steward. He appeared only briefly at lunch and coldly declined her request for a moment of his time. Diantha congratulated herself on not giving in to such an unreasonable man and sailed off to the morning room to attend to the correspondence she had neglected for that day's riding lesson.

The appearance of a footman two hours later, bearing a telegram on a salver, sent all worries of whether she and Kieran would ever make up out of her head. She accepted the envelope and nodded to dismiss him.

Once alone, Diantha tore it open with shaky fingers and read the contents. Her face went numb as the blood drained from it. Wishing she was the type of female who kept a vinaigrette by her side, she read the message again.

After she patted the sheen of cold sweat off her forehead and took several deep breaths, she arose and made her way on rubbery knees to Kieran's office in the opposite wing. Grasping the telegram, she knocked on the door.

"I am very sorry for interrupting you, Kieran, but I must speak with you. At once."

"Come in." Kieran stood as she entered, then seated himself behind an ornate desk. Bookshelves lined the walls, filled with narrow ledgers of varying colors. The smell of leather mingled with that of musty paper despite the multipaned window propped open behind him.

"Yes?" His voice sounded as though he wished her to conduct her business and disappear. Diantha swallowed and held out the crumpled yellow sheet.

As soon as he saw it, he came around the desk. With an arm around her shoulders, he guided her into a chair. "My dear, what is it? Has something happened to your grandmother?" He knelt in front of her, enfolding her hands in his. "Tell me what's wrong."

She searched for a way to break the news gently, then gave up. "My parents are coming."

Chapter 11

Given what he'd learned of his in-laws during his betrothal, this information did not surprise Kieran. While he hardly fancied close proximity to them, he did not share the apprehension that radiated from his wife. Her implication of the previous night still rankled, but her trembling lips undid him.

He tucked a wayward brown tendril behind her ear, allowing his fingertips to linger on its softness. "It won't be that bad."

"'Won't be that bad?'" Her eyes changed from fearful to furious and she shoved his shoulder so hard he nearly fell backward. "You've never had to live with them!"

He scrambled to his feet, aware of how undignified he must look, but Diantha did not appear to notice. He stepped back as she stood and paced across the room.

"This is nothing but an inspection tour." She crossed back to him, still clutching the telegram. "And they're all coming! My parents, my brothers, even Granny."

Kieran plucked the wadded sheet from her hand and smoothed it out. He frowned as he read the long and sharply worded message. "You'll enjoy seeing your grandmother again, surely?"

"Yes, of course." She sighed. "But what will I do with the rest of them?"

He shrugged. "I suppose I'll take your father and brothers in hand. They'll be here when grouse shooting starts."

Diantha gazed up at him, eyebrows raised. "You'll help? Truly?"

"Of course I'll help. What kind of bounder do you think I am?" His lip curled. "Oh, wait! You did make that clear last evening."

She cringed. "I'm sorry. Your offer is especially kind in light of my remark last evening. It was un-called for. You've always treated me with the utmost consideration." A dry note entered her voice. "In the bedroom, at any rate."

He crossed his arms. "I beg your pardon, but I was unaware of mistreating you anywhere else. I am sorry, Diantha, but this is my home and I am enti-tled to some privacy."

She turned away from him and walked over to the bookshelves. Staring at them as if they fasci-nated her, she said, "And I am not? I suggest you do not plan to come to my room the next time you want a—a tumble. This is supposedly my home, too." He could barely hear the choked-out words.

"You've never complained of my touch." Following her, he ran his palm over the warm column of her neck. "And I think you know that you please me."

She shivered, then jerked away. "That is irrelevant!

I am reasonably sure we would enjoy conjugal relations in your bed as much as we do in mine."

A laugh escaped him at the absurd remark. She glared at him over her shoulder, then bit her lip in a not entirely successful attempt to repress a smile.

Relieved that the tension between them had eased, he leaned against the shelves. "This is not directed at you personally, Diantha. My room is off-limits to everyone in the house but my valet. It was during my father's time as well."

She faced him fully. "I find that difficult to believe. Your mother always speaks of him with great tenderness. I doubt she'd do so had he fenced himself off from her."

"It's for the best." Kieran retreated to his desk and stared down at the worn leather surface. "She did love him, and I think he cared for her in the beginning. But later—it was exceedingly painful to watch." He struggled, then said what he had to. "It would be best if we avoided that mistake."

He looked up, half expecting to see tears after his harsh words. "I'm sorry."

She returned his regard, her expression unreadable. "Don't be. The one thing I learned from my family is that a person cannot control who they love, or force someone to love them back. Perhaps you're right. We should not become overly attached to one another."

Instead of relief, her words triggered an inexplicable sense of loss. "We could at least try to remain cordial with one another."

A bleak smile twisted her lips. "Given your continued interest in my bed, that would be preferable. And we still have my family to deal with."

He invited her to a chair, then seated himself. "I wonder if we should not seek safety in numbers. We could invite some of my Rossburn relations to join us while they visit. You'd need to meet them anyway."

She tilted her head, considering his suggestion. "I think that might work."

They brought up the impending visit over tea. To Kieran's surprise, Iona protested even a small house party.

"Your first social event of this sort should mitigate concerns about the family's current connections, not increase them."

Seeing Diantha's murderous expression, he rose to his feet. His father had always advised against dictatorial behavior, but he doubted anything less would quiet his aunt. "I can hardly tell the Quinns to stay away at this point. Their telegram announced their arrival in ten days."

Lounging in a wing chair near the fireplace, Barclay raised his eyebrows nearly to his hairline. "They invited themselves? I say, that's rag-mannered. Tell them we're not at home."

"We could, but I assure you they would ignore the message." Diantha sat stiffly and held her untouched tea in her lap, but spoke calmly.

Kieran caught her eye and nodded his approval. "Despite the short notice, I think some of our nearby relations might accept an invitation."

Iona looked at them askance. "By now they will have either accepted invitations or issued their own. Unless you plan to inflict the likes of Cousin Francesca upon us." She shuddered.

"That archwife!" Barclay winced. "I beg you,

spare us." He glanced at Diantha. "Her mother was a Rossburn, and her own birth is impeccable, but she made a horrible *mésalliance*. Her husband is dead and can no longer trouble us, but she remains an embarrassment."

"I was always quite fond of Francie, and yes, I should like to invite her." Kieran glared at his relatives. "I trust there will be no further comments."

Neither Barclay nor Iona spoke for a moment. Then the latter set her cup down with an emphatic clink. "I have just recalled that I have some correspondence which needs to be completed before dinner. Please be so good as to excuse me." Rising, she sailed out of the room, closing the door behind her with a bang.

Barclay cleared his throat. "I don't think you're going to prevail on her to provide much assistance. I know that stubborn expression on her face." His voice held barely suppressed triumph.

Diantha finally took a sip of her tea. "That hardly matters. I should certainly be able to plan a small house party."

Barclay stared at her. Kieran said nothing, but he harbored doubts as well.

He need not have worried. Immediately after breakfast the next morning, Diantha disappeared into the morning room with MacAdam and Jarrard, emerging only to ask Kieran for the directions of those persons he wished to invite.

Ten days later, he and Diantha stood at the top of the steps and watched three traveling carriages clatter into the main courtyard. A truce had developed between them, but she remained distant. He had gone to her bed once in the days since their conversation in his office, but even while her physical reaction sated him, she seemed to hold part of herself back even as she moaned in pleasure.

He attempted to flirt with her in the hope of coaxing out her impish sense of humor, but she answered his teasing with composed civility.

He glanced down at her. Just now she looked pale and tense, despite her daily riding lessons. And she'd barely touched her meals for the last few days. He stroked her arm. "I'm sure everything will go well."

She responded only with a tight smile and returned her attention to the approaching vehicles.

The servants' coach, encumbered with luggage, swept around the house toward the stables. The other two rolled to a stop at the bottom of the broad steps. The first disgorged Diantha's father and brothers, while footmen assisted her mother and grandmother out of the other.

"Papa, James, Thomas—how agreeable to see you again." Diantha held out her hands as her brothers ascended the steps.

Thomas turned to take in the valley's expanse. Late afternoon sunlight and shadows chased each other across fields and hills. Crofters made their way along the road to their homes. The cottages stood out in the distance as the light touched their whitewashed stone.

"I do believe we've discovered the edge of the world, James."

His brother, who had not gotten any thinner in the last months, puffed up behind him. "Never seen so much empty space. However do you occupy yourself, Rossburn?" He gave Diantha's outstretched hand a perfunctory peck.

"Should have told us to bring more than a paltry newspaper to read on the way." Mr. Quinn brushed past his daughter. "My regards, Rossburn. I take it refreshments are inside?"

Appalled, Kieran gave a curt nod. "Tea awaits us in the drawing room."

Diantha stepped forward. "We also have coffee if you prefer, along with scones and sandwiches."

"Mouse food." Her father grumbled under his breath as he waited for his wife. She, engulfed in an ecru serge mantle, bustled up the steps and scrutinized Duncarie's classical façade. "I expected a lord's house to be more impressive."

Before Kieran could say a word, she grasped Diantha's shoulders and held her at arm's length. "Let me see you." Her lips pursed. "You should be increasing by now."

Diantha's face turned bright red and her hands fluttered defensively to her still slender midriff. Kieran placed an arm around her waist.

"As my wife's health is excellent, I am not overly concerned about our immediate prospects for a family."

Mrs. Quinn gasped at his hostile tone.

Diantha gave him a brittle smile. "Would you be so good as to assist my grandmother, dear? I shall escort the others inside."

He stared after them as Mr. and Mrs. Quinn entered the house without an embrace or an affectionate word for their only daughter.

Mrs. Helford did not display her usual vigor as

she climbed the steps with the aid of a footman and a silver-headed cane. Going to her side, Kieran dismissed the servant and offered his arm.

The twinkle in her eyes remained undimmed. "I never refuse the chance to walk with a handsome young man."

He chuckled. Here was one in-law he sincerely welcomed. "We shall do everything in our power to make you comfortable, ma'am."

In the drawing room, Kieran introduced the elderly woman and helped her to a comfortable chair. His father-in-law had already buried himself in a periodical, while Mrs. Quinn and Iona had already locked horns.

"Here is your tea, Kieran." Iona handed him a porcelain cup and saucer. "You're just in time to hear our guest expound upon several unusual theories of interior decoration."

Amalthea nibbled on a watercress sandwich. "Having lived in a backwater for several years, one can hardly expect Lady William to be *au courant* with the most fashionable styles."

"Fortunately, persons of quality have no need to follow the whims of the lower classes." She offered a small plate to her newfound adversary. "Scone?"

Seated on a sofa nearby, Diantha focused her gaze on the floor, just as she had during their betrothal. His heart sank. Hoping to ease her discomfort, Kieran took the seat next to her. She said nothing, but edged infinitesimally closer to him.

Strolling toward the gallery before dinner, Diantha gave thanks that no one else would arrive before the following afternoon. Kieran's refusal to accept anything but physical intimacy in their marriage devastated her, and she had thrown herself into the house party preparations as a way to numb her aching heart.

Her anger at her husband had dissipated. The tortured expression on his face when he had apologized for not wanting an emotional attachment between them still haunted her. She wished that she knew how to reach him.

He had relaxed in her company since then, even asking to join her in bed one night. Horrified by the realization that she craved his touch like an opium-eater's desire for his drug, she had tried to detach her feelings from their coupling. Although her climax left her limp and breathless, the experience ultimately lacked the intensity she yearned for.

Now, with nothing more to plan and in the face of her family's usual indifference, she needed a respite to gain control over her jumbled emotions.

She found everyone else already gathered in the long room. Abashed at her tardiness, she stammered an apology.

Kieran, with the rest of the men, had risen to his feet as she entered. Now he came toward her. "Your regrets are unfounded, my dear. We have several minutes before dinner. Your family has asked what activities are devised for their visit. As the one who took charge, you are entitled to their thanks."

Some of the tension across her shoulders eased at the approval in his voice. He had shown no rancor since their harrowing conversation ten days ago. Just the opposite, he treated her with a cordiality that their relationship had previously lacked.

He just couldn't—or didn't want to—give her what she wanted most.

Meanwhile her mother regarded her with a furrowed brow. "That gown isn't from your trousseau."

Diantha groaned inwardly. She had selected the ensemble of bright blue sarcenet and taffeta because the color cheered her up. Trimmed with black lace instead of the predictable white or pink, it also helped her feel pretty and elegant.

"I purchased it from Monsieur Worth during our stay in Paris." As things stood with Kieran, she could not bring herself to utter the word *honeymoon*.

Mama sniffed. "Blue is so insipid."

"Monsieur Worth selected it for me." Diantha's bland comment spiked her mother's guns until dinner was underway. Mrs. Quinn eventually rallied, however, and addressed Kieran over the entrees.

"Mr. Quinn and I were surprised, to say the least, when we arrived in London only to find you had left weeks before the Season ended." She accepted a portion of the chicken offered to her, then peered at it suspiciously. "Er, what might this be?"

"Chicken stovie." Diantha and MacAdam had included at least one traditional Scottish dish in each dinner menu. She took a bite of parsley-covered potato.

At her right, her father sampled some from his plate. "Very nice. I wouldn't mind having this at home."

"Mr. Quinn, it contains entire slices of onions." Her mother ate a morsel of chicken after examining it for any trace of the dreaded vegetable. Then she returned her attention to Kieran.

"I fear my digression interrupted you, dear Lord Rossburn. I suppose you have an explanation for leaving the gaieties of the Season before it ended."

"No." He regarded her with half-closed eyes. "Why would I need one?"

"We expected to spend at least part of the Season with our daughter during her first months as a peeress."

Diantha's hand clenched around her fork. Her parents had evidently not milked enough attention from the marriage they had engineered.

"After months of being away from my home, London held little interest for me." Kieran drawled the words with every evidence of boredom.

Papa harrumphed. "And what about our daughter, sir? As her parents, we are entitled to her company when we want it."

"Ah, but the law gave that privilege to me upon my marriage."

Livid at being argued over like a parcel, Diantha confined most of her conversation for the rest of the evening to Barclay.

Her sense of ill-use lasted to the next day. The weather did not help, turning to a chill mist that veiled the distant hills. She ordered a fire built in the winter salon, a comfortable room lined with golden oak. Iona grumbled about lowered standards at Duncarie, but wasted no time availing herself of a seat near the fire. Granny had already settled into a wing chair opposite with an old-fashioned lapdesk.

Kieran entered shortly afterward. "Jarrard said

everyone had gathered here. A capital idea on such a *dreich* day."

"If that means dismal, yes, I thought it would be cheerier to welcome people here." Diantha did not look up from her needlepoint.

Her brothers, playing a listless game of backgammon in the corner, greeted him more enthusiastically.

"I say, old boy!" Thomas's poor imitation of a British accent grated on her ears. "Rotten weather today, isn't it? I hoped to go out for a day's shooting. Maybe we'll have better luck tomorrow."

"Grouse season commences on August twelfth." Kieran smiled, but his voice brooked no argument.

Thomas chuckled. "What's a day or five early matter when you're the landowner? It's not as though anyone is going to turn you in."

Barclay entered in time to hear both men. "Shooting before the twelfth is out of the question. It's not done." He sauntered over to the table at Diantha's elbow and picked up a book. As he sat down across from her, he mouthed "my sympathies." She bent farther over her canvas so no one would see her struggle not to laugh.

Kieran overrode her brother's protest. "I fear the matter is closed."

As Papa's favorite, Tom normally got what he wanted after a minimum of teasing. She would have to watch his mood now, for he often lost his temper when balked.

Kieran frowned as his glance fell on Barclay in the chair nearest to Diantha. Changing course, he moved to sit down near her grandmother. "And who are you writing to, Mrs. Helford?"

"The Dowager Comtesse de Pontrevault." She blotted her letter. "She's invited me to winter with her in the south of France and sends you her love, Dina."

Iona and Barclay's jaws dropped. Diantha pushed her needle into the canvas. The day might not be as bad as she dreaded.

That day's guests lived nearer than Aberdeen and arrived after luncheon. The maligned Cousin Francesca proved a particularly pleasant surprise. Instead of the middle-aged dragon conjured by Iona and Barclay, a woman of perhaps twenty-eight years swept into the hall on Kieran's arm.

"Thank you so much for inviting me, Lady Rossburn. Kieran has never snubbed me, but I did not know if you would be willing to have a mere colonel's widow under your roof." She accompanied the words with a dazzling smile.

Diantha liked her at once. "As the daughter of a mere 'mister,' I can hardly object."

"You're very kind." She removed her mantle, bonnet, and gloves, handing them to Jarrard. She wore a neat poplin gown in the gray of half-mourning.

The butler bowed. "If I may say, it is a pleasure to see you again, Lady Francesca."

"I am delighted to visit Duncarie again after so many years. But I prefer to be called Mrs. Urquhart."

"Lady Francesca?" Diantha looked from her to Kieran.

"My father is the Earl of Turbury." Her lips thinned. "He cast me off when I eloped with the man I loved and refused all contact with me even after my poor William was killed five years ago."

"Iona and Barclay are doubtless having palpitations

at this moment." Kieran chuckled. "However, my mother wishes to see you during your stay."

"They have never found me sufficiently servile." She and Diantha fell into step behind Kieran. "I do hope you stand up to them."

While Iona made no secret of her disapproval, she did not cause any ugly scenes in front of the other guests.

Two days later, her glacial calm cracked as she hastily entered the drawing room. Several ladies had enjoyed a lively game of lawn tennis and now occupied themselves with gossip and fashion periodicals.

"Diantha, there is a tradesman in the front hall! And he is opening several crates that he insists are paintings and are nothing but blots! Send him about his business at once!"

"Splendid!" Diantha brushed past her and scurried to the main stairway as quickly as one could in a bustle and corset. She paused at the landing that overlooked the entry hall and grinned.

Sir Harry Emerson stood in the middle of a pile of wood and packing material. Two paintings leaned against the wall and two footmen lifted another out of the last crate under his supervision.

"Oy, careful! That's canvas, not a piece of steel."

"What an intriguing man." To her surprise, Francesca stood at her side. She replied to Diantha's raised eyebrows with a shrug. "You didn't think I was going to stay for another of Iona's lectures, did you?"

Diantha chuckled. "Come along then." She descended the rest of the stairs. "Harry! You're making a mess."

"I expected you needed a diversion." His easy smile widened to include her companion. "Besides, you brought reinforcements."

"Francesca, please allow me to present Sir Harry Emerson, a dear, if untidy, friend of my family's. Harry, Lady Francesca Urquhart."

He bowed. "My pleasure, your ladyship."

A flush spread across her new friend's face, but she kept her composure. "Don't let Diantha frighten you off with my title. Your accent tells me you are from Yorkshire, sir."

Harry straightened, his face neutral. "Aye."

"I grew up not far from Helmsley." Francesca bestowed one of her wonderful smiles on him.

The industrialist gave her one in return that Diantha could only describe as foolish. "I'm from Hull myself."

"Harry! I thought I heard your voice!" Her father emerged from the billiard room at the back of the house, looking genuinely pleased for the first time since his arrival.

Kieran followed him, a frown marring his face. "Emerson. I did not know Diantha invited you."

She had prepared herself for this reaction. "I invited him for Papa's sake."

"Thankee, my girl." Her father patted her shoulder in an awkward gesture of affection.

"What do you think?" Harry waved a hand at the paintings. "Dina commissioned me to purchase these before she left Paris."

Papa peered at them. "Can't tell what they're supposed to be."

"They do seem to have rather a lot of daubs." Francesca tilted her head to one side.

Kieran came to Diantha's side. She could smell the lavender and bay of his soap. "That's what you asked him about at the Opera?" His eyes twinkled. "Dina?"

Her father harrumphed. "Silly pet name, Mrs. Quinn's mother started calling her that in the nursery."

"Hetty always swore the name suited her." Harry cleared his throat. "My late wife."

"It's called impressionist painting. Step back here." The words all but squeaked out as she led them nearly to the front door. At a distance the paintings resolved themselves into outdoor scenes that captured sunlight and shadow as it fell on buildings, meadows, and people.

"How clever." Francesca sighed wistfully. "It's been ages since I've been to a proper gallery."

Kieran nodded. "We'll have to find a place to hang them where they'll show to best advantage. For now, we should put them in the study and let the rest of our guests take a look at them."

"I am so gratified that you like them." Her heart danced at his approval, though, of course, she did not dare throw her arms around his neck as she wished. "Of course, Harry deserves the credit for finding them."

"Indeed." Kieran held out his hand. "You're quite the connoisseur, Emerson."

"Self-taught, no more." Despite the gruff words, the Yorkshireman failed to hide his pride.

Her guests occupied her time over the next days. Advised by Kieran's mother, she had prepared activities for both sunny and inclement weather. Sunny days brought walks through the garden, and sketching parties for the ladies. Kieran oversaw fishing excursions and practice shooting sessions for the men.

On rainy days and in the evenings, guests occupied themselves with cards, charades, or games like "Twenty Questions." Others played the piano in the drawing room or sang.

The day before grouse shooting started featured a picnic near the estate's fishing village. The community welcomed Mr. Quinn particularly, and he responded by becoming as human as Diantha had ever seen him. Under her mother's horrified eyes, he and Harry examined the existing fleet of boats and bantered with their crews.

Mrs. Quinn pressed a scented handkerchief to her lips. "Everyone else is staring! I shall die of mortification!"

Diantha barely heard her, for she could not take her eyes off Kieran.

He spoke to nearly every man, calling them by name and asking after their families. The wind blew his dark waves of hair around his perfect profile as he spoke to one of the youngest fishermen.

They seemed to be arguing about something and she wondered what the trouble could be.

Iona bustled up, scowling. "Come away, it's time to leave."

Diantha's brows snapped together. "I do beg your pardon, Aunt, but as hostess I believe that is my decision."

Barclay, following his mother, attempted to placate both of them. "That was a bit abrupt of Mother, but indeed, there's no need to linger. I daresay

Kieran can bring your father and Sir Harry along after they've finished with their new acquaintances." He drew the final word out in a sarcastic manner that set her teeth on edge.

She dug in her heels at his condescension until she caught sight of the others aimlessly sitting and standing near the carriages. "Very well, Barclay." She stretched her lips into a saccharine smile. "You may escort my mother."

She took Iona's arm, which she knew the other woman would detest. "Shall we go, Aunt?"

Several of their guests looked askance when Kieran arrived at the picnic site with Papa and Harry, but the three men ignored the stares.

After the meal, Kieran signaled the footmen. Grinning, they produced several long bags from under carriage seats. Their owners pulled out long clubs that ended in thick wood knobs or narrow iron blades. Alarmed, Diantha wondered if the Scots were about to engage in some sort of ritual combat, like fencing.

One of the friendlier Rossburn relatives rubbed his hands together. "Now for the entire point of the day! Did you bring the gutties, laddie?"

With a grin, her husband opened a box filled with small, pale spheres. "Hard to play golf without them."

They offered to teach the game to those unfamiliar with it. Diantha declined, but her brothers tried their hands at it. To Diantha's amazement, the Scots, male and female, spent the next hours whacking the balls into a series of holes among the heath that grew just beyond the seashore.

"That is the most absurd thing I have ever seen." She addressed the remark to Mama as they sipped lemonade some distance away from the course.

"Lawn tennis is more enlivening. But I'm told that royalty patronizes some golf clubs. Perhaps you should take up the game."

Iona sat nearby, watching Barclay play. "That would be most suitable. The dowager baroness never did take up the game."

Which only demonstrated her mother-in-law's good sense. Diantha kept the words to herself to preserve the rare accord between the two women.

Chapter 12

Buoyed by an afternoon of fierce competition on the links, Kieran decided to look in on his mother. Poole beamed at him when she opened the door.

"Her ladyship will be pleased to see you, my lord. Will you be joining her for tea?"

"If your wife can spare you." The dowager set aside the book she had been reading and held out a hand to him.

He kissed her cheek. "You look very well this afternoon."

"I took advantage of the empty house to spend some time on the terrace."

"I'm sorry, do you feel terribly hounded?" He took the seat next to her daybed.

"Not at all. If any of the more encroaching guests stop by, I simply feign a bad turn."

He chuckled at the mischievous twinkle in her eyes. She patted his hand. "Never mind, my dear. Nearly everyone who has visited me commends Diantha's skill as a hostess. Once that piece of gossip makes the rounds, she will be much in demand next Season." She quirked an eyebrow at him. "Unless she is occupied with more *domestic* matters."

Kieran helped himself to a scone. "You are quite as bad as Iona and Mrs. Quinn."

She straightened against the pillows at her back. "And why not? You are nearly thirty. Surely it cannot be a lack of attraction between the two of you."

Kieran choked on his tea. Once the pain caused by the hot liquid in his nostrils receded, he glared at his parent. "Mother! That is a highly improper speculation."

She sniffed. "Pooh."

He escaped shortly after that, torn between exasperation and amusement. His amusement abated as he rounded the corner to the corridor leading to the best bedchambers. A series of muffled thumps greeted him. Sprinting, he reached the room the noise came from and wrenched the door open.

And jumped aside as Thomas Quinn erupted into the hall and landed on the crimson runner carpeting the floor. Blood oozed from a split lip. Colin, the footman, stood in the doorway panting and nursing the skinned knuckles on his right hand.

Kieran peered past the servant. A maid sat crumpled on Thomas's bed, cap askew as she wept. That and the torn dress gaping open from her neck to her waist told Kieran all he needed to know.

"I'll have your job for that, you insolent bastard!" Thomas, having climbed to his feet, bellowed the words as he flew toward the footman, hand raised to strike.

He staggered backward as Kieran's fist drove into his solar plexus. Thrown the width of the corridor, he slammed into an occasional table and collapsed against it, gasping for air.

The noise brought observers. Kieran found himself the cynosure of the rest of his wife's family. Diantha hurried to his side from the opposite end of the hall, followed by Iona and Barclay.

"What is the meaning of this? Thomas, are you all right?" Mrs. Quinn pushed forward to inspect her son.

Catching his wife's eye, Kieran jerked his head toward Thomas's chamber. She took one look inside, shooed Colin out and entered, shutting the door behind her.

"That scum attacked me." Thomas spat the words out as he pointed a shaking finger at the footman. "I want him dismissed. Now."

Colin broke his silence. "I did naught but lairn the muckle feardie not tae lay hands on a poor lass."

Kieran crossed his arms and stared the younger man down. "The only thing that is going to happen now is that you are going to wait until your sister can ascertain how badly you hurt that girl." He did not bother to hide his contempt.

Mrs. Quinn drew herself up. "Lord Rossburn, you cannot mean that you would take the gibberish of an ignorant menial over the word of a gentleman."

"On the contrary, I'm taking the word of the only gentleman involved in your son's disagreement." He turned to the servant and grasped his shoulder. "Brawly done, my lad."

While the Americans stared in confusion, the footman relaxed. "Thank you, my lord. It's Gaira Wallace, we grew up together."

His father-in-law blustered. "This is an outrage!

No doubt the girl threw herself at my boy. Pay her off and haul this miscreant to jail."

Diantha emerged in time to hear her father. Her face paled, but she remained composed. "On the contrary, Papa. Tom tried to force himself on the poor girl and would have succeeded had Colin not intervened."

Her mother's narrow face contorted. "Diantha! She's a servant, for heaven's sake."

"And that makes Tom's action somehow acceptable?"

Quinn's face took on an ugly red hue. "By God, Rossburn, we'll see what the authorities have to say about this."

Despite the serious situation, Diantha bit her lip to prevent a smile.

Kieran twitched his cuffs into place. "This is Scotland, Quinn. I *am* the local authority." He nodded to the grinning footman. "I think this calls for a bonus, Colin. Now get downstairs and have someone look at those knuckles."

With a tug of his forelock, the servant took himself away. Kieran fixed his gaze on his furious brother-in-law. "I ought to turn you over to the courts and request transportation for you."

Mrs. Quinn turned to her daughter. "How can you permit him to speak to us so? Have you no proper feeling for your own family?"

Diantha stepped past Kieran and planted herself in front of her mother. "After you invite yourself to my home and accost my servants?" Her voice shook. "The only reason I am not ordering you to leave at once is because doing so would worsen the scandal Tom created."

"You do not give orders to me, my girl." Mrs. Quinn's hand whipped out to slap her daughter, hard.

Kieran pulled Diantha back against him. Keeping one arm around his trembling wife, he gripped the older woman's wrist until she cried out.

"I suggest you exercise some self-restraint, madam." Or he'd kill the bitch before he let her strike Diantha again.

Like every other bully he'd come across, Mrs. Quinn backed down at the first threat of danger to her person. "No gentleman would think of harming a lady!"

Diantha, large-eyed, slipped to her grandmother's side.

"I've never harmed a lady in my life."

Mrs. Quinn gasped at the insult and he released her. "I suggest that everyone dress for dinner. I have no intention of putting the meal back for the likes of you."

Iona had watched the entire scene in silence. Now she stepped forward. "I shall accompany Gaira to Mrs. Menzies and issue an order that no female servant waits upon either of her ladyship's brothers."

She gave Diantha a withering glance. "Then Barclay and I shall attempt to curtail the damage you and your dreadful family have caused ours."

Kieran rounded on his aunt. "By all means do what you can for the poor girl, but if you belittle my wife one more time, you can pack your bags as well."

Barclay took his mother's arm. "I say, that's out-of-bounds!"

"What is out-of-bounds is the stream of insults

Diantha has suffered from all of you under her own roof." He glared at everyone impersonally. "The matter is now closed."

"Go get dressed, Granny. I have some things to attend to." Diantha made her way toward her room. Her unsteady voice alarmed him, but he stared down the others until they retreated to their rooms.

Only Mrs. Helford remained, her habitual vigor extinguished. One hand clutched the door frame for support. "This is all my fault," she whispered.

Kieran helped her into her room and onto a chaise. He sat down at her side. "How can you be to blame here?"

The old woman pressed her fingertips to her eyes. "Don't you understand? I failed my daughter, and she failed hers." A sob escaped her.

Kieran rather desperately wanted to go to Diantha, but he could not turn his back on her grandmother. He tried to think of comforting words. "I do not see any of you in your daughter's nature."

Tears slipped down the wrinkled cheeks and she sought her handkerchief. "No, you see her father." To his relief, some color returned to her face. "Although he could be charming in public, my husband was a beast. Amalthea was our only child, and he alternately praised and intimidated her.

"I wanted to protect her but my husband beat me when I tried to interfere." She pressed the lace-edged square of white lawn to her lips. "I was too cowardly to protect my own child. Needless to say, Mally handled her children the same way her father treated her."

Kieran patted her shoulder as she dried her eyes. "I'm sorry. You must have been terrified for years."

"Did Diantha ever tell you she tried to run away before the wedding?"

Stunned, he shook his head. His wife disliked him that much?

Mrs. Helford sighed. "She bribed a servant to purchase a train ticket to Boston. When her father and brothers caught her, they found she'd forged her own references to teach French at an academy there."

A weight settled in his gut. "What did they do to her?"

"Her mother took a dogwhip to her to force her to name her accomplice." She shuddered. "When that failed to work, her parents locked her in her room and did not let her out alone until the day she married."

Unable to bear immobility when he wanted to pound her family to a pulp with his bare fists, Kieran pushed himself off the chaise. "How could they do that to their own child?"

"She was never a child in their eyes, only a bargaining chip to be used to their best advantage." Her mouth twisted. "I tried to make up for my sins by providing her with the affection they should have given her."

Kieran paused before the old woman. "You succeeded in that much, ma'am, I assure you."

She shrugged, a barely discernable lift of her shoulders. "I supported her marriage to you because I hoped it would take her far away from that house." She lifted her gaze to his. "I hope I was right."

Under the intensity of her silent plea, he retreated to the bellpull and tugged. "Do you feel well enough to remain alone until your maid comes? I should go to Diantha."

He left before she finished nodding yes.

A bitter smile twisted his lips as he strode through toward Diantha's chamber. He hadn't the least idea what to say to her. *I know you don't want me, but I'll look after you anyway* sounded as if he'd adopted a stray dog.

She deserved a true husband, one who did not have infidelity in his blood.

He realized he stood before her door and still did not know what he could say or do that would offer her comfort. He had to try, though.

She replied as soon as he tapped on the wooden panel. "Come in."

He squared his shoulders and entered.

She sat at her dressing table. Her glance flickered to his reflection in the mirror, then back to her swollen cheek. "I don't know how I'm going to hide this at dinner."

"Never mind dinner." He approached her gingerly, prepared for tears. "May I?"

She allowed him to turn her about on the chair until she faced him. A livid, hand-shaped welt rose on her fair skin. His throat closed. "Oh love, I'm so sorry."

"For what? You're the one who stopped her." A half-smile faltered on the undamaged side of her face. "Luckily I don't bruise easily."

He eased her to her feet and into his arms. He stroked her hair as he murmured, "For everything. For ruining your life with a marriage you didn't want. For not telling your family to go to the devil when they sent that arrogant telegram. For permitting Iona to run roughshod over you."

She rested her head on his shoulder, unmoving. Then she took a deep breath. "You're not the man I thought you were."

Kieran swallowed. He deserved no better, but the assessment still hurt. "I know, but perhaps we can come to some arrangement where you would not have to see me—"

Her finger against his lips stopped him. "You don't understand. I thought this marriage would be hopeless. It's not. You don't tell me what I must do or say or wear. This house party proves that we can work together when we need to."

She touched her cheek. "You stopped Mama from hitting me. Even Granny could never accomplish that."

Then she sighed. "Speaking of the house party, I must find a way to cover this up. Florette is bringing ice, but I'm not sure it will work quickly enough."

"I shall tell our guests you're indisposed."

She nibbled her lip, an expression of longing on her face. "An evening alone sounds tempting."

"Then turn around. I'll unfasten your stays and you can crawl into bed. MacAdam can send up a tray."

"Kieran, I did mean an evening alone. By myself." She regarded him anxiously. "My face hurts and I truly have a wretched headache."

He brushed her mouth with his. "That is exactly what I meant, my dear. With a houseful of guests, one of us has to appear at dinner."

He freed her from her corset and even helped

her with her nightgown, amused at the idea of helping his wife *into* her garments.

When Florette arrived, bearing a bowl of ice and a clean towel, she gave a nod of approval. "It is very good, milord. Her ladyship needs a night of quiet. I shall convey to MacAdam the request for a tray and bring it up later."

"Would you also ask Poole for some of the dowager's salicin? We always keep a good supply on hand and it will ease her ladyship's headache."

He left her to change for dinner, then returned. Diantha drowsed, curled up on her side beneath the sheet. On a chair beside the bed, the ice-filled towel now rested in the bowl in easy reach of her hand.

"Is there anything else I can send for to make you comfortable?"

She lifted her head slightly. "Would you—would you mind brushing my hair?"

Wordlessly, he collected her brush and seated himself on the other side of her bed. She closed her eyes and sighed as he carefully drew the bristles through the long brown strands.

"That feels lovely." A smile played about her lips. "I thought so the first time you brushed my hair."

The morning after their wedding, when he'd decided to seduce her. As her shoulders relaxed under his ministrations, he realized that he found the action far more gratifying this time. Perhaps he should brush her hair more often. His cock hardened as he recalled the sensation of warm silk flowing over his skin when they made love.

A soft snore broke the silence. Diantha had fallen asleep.

* * *

He looked in on her again before retiring, expecting that she slept on. Instead she sat up in bed, working on her sketch pad. She closed it and tucked it beside the bed. "I was sound asleep for hours, now I'm wide awake."

"Have a brandy." So saying, Kieran slipped into his own chamber and filled two snifters with the amber liquid. He returned, giving one to her.

"You look much better." As she had predicted, the mark had faded without leaving signs of darkened skin.

"I feel better." She sipped carefully, then sighed. "But I don't look forward to spending the day with my mother and Iona tomorrow."

"You could come watch the shoot." He blurted the words out without thinking, but the idea pleased him considerably. "If you are not too squeamish."

"I fear I've never fainted at the sight of blood. Most indelicate of me." Her face clouded. "But I cannot leave the other ladies, it would be uncivil."

"It would guarantee a reprieve from the two dragons." He leaned forward, using his most coaxing smile. "I'll make it clear that I, the lord and master, insist that you come watch."

She wavered. "I should feel more comfortable if I had another female. Could I invite your Cousin Francesca?"

"A first-rate idea! She herself learned to shoot as a girl; she can tell you what's going on."

"Never mind that, she can tell me what to wear."

* * *

Diantha woke up in a much better mood than she had expected. Her face still felt stiff, but all visible sign of her mother's abuse had disappeared. The quiet evening and Kieran's kindness had restored her peace of mind.

She needed it, for when she went down to breakfast, she discovered the exquisitely appointed salon awash in tartan. Her Scottish guests nearly all sported some form of the pattern, in a variety of colors. The women wore sashes diagonally across their torsos and pinned at the shoulder, which was unexceptionable. The men however—

Diantha swallowed. She had seen portraits of Kieran's father and grandfather in their kilts, but that did not prepare her for the sight of an entire room filled with males in a state of half-undress. Even covered with stockings, the myriad of calves exposed by the knee-length kilts unnerved her.

Someone tapped her shoulder. She turned her head to find Francesca Urquhart regarding her with twinkling eyes. "If you're just going to stare, don't block the entry. Some of us wish to eat."

Diantha accompanied the other woman to the sideboard. "Is someone playing a joke?"

Francesca repressed her laughter. "Don't say that too loudly. Wearing tartan on the first day of shooting is a Duncarie tradition." She helped herself to eggs and smoked salmon. "Gives the Scots a chance to show off before the English."

Diantha nodded at the sash of muted blue and green draped over her friend's shoulder. "You're from Yorkshire."

"But my husband was an Urquhart." The other woman stroked the woolen length tenderly. "He had this cut from his own plaid and gave it to me after we married. It means as much to me as my wedding ring."

They found places beside Diantha's grandmother. Due to her age, she was the only person waited on at breakfast. As the footman presented the elderly woman with a heaping plate, Diantha realized even the servants wore kilts. "This is dreadful! I don't know where to look."

Granny's gaze rested on the retreating servant's legs with every evidence of pleasure. "I think it's a splendid notion."

Francesca nudged her. "You could try looking at your husband."

Diantha did, and forgot about food. The gray background of the Rossburn tartan suited his dark hair. The plaid on his upper body emphasized his broad shoulders and the belt at his middle showed off his narrow waist.

As he strolled to the sideboard, she noticed nearly every other female eye in the room riveted on him as well. Diantha stabbed at a kipper. She was not leaving her husband unwatched until he changed into something that inspired less attention.

Some of her guests expressed surprise or even outright disapproval when he announced that Diantha would accompany the men. He ignored everyone, however, and at ten o'clock sharp, a footman assisted Diantha and Francesca down from the carriage onto the immense moor.

The shooting party itself disappointed her. Kieran and his guests stood at designated spots and waited for the beaters to drive the birds in their direction. The constant blasts nearly deafened her and smoke from the powder used to fire the cartridges formed a miasma around the gunners.

"How can you stand the noise?" She had to raise her voice to ask the question of Francesca.

"I got used to volleys of all sorts while married to a military man." She shook her head. "And this is only a small party. It's amazing that the entire sporting community of Britain can hear anything at all."

The two women wandered far enough behind the guns for rational conversation. Diantha occupied herself with her sketchbook while Francesca pulled a crochet hook and thread out of her pocket. When he approached them some time later, Kieran burst out laughing.

"The ground doesn't look very suitable for such ladylike occupations."

Diantha grasped his outstretched hand for assistance as she got to her feet and waited for him to help Francesca. "Nonsense. We had this comfortable blanket to rest upon."

"I hope you aren't too bored." He offered each of them an arm. "I should have thought before I invited you."

"A morning spent in fresh air is far more attractive to me today than staying in the drawing room."

Kieran grinned down at her. "I thought you might say that."

They approached a small table set with cold meats and bread. Everyone would gather for a picnic lunch later, but the men hailed Diantha for considering their masculine appetites. Archie and the loaders relaxed and ate near a cart set aside for their use. At the other end of the moor, the beaters ate a similar snack.

Afterward, servants packed up the remains of the meal. Kieran escorted her to a line of unloaded guns with their breeches open. They had been cleaned during the break. "Would you like to shoot one?"

"Mama will be horrified when she finds out." She hesitated. "Would it be safe?"

"An excellent concern. We'll be sure to point you away from the others." He picked up a shotgun with an inlay of polished steel on the butt. "My father gave me this one."

Barclay strolled up, holding his own weapon. "Kieran said he might try to coax you to fire a round. Bravely done, Cousin." He eschewed a kilt, but looked very fine in trousers and a tailored shooting jacket. He fell in with them.

After showing her how to carry it safely, with the barrel pointed to the ground, they guided her to a spot several feet away from the others. Nervous at the stares in her direction, she drew comfort from Kieran's solid warmth as he walked beside her.

While she watched, the two men showed her how the breech mechanism worked, and how to load and unload cartridges. Finally Kieran handed her his gun. Diantha did not expect it to weigh so much, but managed to hold it properly.

Barclay held out his own. "That's rather heavy for a lady, Cuz. Would you like her to use mine?"

"Good of you, Barclay, but she'll need help bracing any shotgun correctly. I'd prefer to handle the one I'm familiar with."

Kieran pushed a cartridge with a handpainted B into the chamber. "This is a blank, so you needn't fear hurting anyone. Now, keep your finger away from the trigger and lift the gun to your shoulder."

Diantha did so as Kieran moved behind her. His arms came around her to help steady the piece. "Ow! It's digging into my shoulder."

She felt his chest shake with laughter. "It's supposed to. If a gun recoils against your shoulder the pain is far worse. Take a breath, put your finger on the trigger, and squeeze."

An explosion thundered in her right ear so loudly she thought she saw flames and smelled something dreadful. The next instant someone ripped the gun out of her hands and threw Diantha flat on her back. Before she could protest, folds of heavy cloth smothered her face and upper body.

Through the ringing in her ears she heard indistinguishable shouts.

"Dina! Oh God!" She clawed her way out of the encompassing wool to find Kieran kneeling beside her.

"Stop that!" She tried to bat his hands away as he pressed his plaid against her.

"Lie still, love!" White-faced, he spoke gently but forced her back to the rough grass. "I have to smother the sparks."

Kieran ran his hands over her neck and down her arm before hauling her onto his lap. Scorch marks darkened his plaid and she realized that the gun must have misfired. Looking down, she traced burnt material to the shoulder of her gown. Exploring further, her fingers encountered a singed clump that had once been a curl.

"My hair!"

Francesca placed an open flask to Diantha's lips and urged her to drink. She smiled in between gasps of breath. "I'm sure that clever maid of yours will be able to do something modish with it." Shivering, the older woman handed the flask to Kieran. "I saw it from a distance. Thank God you have nothing worse than a ruined coiffure."

Normally Diantha enjoyed it when Kieran held her close, but not when he shouted in her ear.

"Green!" She cringed as he roared the ghillie's name in a voice that echoed across the moor.

Archie pounded up, his face gray. "Dear Jesus, is Lady Rossburn safe?"

"No thanks to your carelessness she is." He bit the words out. "It is impossible that so much flame could be produced by one blank cartridge."

"No, my laird." The ghillie wrung his cap in his hands. "I swear, I looked over your piece myself in and oot and there was naught in it."

"Well, something bloody was, and it near killed my wife!"

"Kieran! That is enough."

He finally looked down at her.

"You checked the barrel yourself. So did Barclay. I distinctly remember watching you." She cupped his cheek, her heart melting at the anxiety in his aqua eyes. "It was a frightening accident, but I don't see how anyone could have foreseen it. And we are both whole, if somewhat crispy."

Kieran's arms tightened about her for a moment. "Thank God." He looked around and raised his voice. "Fetch a carriage. I'm taking Lady Rossburn home."

Despite her repeated demands to walk, Kieran did not let go of her until he placed her on her own bed at Duncarie. He sat beside her, silently stroking her hair until Florette arrived. Still without a word, he leaned forward and kissed her, then left for his own room.

Diantha watched him leave, wishing she knew what his silence meant. She turned on her side and stared at the brocade curtains covering her windows. She had not told him the entire truth the previous evening. Difficult as he was to reach, and as much as she feared what his eventual rejection would do to her heart, she had fallen in love with her husband.

Chapter 13

Although no more untoward events occurred the house party could not end soon enough for Diantha. As she waved good-bye to the last of their guests, she could not repress a sigh of relief.

"It does feel good to have the house to ourselves again." Kieran took her arm as they returned to the entry hall.

"Indeed, although I'm spoiled by all the recreation we've indulged in over the last weeks." Diantha's heart turned over as Kieran kissed her cheek.

"If you say so, but I think getting shot is a drastic excuse to change your hairstyle." He grinned as they climbed up the grand staircase. "I have a lot of work to catch up on, but we could go riding on occasion."

Archie took a dim view of the idea. The first time she and Kieran rode out together he ordered her husband not to tire her. "You leuk ower her well, you scamp! She's not been a'horseback that long." Touched, she realized that for once the ghillie spoke of her safety, not Dancer's.

The only roads on Duncarie traveled from Ulladale, a village just beyond the estate, to Cariford on the coast; and one from the house to the far side of the valley, where several tenants lived in stone crofts.

Diantha expressed concern over the often primitive houses the first time they visited the far side of the valley. Kieran nodded his agreement as he rode beside her on his black hunter. "I hope to use some of the increased funds at my disposal to improve them." He sighed. "My forefathers didn't engage in the wide-scale clearances that so many others did. I'm sure it's a credit to our family motto, but it means there are a great many crofts to repair."

"'We guard our own.'" Diantha repeated the words carved around every stone fireplace in Duncarie House. "It's a worthy goal." She enjoyed meeting the crofters, although the knowledge they seemed to have of her activities astounded her. Kieran explained with a chuckle that several of them had relatives working at the house.

They explored more of Duncarie as her riding improved. A cleft at the far end of the valley opened to a narrow glen on the way to the seashore. On one side of that dark valley, a promontory etched its top against the sky.

Kieran glanced up at the cliff as they passed. "Eventually, several Rossburn tenants rebelled against the attempts of the English to burn them out of their crofts. The local commander ordered every man arrested or captured to be thrown over the edge."

"Arrested or captured? He didn't even try them?" Diantha shuddered as he shook his head. "That's barbaric!"

"And several other innocent families were burned out, marched to Cariford and told to learn fishing or be deported."

"Is that the origin of the village?"

"There were a few fishermen there before. It's a natural harbor. There are still descendants of some of those families living there." He glanced at her. "They regard you in the light of a patroness due to the boats your father is sending."

Her heart leaped for a moment at the tenderness in her husband's voice, but she told herself she only fancied hearing it. As she stared blindly ahead, she ruefully reflected that she would rather have the affection of Duncarie's lord than that of its people.

Another day they rode to one of the hill lochs, small cold lakes teeming with fish. She spent the afternoon on the shore sketching while Kieran fished.

As he cast his line out again and again, a mischievous smile curved her lips. Under her fingers, a rough drawing of her husband's muscled back came to life. The pencil moved lower, outlining the firm rear end and long legs.

A splash and a tiny fountain of white marked the attempted escape of a trout from his hook. Reeling the line in, he waded into the chilly waters to grab the fish and tuck it into the wicker creel slung over one shoulder.

She closed the pad and set it down on top of her jacket, discarded in the muggy afternoon, content to watch his strong body wading back to shore. "You look like a kelpie."

He looked down at himself and roared with laughter. "I've never heard of a kelpie with a fishing rod. They take the form of horses."

Diantha gurgled with merriment at the wet legs of his breeches and muddy feet. "I found a book in the library which says that once a kelpie sought a woman for warmth and companionship." He gave her a sharp glance.

Leaning back on her elbows but looking straight ahead, she went on with the story. "The girl he courted was clever and consulted a wise man about the handsome stranger who always met her with a string of fish and wet hair. The two of them captured the kelpie and put him to work until he learned the meaning of compassion."

She tilted her head back. To the northeast, a bank of dull clouds stretched across the sky. "At the end of his servitude, he was given the choice of returning to his loch or drinking a potion that would make him fully human."

The heavy air seemed to suffocate her. "By then he had fallen in love with the girl, so he chose to stay with her."

Kieran seated himself nearby, drawing up his legs and resting his hands on his knees. "The version my nurse told me was slightly different. Instead of capturing him, the girl tells him she knows what he is."

He too stared into the distance as he spoke gently. "Although he craves her human warmth, he is a water spirit. He leaves her rather than break her heart."

"That certainly proves his gender." Diantha scrambled to her feet. "Only a male would reach such an idiotic conclusion." Unable to bear the sight of his beautiful body without touching him, she strolled away, giving him one glance over her shoulder.

Kieran stood as well, but stayed in place. "He was trying to be noble!" His voice followed her as she walked. "Just where do you think you're going?"

By the time she turned to face him, she had unbuttoned her blouse. "I don't want to get captured by a kelpie."

He eyed her hungrily as the white garment fluttered to the ground. "Can you swim?" His hands dropped to unfasten his breeches.

She sucked in her breath and shook her head. "Mama considers it even more unladylike than riding."

His trousers hung loosely off his hips as he strode toward her. "She may be right. And you never know when you may meet a dangerous water creature."

Diantha shrieked and tore across the turf. With a roar, he caught up with her in no time, carrying her to level ground. Laying her flat on her back, he swept her skirt and petticoats up to expose her drawers. Using both hands he widened the slit in the undergarment, then bent forward to brush his mouth over hers.

Heart pounding, she nibbled his lower lip. "I thought the kelpie enticed maidens to ride him."

His eyes darkened to green above her as he sucked in a breath. "I believe they do." Rolling onto his back, he pulled her on top of him, his hands scrabbling to shove cloth aside. "Ride me, my clever girl."

Reaching down, she felt hot hard flesh in her

hand. She squeezed and stroked him until he shut his eyes, groaning. Only then did she raise herself up on her knees to straddle him. As the thick length of him slid up inside her channel, he worked her breasts free of her corset. She threw back her head with a hoarse cry as his mouth closed over a stiff pink nipple.

Yes, she would ride her dark lover. Perhaps she could capture him after all.

Much later, she shivered as she lay on his chest. His arms held her securely as one hand stroked her hair. Silently, her fingers traced his high cheekbone. She shivered again. The wind had turned cold, she realized.

Kieran raised his head. "Damnation!"

Disoriented, she rolled off him. "What?"

"I think we're about to get caught in a storm." Sure enough, the clouds in the distance approached steadily now, with unmistakable slants of rain beneath them.

It hit them halfway back to the manor. Not just rain, but battering winds, lightning, and thunder. "A gale!" She could hardly hear him over the rain beating over them.

They clattered into the stable yard only to receive a dressing down by a furious Archie Green as their steaming beasts were taken away by the grooms. Slipping through a side door, they squelched their way across the kitchen, ordering cans of hot water to be brought up to their rooms for baths.

A chill shook Diantha's body. "I fear we may have to set dinner back."

Kieran hugged her to him, although he was not

much warmer. "That would hardly be fair to Iona and Barclay." He shouted down the narrow stairs after the scurrying servants. "Send up dinner for two to Lady Rossburn's room."

A worried Florette hurried her out of the sopping wet habit and into a heavy robe after Kieran had pushed her into her room. Even huddled in a chair next to the fireplace, her teeth chattered until hot water arrived for her bath.

Finally warmed through, she dressed in a long-sleeved tea gown and relaxed until a footman brought in a small table, followed by another bearing a tray filled with covered dishes.

Knocking on his door, she told Kieran their meal awaited, then dismissed Florette and the other servants.

Much later, she sat back in her chair, stomach full. The gale had blown inland by then, leaving only a steady rain to tap on the windows. "I think this has been the most enjoyable dinner I've eaten at Duncarie."

Opposite, her husband's eyes gleamed in the firelight as he rubbed a finger on the rim of his wineglass. "MacAdam won't care for that remark." Under the table one of his bare feet slid up her unstockinged leg under the tea gown's loose skirt.

Pushing her chair back from the table, she rose to her feet. "I referred to the company, not the quality of the food. MacAdam always excels."

He stood too, clearly prepared to pounce. Her heart pounded and she bit her lip in anticipation.

They both jumped when someone pounded on her door. "Open up!" Barclay pounded again.

"Word just came from Cariford that the fishing boats were caught in the storm."

Kieran closed his eyes. "Oh my God." He called to his cousin through the door. "Were any lost?"

"All of them."

Chapter 14

Kieran gripped the back of his chair, ashen-faced at the news. Only the soft snaps of the fire and the rain striking the windowpanes filled those few seconds of silence.

She took a step toward him, but he lifted a hand, sharply, to fend her off. "No!" He regarded her as though he could not focus clearly. "I'm sorry, but I have to go now."

Hurt at his rebuff, Diantha swallowed. "Of course, I understand. Is there anything I can do to help?"

He sighed, and it seemed to her that a burden of immense heaviness settled on his shoulders. "Pray for the dead."

She nodded, unsure of her next course of action.

Barclay's voice burst through the door. "Kieran!" Anger shaded it now.

She wanted to hold him to her, to comfort him, but he only turned and disappeared into his room. His departure released her from her own state of suspended animation. Going to the bellpull, she jerked it imperiously.

By the time Florette entered, she knew what she wanted to do in the immediate future. "I need to dress, and the table must be cleared away. I should find out if the house has any supplies which can be sent along."

The Frenchwoman nodded soberly. *"Oui, milady."*

Diantha dressed as quickly as she could, feeling remarkably useless. Her father's company had lost ships only twice in her memory. They had been serious occasions, but had involved no more action on her part than attending the memorial services with her mother.

This would not do. Rising from her dressing table, she moved to her writing desk and pulled out a sheet of paper. She needed a list.

For a while, the only sounds in the room were the soft scratching quill on paper and the clink of dishes. She lifted her head and swiveled around in her chair. Florette had quietly stacked the dishes and stood prepared to pick up a tray.

Diantha regarded her lady's maid in amazement. "Whatever are you doing? We can summon footmen."

The older woman's hands stilled. "I know, milady, but this news has affected many of the servants. Several had friends or relatives on the boats." She sighed. "Not only that, many large waves hit the town. They fear the town itself may be badly damaged."

Diantha shuddered, then recollected herself. "I shall leave you in charge of removing the dishes, then. I shall make sure messages have been sent to the rest of the estate and Doctor Andrews. If you need me I shall probably be in the gallery or the drawing room."

She left her chamber to find signs of panic immediately. Charles, the footman, rushed up the stairs with a housemaid in tow. Seeing her, both came to a halt. The footman apologized for not fetching the dishes from her room earlier, while the young girl beside him tried to choke back her tears.

Diantha took command. First asking Charles if he knew anyone on the missing vessels. At his negative answer, she asked him to take a note to Dr. Andrews in Ulladale. "You will notice it on my writing desk. When you get back from your errand, please come find me."

He nodded and gave the girl a sympathetic look. "Beattie here is from Cariford, your ladyship."

As he hurried off, she put her arms around the girl's shoulders. "My dear, I am so sorry. Did you know anyone on the boats?"

A sob escaped the servant. "Me dad's a fisherman—and Jamie Cruikshank—we were supposed to be married in the fall." A lump rose in Diantha's throat as the slight body shook with weeping. "Please, I must go home. Me mum needs me."

"Of course, I understand." Leading the girl to a bench, she held her close and rocked her while she cried.

The door to Kieran's bedroom opened. She scarcely recognized her husband in the grim-faced man that stalked down the hallway. Dressed in heavy trousers and a thick jumper, he resembled a villager.

For the sake of the girl sobbing on her shoulder, she softly called him. "Kieran?"

He looked at her absently, the way he had when they were first engaged. Her heart failed her before she reminded herself that he had just suffered a shock.

She told the girl's story briefly. "I told her we could spare her for a few days to go to Cariford."

"No!" He nearly shouted the word before hunkering down to the servant's eye level as she sat next to Diantha. He took her hand until she lifted her gaze to his. "Beattie, I know you want to go to your mother, and I think you have two sisters as well?" He spoke firmly, but gently. "Think: all will be confusion for the next few days, and you won't be able to help.

"Now, if your family needs you, perhaps we can find a place for them near here. Don't you think that would be better?" She hiccupped and nodded. "Good girl. Now, go downstairs and have a cup of tea to compose yourself. I'm going to Cariford now and I promise to send word of what has actually happened."

The small maidservant heaved herself to her feet. "Thank you, your lordship." Hanging onto the wall for support, she slowly made her way toward the stairs.

Kieran's gaze followed her for a moment before he took Diantha's arm. "Come with me, please." Opening the door to the nearest room, he drew her inside.

Alarmed at the tightness in his voice, she turned to him as soon as he shut the door behind them.

They stood in an unused bedroom. All about them furniture lay shrouded in Holland covers.

He held up a hand before she could utter a word. "I understand you want to help, but under no circumstances should any of the staff be allowed to return to Cariford just now."

She gaped at him in disbelief. "That is the most inhumane thing I have ever heard!"

He scrubbed his face with his hands. "Diantha, have you ever seen the aftermath of a shipwreck?" She shook her head. "It's hideous. That poor child is suffering enough. Do you think the sight of her father or her sweetheart after three days in the water will ease her grief?"

His words brought her up short. "I'm sorry, I was stupid." She grimaced. "I suppose this means you don't want me there either?"

He placed a hand under her chin and lifted it until she looked into his eyes. They were red-rimmed. "Not stupid. You just didn't know." He took a shaky breath. "You have no idea how much I will want you there, sweetheart. But I need you here."

She did not want to cause a scene, but he was pushing her away once again. "Iona can run the house. Surely there is something I can do to help."

"There is." He pulled her into a hard embrace as his lips grazed her hair. The rough wool sweater prickled against her cheek as he took a near-sobbing breath. She wondered why as he spoke. "Look after my mother. And stay here. I need you safe."

He tilted her head back, fingertips brushing her cheek. Kissing her deeply, as if he wanted to take her breath with him, he then let her go. With a last look and a shaky breath, he left.

The next morning dragged past. Diantha divided her time between her mother-in-law's room and the gallery, where Iona sat near the great window at the far end. Barclay disappeared into the estate office.

When he did emerge for luncheon, he spent most of the meal frowning down at his plate. Only the two of them sat in the main dining room, for Iona had retired with a headache. Further, she had ordered that until the household returned to normal, servants need only wait on the family at dinner.

Polite conversation struck her as frivolous under the circumstances, so Diantha too ate in near silence.

She eventually brought up the possibility of preparing a wagon of supplies from the house to send on to Cariford.

Barclay stared at her abstractedly before giving an impatient shake of his head. "Unnecessary. My cousin will send for them if they are required." With that, he returned to his cold chicken.

His snapped reply nettled her, but she reminded herself that the loss of the fishermen would hit him harder than it had her. Before leaving the dining room, he apologized in his usual quiet manner.

Diantha regarded him sympathetically. "I beg you, not to dwell on it. We must all feel for those poor men and their families."

He stood looking down at her as though he

wanted to say something. With the air of a man making up his mind, he took a deep breath. "I fear Kieran's involvement in the village is far more personal than mine."

She cocked her head, confused. "I'm sure it is; he cares greatly for Duncarie and its people."

With a harsh cry, he gripped her shoulders. "You don't understand! Kieran has near relatives in Cariford." He looked at her meaningfully. "Young relatives."

Feeling faint, she pushed back from him slightly. He released her shoulders at once and helped her to the nearest chair. Pulling another out, he faced her, taking her hands in his.

He closed his eyes, a pained expression on his face. "My dear Diantha, forgive me. To have given you such a shock on top of this disaster is unconscionable."

Her entire face seemed to have coalesced into stone. Removing her hands from his grasp, she straightened her back. "Tell me."

Barclay spoke gently. "My cousin takes after his father, not only in how he manages his estate, but in his fondness for women of a certain class."

Her heart beating painfully, she nodded. "I see."

He sat back with an expression on his face that she would have described as ludicrous at any other time. "You do?"

Almost violently, he pushed himself to his feet and paced away from her, knuckles pressed against his mouth. "My God, that swine." Whirling, he faced her again. "I have felt a certain amount of sympathy for you ever since he brought you here. The man has some appetites that hardly bear thinking of, and that a lady should be subjected to his rutting—it is unconscionable."

Remembering the lovemaking she and her husband had shared yesterday by the loch, she kept her gaze fixed on her clasped hands. "In other words, it may be for the best that he goes to common women to relieve his more base wants."

His footsteps halted, and he cleared his throat. "I suppose. I had not thought of it from that perspective."

Composing her face into a serene mask, Diantha lifted her gaze to him. "Suppose you tell me about his illegitimate children."

Barclay's cheeks flushed. "Oh, they aren't even recognized as that; he's far too clever. But the resemblance is undeniable! Forgive me for speaking of something so distasteful, but I've had the misfortune to come across them more than once. It is why I so seldom visit Cariford."

It occurred to her that her husband's cousin rarely visited any of the tenants. "I see. I am sure your sentiments on all that are correct." She stood up, smoothing her dress. "I gather part of my dowry is going to the support of these unfortunates?"

He flinched. "Your tranquility in the face of such sordid disclosures is a credit to you, madam."

A humorless laugh escaped her as she walked to the door. "It rather is, isn't it? Until later, Cousin."

Crossing the entrance hall, she mounted the main staircase and went to her room. Tugging the bellpull, she waited until a chambermaid appeared and sent for a pot of tea.

She had a great deal of thinking to do.

An hour later, she tapped on her mother-in-law's door. When Poole opened it, she asked if the dowager felt well enough to see her again.

Poole's plain face broke into a smile. "That would be grand. The news about the boats has flattened her and you were a great comfort to her this morning." She led the way into Lady Rossburn's bedroom.

Her mother-in-law opened her eyes and tried to move up on the pillows. "My dear, thank you for coming to see a decrepit old woman twice in one day."

Diantha and Poole flew to her assistance. "I beg you, let us help, dear ma'am." The two of them carefully moved her ladyship into as comfortable a position as she could find. Although sweat broke out on the wrinkled forehead, the dowager thanked them when they had finished.

Reaching for the pitcher of lavender water that habitually sat on her bedside table, Diantha dampened a lawn handkerchief and blotted the droplets from her mother-in-law's skin. Poole handed her a glass of water and salicin, which she held to the older woman's lips. In the face of her mother-in-law's pain, she decided she could not add to her discomfort.

However, after she drank her medicine, the dowager looked at her with sharp eyes. "Something has upset you."

Diantha brushed the remark aside, but the other woman pressed her until she gave in. "Ma'am, may I ask you some questions about your son? I had a very disturbing conversation with Barclay over lunch."

The withered lips pursed and she signaled Poole

to leave. After the maid departed, she spoke, choosing her words carefully. "My sister-in-law has always had a strong attachment to her childhood home. I often think she wishes she could have been a male so that she could have inherited instead of her younger brother."

Diantha frowned. "Kieran's father?"

The older woman smiled grimly. "Exactly so. She often criticized his management of the estate when he was alive, and I would not be surprised if she has passed her attitude on to her son."

Diantha played with her wedding ring, turning the golden circle around on her finger. "I'm afraid this conversation revolved around more personal subjects."

Lady Rossburn's misshapen hand covered hers. "Please tell me what that horrid boy said about my son. And don't waste my time by wrapping it up in clean linen."

She looked into the dowager's concerned face. "He tried to tell me Kieran has had liaisons with a female in the fishing village, and fathered a child who lives there."

"Oh no!" Tears rose to the old woman's eyes.

Diantha cursed herself for her insensitivity. She should have known this would be too much for her mother-in-law to bear. "Indeed, ma'am, I do not believe it! Kieran is attracted to—"

She stopped awkwardly, but the older woman finished her sentence. "—To a more sophisticated level of female company."

She looked at the dowager nervously. "Precisely. But how do you know?"

The other woman raised her eyebrows and looked

pointedly at the door that Poole had closed behind her a short while ago. "I do pity the woman without servants. How else does one know what is happening under one's roof?" Her hands moved restlessly on the satin counterpane. "But I digress."

She sighed. "There was an illegitimate Rossburn in that village. But not my son's."

The woman's candor robbed Diantha of speech for several seconds. Finally, she collected herself. "Then whose?"

The dowager stared at her bedpost. "My husband's."

Diantha did not know what to say. "Ma'am, I am so sorry. Forgive me for bringing up a painful episode."

"Just listen, I pray you." Her mother-in-law spoke sharply and she subsided. "My husband loved me. Always. But he was a man of great physical appetites, and eventually my pain became so intense that I could not bear the marital embrace." She could not seem to meet Diantha's eyes. "I am sorry to shock you, but I told him I would understand if he needed to seek physical comfort elsewhere."

She took a shuddering breath. "I wanted to satisfy him as much as I had in my younger days, but he, dear man, could not bear to cause me pain."

Diantha reached for a clawlike hand. "How terrible for both of you."

The dowager waved her pity away. "He still spent most nights at home with me. For the rare occasions when he needed something else, he came to an arrangement with a widow in Cariford. Unfortunately, a child was born of one of his trysts with her.

Kieran and I didn't know about the boy until my husband died and left him a small inheritance."

Grim pride filled her voice. "The young fellow is enough of his father's son to have rejected any help from Kieran or me, save for a generous sum on his marriage last year. Or he was," she finished sadly.

"He was a fisherman." Diantha closed her eyes at the other woman's nod. They sat in silence for several minutes before she stirred. "But none of this explains why Barclay wants to drive a wedge between Kieran and me."

Her mother-in-law pondered her statement. "No, it does not. That boy always has had a sly streak."

Diantha stood. "Just now I need to go to Cariford."

The older woman arched an eyebrow. "I understand Kieran told you to stay away."

Diantha paused before she opened the door. "The best way to keep Barclay from coming between us is to stay close to my husband."

Lady Rossburn's eyes twinkled. "Wear warm clothes."

Diantha sent for Florette first and asked her to pack a valise with her plainest, heaviest garments. Then, remembering the dowager's comments about servants, she asked the maid if she could quietly locate Archie Green and send him to the library.

The Frenchwoman's face did not so much as twitch. "But of course, milady."

Diantha went to the library to wait. Knowing the ghillie had more to attend to than usual, she did not expect him soon. She opened a thin drawer and pulled out the architect's original plans for Duncarie House. She could pore over the sheets for hours, fascinated by the measurements and notations.

Today she needed something to occupy her mind fully, though. Tucked into the aged vellum were several new sheets of paper. She removed these and carried them to the massive desk facing the door to the gallery. Pulling out a ruler, pencils, and a piece of India rubber, she continued working on plans of improved cottages for the estate.

As a woman, her knowledge of architecture came only from what books she could find on the subject. She had not dared to show her drafts to Kieran or anyone else, hoping only that someday she might at least use them as a basis for suggestions.

When the door opened, she automatically turned over the sheet she was working on. To her relief, Archie Green stood in the doorway, his usual irascible expression subdued by the unfamiliar surroundings.

She beckoned to him. "Come in, and please shut the door behind you."

He tramped forward as she gathered her papers into a neat pile. "And wha' can I do for your ladyship?"

Replacing the papers among the plans for Duncarie, she closed the narrow drawer and turned to the burly Scot. "I'd like to go to Cariford, as discretely as possible. Can you help me?"

He nodded in approval. "A fine idea. Dinna fash yourself, my lady. My brother Billy is settin' out with a cartload of food for the poor souls in just a bit. How long before you're ready?"

Ignoring his last question, she crossed to him. "His lordship sent word from the village? Is he well? How bad is the damage?"

The ghillie held up a hand. "Wheesht! I canna answer everything at once. Of course, his lordship sent for supplies, and they're ready no thanks to Master Barclay."

He made a disgusted sound. "Luckily Mr. Mac-Adam ain't one to sit and wait when he knows what needs to be done. His lordship is as good as we can expect, and there's but a bit of damage to the village." His face stiffened. "At least to the buildings. Near every man in Cariford between twelve and fifty was on those boats."

"My God. I had no idea it was that bad." Diantha shook her head.

Archie, his eyes brighter than usual, patted her arm. "No reason you should. You're still new to Duncarie." Pulling a handkerchief out, he blew his nose. "If you still want to go, don't expect a lot of bowin' and scrapin'."

Diantha tried to grasp the magnitude of such a loss all during her ride to the seacoast. She sat beside Billy Green on the seat of a wagon as it bumped through small Norpen Glen between the manor house and the cove.

As soon as they passed through the north end of the glen, the tang of the sea scented the air. Cariford lay only a few miles down the road by then.

From a distance, she found it difficult to consider it devastated by tragedy. Puffy white clouds filled the sky and the sun shone. But no boats floated beyond the rocky waterfront, only pieces of debris. Planks, crates, and a few bundles lay on the shingle beach and narrow walkway nearest the water. Only a few figures stirred to pick them up.

A group of men labored on a collapsed wooden building at the end of town, led by a lean dark-haired man with windblown curls. Only when they approached near enough to hear the work crew's voices did she recognize her husband's cultured pronunciation. Unadulterated pride filled her as she watched him join another man to pull a heavy pallet of wood to one side.

Billy cleared his throat. "D'ye want to go see him, your ladyship?"

She shook her head. "He's busy. I should make myself useful."

He guided the cart onto a muddy path leading to a scattering of houses above the harbor. "I'm taking you to Doctor Andrews."

They found the medical man inside the church. In his shirtsleeves, he and the rector moved the pews against the walls. Billy murmured in her ear that any bodies washed up on the shore would be brought here.

Dr. Andrews did not look particularly happy to see her. "Your ladyship, I'm not sure but that your presence here is a hindrance rather than a help. You're very good to show up, but what can you do to assist?" He spoke without rancor, but his bluntness took her aback.

The rector spoke up. "My wife is in the Herring House trying to comfort the bereaved. Perhaps you could be of assistance there."

Diantha mentally cursed her sheltered upbringing for not giving her more practical skills. "Of course. I just need someone to show me where it is."

Billy told her about the Herring House, a two-story stone building not far from the church, as he drove his wagon load of food, blankets, and clothing to its single door.

Built to shelter the young women who migrated from town to town along the Scottish coast following the herring runs, it was a dormitory built by a previous Lady Rossburn. At the moment it stood waiting for this summer's crew of girls who gutted and filleted the catches.

Diantha regarded it with interest. "That was kind of her."

Billy snorted. "No' likely. She didna want immoral creatures from outside the estate to corrupt Duncarie folks."

She ordered Billy to start unloading the cart and stepped through the low door. Finding herself in a low-ceilinged, shuttered room, she located the rector's wife, who sat reading from the Book of Job to a few silent women and children.

A few looked in her direction, but most of the occupants stared straight ahead. Some cried, most did not.

Diantha took a deep breath and introduced herself. A stir of interest awoke on some faces, almost immediately extinguished by grief.

She wasted no time. As Billy brought in the first load, she conferred with the rector's wife. The good woman explained that times like this provided excellent opportunities to remind sinners of their own mortality and hopefully save souls.

Diantha looked at her for a long minute. "Indeed?"

Turning her back on the woman, she saw a boy

of about ten huddled next to his mother on a hard wooden bench. He stared at her with vacant brown eyes, but she approached him anyway. She stooped to his level and spoke softly. "Good afternoon. I am Lady Rossburn."

He blinked, but gave no other response. Very gently she asked, "Was your papa on one of the boats?" The boy's lips moved and tears filled his eyes, but did not overflow. Her own vision blurred at the sight, but her tears would not help any of these people.

Reaching out, she took hold of a grubby hand already tough with calluses. "I am so terribly sorry for your loss. When did you last eat?" One thin shoulder shrugged. "Do you think your Mama would like something to eat?"

Finally focusing on her, he nodded. A few minutes later, she had coaxed him into helping Billy. His mother leaned against the wall, wrapped in her own silent world, but when Diantha touched her hand in sympathy, she felt a twitch from the cold fingers.

The boy acted as the first crack in an ice dam. An old man got up to help unload as well, and when Diantha apologetically asked if someone could start cooking fires on the hearths at each end of the room, a few women stirred.

An hour later, porridge cooked over one fireplace while mutton stew bubbled at the other. Bread from the Duncarie ovens sat on clean towels next to piles of plates and bowls provided by the villagers. MacAdam had sent along more than enough supplies; fewer than sixty souls called Cariford home.

The room had warmed from the fires, and Diantha ordered the shutters opened to let in as much light as possible, both upstairs and down. The sound of forks and spoons scraping tin filled the room, interspersed with occasional soft conversation or sobs.

She and a few other women made up pallets for those men who had come in from other parts of the estate to remove the debris and help repair those buildings that needed it.

She returned to the ground floor as the first of the visiting men entered. The younger women and children had returned to their homes after eating. Only a few older ones remained to help serve and wash up.

One old woman sat by the porridge pot, and Diantha picked up the ladle for the mutton stew. Most of the visitors knew her by sight and murmured amazed thanks at being handed their supper by a peeress. After working all day without hot food, they wolfed down seconds and thirds. She filled bowl after bowl, scarcely noticing the faces above them.

One bowl stayed in front of her after she put in not one, but two ladlefuls of stew. "What the devil are you doing here?"

Startled at the furious whisper, she looked up to see Kieran's scowl. After witnessing the devastating grief of the people around her, she welcomed even his anger. "I'm serving mutton stew. And you're slowing everyone down." She smiled for the first time since arriving at Cariford as he looked guiltily over his shoulder, then back at her.

"We'll talk later."

Still smiling, she gave thanks that her husband stood glaring down at her, breath flowing in and out of his lungs. "Very well, Kier."

He stalked away and she dipped her ladle into the mutton stew to serve the next man.

Chapter 15

Kieran paused to thank each man as he made his way across the room. He took a place by Dr. Andrews on the hard bench against the wall. He all but groaned in relief as he leaned back against the unyielding wood. Holding his bowl, he slowly ate the mutton stew, relishing the warm food as it slid down his throat into his stomach.

The two men ate silently for several minutes before the doctor spoke. "Lady Rossburn did very well this afternoon. I thought she'd do no more than try to dispense tea and crumpets."

His hand tightened on his bowl. "I told her to stay at Duncarie."

The older man raised his eyebrows. "Perhaps you should have been more specific. After all, this is part of Duncarie as well."

He gave the doctor a look. "It's not a part she's used to." His gaze moved to Diantha, standing at the far end of the room, quietly collecting plates to put into the washing-up tub. "And where am I supposed to put her tonight? I planned to sleep with the lads upstairs, but she'll have to impose on some poor woman already suffering the loss of family."

"Begging your lairdship's pardon." Kieran turned his head as an old woman missing several teeth interrupted them.

He sat up at once, giving her his full attention. "What can I do for you, madam?"

Her mouth drooped for a moment. "No' a thing, sir, unless ye can bring back the dead. But that ain't wha' I was going to say. I already offered Lady Rossburn my cottage for the night, and I'd be honored if you would both bide there this evenin'."

Kieran took one work-roughened hand in both of his. "I am profoundly touched at your offer, but Lady Rossburn and I couldn't possibly drive you from your home, especially at a time like this."

The old woman's chin trembled. "'Tis no' a problem for me. I lost my husband to the sea eighteen years ago, and then yesterday my youngest son." She looked down, fighting for composure. "I canna face going back in there yet, so I'll stay here tonight and get breakfast tomorrow morning for this lot."

Diantha glided up and slid an arm around the woman's thin shoulders. "Mrs. Dunn's daughter and son-in-law live in Ulladale. Doctor Andrews is going to take her back to stay with them when he returns home." She smiled at the medical man where he sat.

The old woman told her to come along. "I've just come from lighting a fire in the hearth to warm it, and we can't leave it unwatched."

Diantha lifted a plain wool cloak from a hook on the wall and gracefully wrapped herself up in it.

She looked over at Kieran before following Mrs. Dunn out the door. "I shall see you in a while, my lord?"

The last thing he wanted was company, even hers, but he nodded. "Yes. I have some things to go over with the men first, though. Don't wait up."

His responsibilities seemed to weigh down more heavily on his shoulders after she slipped away. He took his time outlining the next day's tasks, wanting to make sure each man understood his duties. By the time he left the Herring House, he looked forward to a night alone. He needed some time without worrying about everyone's expectations.

Provided, of course, that his wife was asleep. Then again, given her flagrant disregard for his orders, she clearly did not look to him for leadership. Or perhaps she knew his needs better than he did himself, part of his mind whispered as he walked along the dark lane. He remembered the sense of comfort that swept over him on seeing her at supper and sighed.

Mrs. Dunn had given him exact directions to her house. He found it easily, and stealthily slipped inside the door. Light from a kerosene lamp and the dying fire illuminated an immaculately clean one-room cottage.

Diantha slept in a box bed against the wall opposite the fireplace. She left the sliding panel open in invitation. Before the hearth sat a small tin tub and two pails of water sat warming on the hearth itself.

He emptied one bucket into the tub as quietly as possible and stripped, leaving his dirty clothes in a pile on the floor. Stepping in, he soaped the linen washcloth and scrubbed every inch of his body twice. Then he poured the clean water from the second bucket over his body to rinse off, closing his eyes to keep the water out. Blindly he reached for the towel he had noticed on the chair by the tub.

After drying himself off and pushing the tub to one side, he examined the offerings Diantha had left on the table under one of the windows. Two complete changes of clothes and a pile of thick blankets from the Duncarie linen closets. He smiled, unable to recall the last time he'd enjoyed such a sense of well-being. Then he started.

Diantha's eyes glittered in the firelight as she stretched out in the bed, hands behind her head, frankly ogling him.

"What are you doing?"

She grinned. "Enjoying the view." Her manner became more serious as she held out her hand. "Come to bed, Kier."

He approached her, but did not crawl in. Gently tucking the sheets in around her he kissed her eyes and mouth. "I'm not going to be good company tonight, darling. Go to sleep, I'll be in front of the fireplace."

He could feel her eyes on him as he spread out the blankets into a makeshift bedroll in front of the fireplace. She must have been tired, for she soon fell back asleep.

He added some wood to the fire and stared at the flames. He did not expect to sleep tonight, just as he had not the night before.

Twenty-eight boys and men dead. Could he have prevented it?

* * *

Despite the disappointment that Kieran did not join her, Diantha had fallen asleep quickly. His tender good night had eased the sting of rejection, but the sick look in his eyes had disturbed her. She dreamed of watching helplessly while huge black birds attacked him.

She woke up disoriented. Around her was a wooden box and she heard a repetitive booming in the distance. A soft, irregular noise came from somewhere nearby. Throwing out a hand, she hit the edge of the bed. Coming to full wakefulness, she recognized the bed and the hollow thud of waves in the cove, but she could not place the other sound.

Raising herself on an elbow, she looked around the semi-dark room. Her eyes settled on Kieran. Wrapped up in his blankets, he lay before the hearth, breathing in harsh gasps.

Flinging back the blankets, she scrambled out of bed and across the floor. "Kier! What's wrong? Tell me, please!"

Stepping around him, she knelt in front of him to see his face. When he lifted his head to look up at her, she exclaimed at his reddened eyes and wet cheeks. Diantha slid into the blankets next to him. "My dear, why are you crying?"

He answered by holding her close and burying his face in her shoulder. Grateful that he did not reject her, she wrapped her arms around him, one hand stroking his hair.

Finally he spoke. "I feel responsible for their deaths."

She hugged him closer. Her hand dropped to

his back, brushing over tense muscles. "Why do you say that?"

From the sound of his breathing, she knew he fought to say more, and waited. "The boats they use have small open hulls. They're easily swamped. Your father agreed to supply the village with new fishing boats built with covered hulls."

He raised his head and looked down at her. "The new boats are scheduled to arrive next month. I delayed our marriage out of a sense of panic at being trapped. If I hadn't, the boats would have been delivered by now and those crews might have survived."

He released her to roll onto his side, facing her. Diantha remained silent as she digested his words. She hated thinking about his financial reasons for marrying her, but she could not deny they existed.

She adjusted herself to face him, shivering unexpectedly as the blanket lifted to allow a draft on her backside.

He pushed their covering back and slid out. "I'll be right back." She watched him as he squatted on the hearth, seemingly oblivious to his nudity. He built up the fire and returned to the makeshift bed.

She lifted up the top blankets to allow him to crawl back in beside her. Pulling them up over his shoulders, she scooted close to him, warming him with her body as they faced each other side by side. "You can't blame yourself for losing those ships."

He started to protest, but she placed her fingertips against his lips. "My dear, there are too many variables."

"One, we were both out in the storm yesterday. We know how severe it was. Two, it was bad enough to smash wooden buildings close to the water's edge. Is that normal, or worse than normal?" She removed her fingers so he could answer.

He traced her hip with his hand. "Worse."

She snuggled closer to him. "And were the men going out on your orders?"

"No." He shook his head. "They know—" He shut his eyes and swallowed. "They knew the sea better than I ever could."

She brushed his lips with her own. "They thought it was safe. Then that storm blew up too quickly for them to get back. And it was worse than average."

She pushed him onto his back and leaned on her elbow, her face above his. "I don't know how soon my father promised the new boats after our marriage, but I think it's quite possible they would have foundered too."

Her fingers brushed a tangle of dark hair off his cheek. He had not shaved yesterday, and the prickle of his emerging whiskers teased her skin. "And because you are a conscientious landlord, you'd be blaming yourself because they were new and the men were unused to them."

He pulled her down to lie on his chest. Contented, she listened to him speak. "But that's what it meant for centuries for the Rossburns. The clan system was based on ties of blood, not oaths from vassal to lord. When you put on a tartan and badge, it meant you were part of a family and that your first loyalty belonged to it."

She lifted her head. "Ah, yes. You had to swear to love and serve the laird of the clan." She kissed his chest and looked at him. "Why didn't you ask me to take that oath?"

His hand stroked down her back as he smiled. "We have a family tartan, but I'm not a clan chief."

She kissed him again, a few inches lower. "You always think of yourself as responsible for the happiness of others." She flicked her tongue farther down, raising gooseflesh across his skin. "I think you need to let someone take care of your needs for a while."

His eyes gleamed green in the firelight. "And what needs do you think require attention just now?"

Her hand slid down to fondle the rapidly hardening flesh of his erection. "I can think of one I'd like to take care of." Becoming serious again, she placed a hand in the center of his chest. "You've thought enough tonight, Kier. Just lay back and feel."

He did as she asked. He watched her, though, as she moved down his body, kissing and stroking her way to his cock. And she watched him. Watched his chest rise and fall as she nudged his thighs apart to make room for her to crouch. Watched his neck cord as she ran her fingertips over the insides of his thighs. Watched his eyes darken to black as she removed the chemise she had slept in.

When she took the head of his shaft into her mouth, his eyes closed and he sucked in a breath. As she explored the hard flesh with her mouth, he buried his hands in her hair and moaned her name, urging her to go faster and deeper.

Then, panting, he sat up and flipped her over, spreading her wide with shaking hands. "I need to be inside you, Dina." He poised himself at her entrance, but although she was willing, her body had too little moisture yet.

Wild-eyed, he lowered his mouth to the apex of her thighs and used his tongue to tease her nub while slipping two fingers inside her.

She groaned as the familiar tension started to build. As soon as the thick digits could plumb the depths of her body easily, he lifted himself over her, positioning his cock once more at the opening of her channel.

She looked up at his beautiful face, now contorted with need and desire. "Come to me, Kier." And then she gasped as he thrust smoothly inside.

He set an ever-increasing rhythm, pounding in and out of her as he whispered his need of her. She met every movement eagerly, matching herself to him. They mated wildly until he raised himself up on his hands and ground into her with a hoarse cry. His release set off hers and she could only cling to him as tremor after tremor shook her.

They remained joined for a long time afterward. Then Kieran moved to her side and gathered her close, tucking the blankets into a warm cocoon around both of them.

When she opened her eyes again, the shuttered room had chilled and she lay alone in the blankets. She faced the bed.

Golden light came from somewhere, so Kieran must have lit a lantern or candle before he'd left her. She buried her head in her arms, afraid she would start crying.

"Dina? I brought you some breakfast."

She twisted to her other side. Kieran sat, fully

dressed in a fisherman's jumper, corduroys, and boots, beside the hearth.

Amazed, he watched her face light up when she saw him. None of the worldly women he had sought as mistresses had ever looked at him like he brought the morning sun with him. Part of him thrilled at the idea that he meant that much to her.

The rest of him wanted to run in terror.

He nearly hadn't come back to the cottage this morning. He could have made the excuse of needing to get started on the grim task of moving debris and carrying bodies.

But he had used her so violently last night. He knew he needed to ascertain that he had not frightened her, and that he probably owed her an apology. So now he handed her breakfast and hoped she would not throw it at him.

Instead, she smiled her thanks and started to eat, sneaking wee peeks at him as though she couldn't believe he sat beside her. She did not appear frightened at all.

But he had to be sure. "Are you all right?"

She swallowed a bite of porridge. "Of course. Why wouldn't I be?"

He cleared his throat. "I'm sorry I lost control of myself last night."

"Oh." She stared into her empty porridge bowl. "Is it because my behavior disgusted you?"

He sucked in his breath. "No, no, no! Dina, Diantha, look at me." She did, and he was reminded of the day on the *Columbia* when she'd thought he was about to hit her.

He moved to her side and pulled her into his arms, blankets, bowl, and all. Gazing into her worried eyes, he tried to find words to tell her that inexpert as her mouth had been on him, he had never had a woman touch him with such honesty and care.

He shook his head, caressing the silken skin of her cheek. "You did not disgust me." Her intense blue gaze bored into his and she seemed to understand what he did not say, for she nestled her head against his shoulder with a contented sigh. With a sense of shock he realized that his need for her included moments such as this.

Diantha chanced to look out of the Herring House window later that day when Kieran was walking by the cart as it carried a few corpses up to the church. His arm supported a redheaded girl carrying something bundled in a shawl and sobbing bitterly. She finished drying the dish she held and slipped out the door, drawn by the devastated expression on his face.

By the time she reached the church, Kieran had disappeared inside, but the girl stood by the door outside, still weeping. The bundle in her arms gave a squawk and she held it to her shoulder tenderly. Her swollen brown eyes met Diantha's.

She still felt awkward offering sympathy to strangers. "I'm sorry."

The girl's pointed chin dipped in acknowledgment. To Diantha's relief, Kieran reappeared. He took in her presence, but held the door open for the other woman. "He's ready."

His voice sounded strained. Diantha followed both of them inside the dim room. A precise line of covered bodies lay on the floor, awaiting coffins. She stayed by the door as her husband led the girl to a body covered not by a blanket, but by a length of tartan. "It was my father's. I brought it for him when I heard about the boats."

The girl sobbed once more, and then gained control of herself. "Thank you, my laird. He deserves this."

Kieran pulled something silver out of his pocket. "For your son." Diantha thought it was a coin until he pinned the badge on the shawl in her arms. "It belonged to my father as well."

She did not bring the episode up until they lay before the fireplace in the cottage that evening. "That was a kind thing you did for your brother's widow."

He stared at her. "How did you know?"

She chose her words carefully. "Barclay mentioned it to me, and I asked your mother."

He sat up, the blanket falling off his bare chest. "How could you bring up something so painful to her? Has she not suffered enough because of my father's neglect?"

"Please listen." She held up a hand to forestall his protest. "The situation was not quite what you think." She repeated what his mother had told her about his father's liaison.

Something dark went out of Kieran's eyes, but the sadness that replaced it tore at Diantha's heart. She stroked his bare back, cherishing the feel of corded muscles under his warm skin. "What is it, my dear?"

His back rose and fell in a heavy sigh. "I had playmates on the estate as a boy, and friends at school. But I always envied the boys with brothers and sisters. I understood early on that my mother couldn't have more children, so I didn't complain. But I always felt the lack."

She curled up next to him. "This was obviously before you met my family."

He placed an arm around her shoulders. "The discovery of my father's other family made me even angrier at his infidelity. Not only had he hurt his wife, he denied me a brother.

"My half brother refused to approach me or accept anything but the occasional gift. I don't suppose he had an easy time of it growing up as the laird's by-blow." His face stiffened and his eyes glittered with unshed tears in the firelight. "I'll never get a chance to ask him about that now."

Diantha reached for his hand. He gripped it tightly and pulled her closer. After a moment she let go and hugged her knees with her arms. "His son is still your nephew. You could sponsor the boy's schooling." Her voice trembled. "If something happens to Barclay, he may be your only heir, since I can't seem to conceive."

Kieran pulled her down on the pallet and stretched out beside her, leaning on an elbow. She echoed his position, facing him. "That bothers you a great deal?"

"One of my few consolations during our engagement was that I would at least be able to have a child of my own to love." She rested her hand on his hip. "I didn't think I would come to—" She caught herself before 'love' escaped her lips. "To care for you as I have.

"I want to have your child, Kieran." She couldn't see his face in the shadows, which gave her the courage to continue. "Not because it's my duty, but because I've thought about being a mother since I was small." She rolled onto her back. "I wouldn't be like mine. I'd want my children to feel loved for who they are every single day of their lives." She spoke the last words vehemently.

He gathered her close. "If we're blessed with children, I will be thrilled. You would make an excellent mother, I'm sure of it." He grazed her temple with a kiss.

"The difficulty might lie with the Rossburns. My grandfather only had two children, and so did my father."

"One of life's mysteries." Diantha shivered as Kieran's mouth possessed hers.

Against her lips, he murmured, "Indeed. And speaking of life's mysteries, I need you in ways that have nothing to do with getting an heir."

As her body responded to his husky whisper, she allowed herself a tiny bit of hope. Need wasn't love, but it wasn't indifference either. She wrapped her arms around her husband. "Perhaps you should elaborate on your needs."

They left Cariford after two more days. Kieran had overseen the removal of most of the wreckage by then, and the villagers themselves reached the grim consensus that the sea had washed all the bodies ashore that it would.

They returned a week later for the memorial service honoring all those lost. Iona and Barclay came with them. Kieran's aunt proved predictably unimpressed with the rapport that Diantha had developed with the survivors.

"It is not necessary to enter into their every feeling." She declared this after watching Diantha speak with a number of villagers and their children. The older woman stood waiting by the landau which was ready to carry them back to the house.

At tea that afternoon, a tremendous quarrel broke out between Kieran and Barclay.

Kieran wanted to attract fishermen from other villages by offering a share of each vessel's profits, with the chance to take over ownership of the new boats.

Barclay considered that too complicated. He paced the rug in front of the drawing room fireplace. "Why not just tear down some of the poorer crofts and send the families to the village? You're the landlord. Act like it for once."

She and Iona listened to the increasingly acrimonious argument for several minutes, until Barclay flung himself out of the room in a rage.

After he left, Kieran's aunt had addressed him sharply. "Why must you be so excessively rude to Barclay?" She shot a triumphant glance at Diantha's slim waist. "He is still your heir, you know."

Kieran drew himself to his full height. "Then perhaps he should remember that he inherits responsibilities to others, Aunt."

* * *

Kieran decided to return to the village a few days later so that he could propose his plan to the survivors. The night before he left, he assured Diantha that he would be back by dinner the following evening.

Barclay went with him despite their earlier disagreement, much to her husband's pleasure. He thanked his cousin repeatedly for lending him his support.

That afternoon, Barclay returned alone with a message from Kieran that he had been delayed and needed to oversee a few more things in Cariford. "I will be more than happy to carry any messages you might have for my cousin."

Diantha, remembering the lies the soft-spoken man had told about Kieran before, declined to take advantage of his offer.

After hearing nothing from Kieran for three days except vague messages via his cousin, Diantha took matters into her own hands. She wrote her husband a short letter, telling him that she and his mother both missed him, and asking if she had done something to anger him.

Sealing it in an envelope and writing his name on it, she left her room to go downstairs in search of a messenger. She did not trust Barclay to deliver it to his cousin. Perhaps Archie or Billy Green would oblige her. Not wanting to be spotted by either Iona or Barclay, she walked down a narrow hall just beyond the main staircase. It led to the kitchen and stable yard doors, and would hide her from her husband's relatives.

Or so she thought. When she noticed the estate

office door sat slightly ajar, she started to tiptoe past. Mr. Johnstone, the bailiff, might not have any reason to comment on her presence in this part of the house to Barclay, but she did not want to take any chances.

"I dinna want to murder the man." She did not recognize the voice, but the words stopped her in her tracks.

"Odd that you didn't mention your moral objections when I offered to rescue you from the hangman's noose." Diantha pressed a palm against her mouth for fear she would scream, or gasp. That soft contemptuous voice belonged to Barclay.

Hardly daring to breathe, she strained to hear more.

"'Tis no' murder to rid yourself of a cheatin' wife. But to slide a dirk into a man what's always spoke polite to me is. I want more money for it. You'll have enough after you kill his lordship!"

Something scraped against the floor. She guessed it was a chair, for footsteps sounded inside the room. Diantha gathered her skirts to run.

A long sigh sounded. "I should have known better than to set a nincompoop like you to guard him, even for a few days." Barclay's voice became reflective. "The thing is, in order to get the money, I'll have to get rid of my cousin's wife as well, because she'll inherit before I do."

He paused. "What are you willing to do for more cash?"

Diantha did not wait to hear more. Terrified, she inched back in the direction she had come, afraid a heavy breath or a rustle of her skirts would cause Barclay and his henchman to look out of the office.

She had to save Kieran, but had no idea how to do so by herself. If she simply reported the conversation she had overheard to the local authorities, Barclay could charm his way out of an arrest.

She needed advice from someone who knew Barclay and Duncarie, someone loyal to Kieran. Hoping she did not look like someone scared out of her wits, she made her way to the entry hall and out the front door. Going around the side of the house, she headed straight for the stables.

As she hoped, she found Archie Green in the stable yard. Drawing him out to a paddock on the pretext of wanting to discuss Dancer, she repeated in a low voice the conversation she had overheard between Barclay and his henchman. They stood by the fence, careful to watch for anyone who might linger and overhear them.

The ghillie nodded, eyes seemingly focused on a mare frolicking with her colt. "I think you should leave the house before he can do you any harm, my lady."

Her heart leaped at the thought of getting away from Barclay. She frowned as she considered the idea closely, though. "Where can I go where he won't find me? Ulladale is small; he'll find me there in no time. And what about his lordship's mother? I can't just desert her."

Archie's massive eyebrows furrowed as he considered her points. "I'm no' sure Barclay thinks of her as a threat. And once I moot word of this into a few trusted ears, we'll find his lordship afore that yellow git knows what we're about."

He straightened. "Hie yourself to my cottage. The wife and I can keep you there for a few days while I have a look round. But you'll have to walk. Folks will notice you on horseback."

Pushing away from the fence, he tugged a forelock as though she'd just given an order. "You'd better haste."

He was right. She needed a walking dress, not the silk gown she wore right now.

She half-expected Barclay or his manservant to pounce on her when she returned to the house. However, escaping proved to be only a matter of asking Florette to assist her in changing into a serge walking suit and sturdy shoes. Disclosing her plans to the maid, Diantha urged her to find a safe place to hide from the two men as well.

The older woman nodded as she shook her head over the grass-stained hem of the silk gown. "I think MacAdam will help me."

Despite the seriousness of her situation, Diantha raised an eyebrow at her servant. "Oh?"

Florette looked up innocently. "He speaks French *very* well, milady." Only the tiniest of smirks ruined her poise.

Diantha slipped out a side door without the least trouble and set out across the valley.

Tea time found her sitting down to bread and butter across from Lily Green, a short bustling woman who accepted Lady Rossburn's appearance at her front door without turning a hair.

Their son's wife Nan joined them, on Lily's recommendation. A sturdy fair-haired young woman, Nan's steady nature fit in well with her in-laws. She ruled her brood of small Greens with affectionate despotism, from Wee Archie, a nine-year-old ver-

sion of his grandfather, down to ten-month-old
Baby Andrew.

When Archie and his son arrived after dinner,
they brought no news of Kieran, but assured Diantha
that eyes and ears in the house and on the estate
were searching for him.

Archie chuckled. "The household had a bit of
fuss when your ladyship didna appear for dinner.
That Frenchie of yours nearly got that *cailleach* Iona
to send out search parties before Barclay could stop
her. The man looked flat panicked, I tell you."

She took what comfort she could from the news.
But when she crawled into the bed Lily devised
under the eaves of the cottage, she prayed that
Kieran was still alive, and would be found before
Barclay could hurt him.

Chapter 16

The next morning dragged by as she tried to help Lily with the unfamiliar tasks of housekeeping. The small woman demonstrated great patience at Diantha's clumsy efforts, although she chose to prepare the meals without assistance.

Lily did permit her to help with the washing up, a procedure which caused Diantha to make a mental note to increase wages for the scullery maids.

They had just put away the clean dishes after the midday meal when Nan rushed into the cottage, holding her baby. "Master Barclay is coming with that bully boy of his." Although pale, Nan spoke calmly. "I'll collect the bairns." She hurried out again, calling her children.

Diantha looked round the cottage. The only door faced down the road. If she left that way, he would see her.

"Quickly, your ladyship, climb into the best bed." Lily pulled the curtains to the master bed aside. "You can slip out the side window. If you stay low, the trellis will hide you all the way to the back gate."

Wee Archie entered, holding his youngest sister by the hand.

"I'll take care of Mairi." Lily picked up the toddler and a clean washcloth. "Lad, go find your grandpa and tell him Mr. Barclay is here. Dinna say anything else, ye ken? Go out the window and through the back."

The boy nodded as calmly as if his grandmother had ordered him to fetch a pail of water.

"How will he know where to find Archie?" Diantha glanced out the window, fearing to see her cousin by marriage standing in the front garden.

Lily chuckled and pulled out a fresh pinafore for the girl. "Those two could find each other in the middle of darkest Africa." She shooed the boy on his way. "And mind you don't get dirty footprints on my clean bed!"

The rest of Nan's daughters trooped in from the garden. Diantha helped change pinafores and wash off grubby hands and faces, mentally shaking her head at the irony. But both women assured her it would be thought odd if they did not clean the children up.

"And that's what we want to avoid. Now get in there, my lady!" Feeling both frightened and foolish, Diantha found herself stepping over the bed, mindful of Lily's admonition about footprints.

Nan whispered last minute instructions to her girls. "So help me, if any of you say one word to Mr. Barclay except 'Good day' or 'I don't know, sir,' I'm takin' my hairbrush to the lot of ye."

Lily closed the curtains just as the sound of hoofbeats reached them through the open front door. Diantha barely had time to slip out the open window and duck down before Barclay's smooth voice floated over the hedge.

"Good morning! What a bevy of beautiful girls!" A few childish giggles greeted his sally. She pressed her lips together. Naturally he would first attempt to coax them into giving him the information he wanted.

After he exchanged the usual pleasantries with the Greens, he finally explained the reason for his visit.

"I fear that there may have been a misunderstanding a few days ago between Lord and Lady Rossburn." He coughed delicately, thus informing his listeners that he referred to an argument of massive proportions. "It left Lady Rossburn, especially, highly distraught. She told her maid she was going to take a stroll to clear her head." A lugubrious sigh followed that sounded overexaggerated even from Diantha's position behind the hedge. "She has not come back."

Appropriate exclamations of shock and pity broke out from the Green ladies. He accepted their sympathy graciously before continuing.

"As I'm sure you understand, the dowager baroness is beside herself with worry. She has asked me to search the estate for her."

"Och, the poor distracted wee thing." Lily should have gone on the stage, Diantha reflected. She could almost see the old woman dabbing at her eyes with her apron. "We havnae seen her, Mr. Upton, but we'll send a message to you right quick if we do."

"That is a shame." His voice took on a mournful quality. "Knowing that she places such trust in your husband, I had hoped she might have sought shelter with you. I'm sure you won't mind if we take a look around your cottage, Mrs. Green."

Silence fell.

"Are you calling me a liar?" Lily's quiet words hissed through the air like cold silk.

"This way I shall be able to assure the dowager baroness that I inspected each cottage. I only want to give her what little ease I'm able to." His voice hardened. "I'm sure you understand."

His fingers snapped before the crofter answered. "MacLeish!"

"Sir." The door to the cottage creaked and Diantha heard heavy steps on the wooden floor. Stifling a gasp, she realized that if he looked out the window, he would see her. The rings of the bed curtains clinked softly as he pushed them aside.

Not daring to breathe, she held herself immobile.

MacLeish must have lacked imagination, for he did not stick his head out the window. She heard him moving about inside, but eventually he left the cottage to report to his master.

"She's not in there, sir."

"Ah." Barclay turned his attention back to the Greens. "You really do have a lovely family, Nan."

He must have given some kind of signal, for the next moment, the woman screamed.

"Mairi! Give me back my baby!"

The crack of flesh hitting flesh sounded as Diantha inched closer to the hedge and risked a peek through a small hole in the foliage. She crouched too low to see everything, but she could see Barclay mounted on his horse. He held Archie's two-year-old granddaughter securely on his lap with one arm. The opposite hand held a pistol at the child's head.

Nan lay at the feet of the bruiser she had heard Barclay speaking to in the estate office. A thin stream of blood trickled from her cut lip, while Baby Andrew screamed in the crook of her arm.

The other girls huddled around Lily, who gathered them protectively in her arms.

"Silence that infant!" Barclay's irritated order cut through the din. Nan pressed Andrew to her shoulder, trying to soothe him between her own quiet sobs.

Lily tried to reason with him. "Master Barclay, you can't really mean to hurt the wee bairn."

Lily's plea fell on deaf ears. "Please listen carefully. I do not for one minute believe you know nothing about Lady Rossburn's whereabouts." He glared at everyone impartially. "Either I leave here with her or with the child."

"Put her down first." Diantha stood up, praying that Barclay had enough sanity left not to harm the child anyway. He would kill her, but she could not risk a child's life.

She wilted with relief when the aristocrat put the gun back into its saddle holster and signaled Lily to fetch the toddler from his arms. The old woman did, careful to avoid contact with his person. Ignoring her, he eyed Diantha with a hint of admiration.

"I could have sworn you had no way out of that cottage. I know MacLeish isn't bright, but this is ridiculous." His servant stirred but said nothing. "If I recall correctly, there is a back gate that I cannot see at all from here. Why didn't you escape while you had the chance?"

"If you truly could not have found me, would you have threatened to kill that child?"

"Of course." A malicious smile curled his lips. "It smoked you right out, didn't it."

At Nan's renewed sobs, a look of disgust crossed his face. "Stop that wailing, you wretched female. I would have done you a favor by removing a mouth for you to feed." He looked pointedly at Diantha. "I remind you that I still have a loaded gun and several targets."

"I'm coming, don't hurt any of them." She hurried around to the gate and stepped into the front garden.

"MacLeish, bind her hands." None too gently, the man tied her hands in front of her with strips of braided leather. She flinched as they bit into her flesh. The man's sour odor assailed her nostrils as he lifted her into Barclay's waiting arms.

"I fear MacLeish doesn't bathe as often as he should." He rounded his horse toward the road while his servant climbed onto his mount.

She twisted to glare at him contemptuously. "It's hard to tell which of you smells worse."

Long fingers tangled in her hair and yanked her head back at a painful angle. "Loaded gun and targets, stupid girl. And at least I don't smell of the shop."

His motions confused his horse, who fidgeted back to face the cottage. "Damnation, I nearly forgot! MacLeish, your neckcloth." He took the sweat-stained cloth handed to him by his hench-man and wrapped it around her head, effectively blinding her. In the instant before the stinking rag covered her eyes and nose, she found herself looking into Lily's terrified face.

Run and hide. She barely had time to mouth the words before they galloped down the lane.

She tried to account for the time and distance they covered, but blindfolded, she had no point of reference. From the way in which the warmth of the sun moved across her head and torso, she guessed they switched directions several times. The pounding of the hoofs beneath her changed as well, from thudding on turf or dirt to crunching on gravel.

The sound of running water and splashing hooves stayed with them for a time, and she tried to remember the streams she'd seen marked on the estate maps in the library. She did not succeed in guessing their direction, but the exercise helped her push back her fear.

She asked once about Kieran, but Barclay only laughed softly. "You'll find out soon enough."

A cold chill ran down her spine at the thought that her husband might already be dead. She bit her lip, hard, to keep from crying out.

At last they halted. Leather creaked and then rushing footsteps approached. MacLeish's already familiar odor filled her nostrils as he lifted her down. She turned her face to one side to keep from gagging. She staggered a few steps, but righted herself as quickly as possible, wanting to avoid the touch of either man.

Someone grabbed her arm anyway and dragged her forward. By the smell, or lack of it, she gathered it was Barclay. The level footing felt springy under her feet. Then she stumbled painfully over something hard.

Barclay's voice sounded in her ear as her feet found purchase on another level surface. "I beg your pardon, I did not think that threshold so high." He might have been standing in the drawing room at Duncarie. Her mind barely grasped that she stood on another level surface before the rag was jerked off her head and she could see. Blinking a few times, she looked around.

She, Barclay, and MacLeish stood in the ruins of a small croft. Incongruous splashes of sunshine entered through large holes in the disintegrating thatched roof and landed on the walls and pounded dirt floor. A couple of baskets near the smoke-stained fireplace held some cooking utensils and dishes. Others containing food indicated that they used this place with some regularity, as did a rickety table.

With a flourish, Kieran's cousin upended a crate and indicated that she should sit down on it. "Welcome."

Diantha ignored him. "Where is my husband?"

Barclay cleared his throat. "About that." Terrified he would say Kieran was dead, a wave of faintness nearly overwhelmed her. "I was wondering if you would care to listen to a proposition."

She mastered her pounding heart. "I don't have the strength to fight you off and win, but rest assured I will resist you."

He winced. "Forgive my poor choice of words. I have no intention of molesting you. Before I go on, however, I do need to see to one detail." He waved to a wooden panel along one wall. "MacLeish."

The big man jerked the panel aside. It emitted a painful screech as he tugged at it again. It revealed a box bed holding only a thin pallet. On it, bound hand and foot, lay Kieran. A yellowing bruise covered one side of his face, his uncombed hair lay in matted curls around his face and he had three days' worth of whiskers. MacLeish hauled him to a sitting position.

His eyes, blinking at the burst of light into his makeshift cell met hers with an expression of combined horror and shame. "Diantha." He could hardly croak her name through cracked lips.

She nearly fainted with relief. He was alive.

Barclay also regarded him with pleasure. "Perfect." He turned to Diantha. "As I should have said, I have a proposal for you."

The sight of her husband gave her courage. She held up a hand. "All well and good, but I should like a drink of water first, and one for Kieran."

"Oh, very well." With a sigh of exasperation, he caught the servant's eye and jerked his head. "See to it."

The taciturn servant picked up a tin pail from beside the fireplace and went outside. A few minutes later, he returned with fresh water slopping over the side of the container. Picking up a battered tin cup, he dipped it into the cool liquid and offered it to Diantha.

The gesture surprised her into a "Thank you." She took the cup to Kieran, holding it for him as he drained it. Then, returning to the pail, she got a drink for herself.

Barclay leaned against the stone wall, watching

her with folded arms and a contemptuous smile. "If I may proceed?"

She set the cup down on the slanting surface of the old table. "By all means."

He bowed. "I have harbored great regard for you since we first met, Diantha. I hope finally to be rid of my unworthy cousin by this evening."

"Finally?" She regarded him in horror. "You've attempted to murder him before?"

"I placed my trust in MacLeish to weaken the bridge that collapsed under your husband." Barclay considered. "In retrospect, I admit it was too grandiose a scheme. The additional wadding I slipped into his gun the first day of shooting was a far better idea. Unfortunately, he used a blank, which had no shot in it."

"He would have bled to death!"

"You bastard, Diantha could have been killed!"

Barclay sighed. "That is rather the point of a murder."

MacLeish hunched a massive shoulder as he left the cottage. "I should hae bashed him in the head tae start with."

Barclay ignored him to address Diantha. "I beg you to preserve your own life by marrying me. I shall be a far more satisfactory husband than my cousin. As my wife, you are constrained from testifying against me, and you will have my undying respect and affection."

She waited for him to finish his speech. "Even though I smell of the shop? Barclay, you are a blithering ass, and I have no intention of marrying you, ever."

Kieran scowled at her. "Diantha, save yourself, please."

She shook her head. "I would rather die."

"Done!" Furiously, their captor grabbed her and dragged her to the bed. Placing a booted foot on Kieran's chest, he shoved him backward, then practically threw her in on top of him. With a few more agonized squeaks, he pushed the door back into place, trapping them in total darkness.

She heard Barclay's boots tramp across the floor before they faded suddenly. "MacLeish!" His voice bellowed from outside the walls.

Kieran struggled to place his ear at the crack between the partitions, and Diantha did likewise.

Barclay said something about "back at sunset" and "have the horses saddled," which she hoped meant they were not far from the manor and Archie.

The two of them scarcely dared to breathe until the muffled hoofbeats died away. Only then did they relax and adjust themselves to lie face-to-face in the narrow space. Keeping their voices to the barest thread of sound, they spoke.

Diantha, at an advantage with her hands tied in front and her feet free, offered to try and untie Kieran's wrists. He told her that the servant stayed in the croft as a guard and warned her to make as little noise as possible.

She placed her bound hands on the rough wool of his jumper and sighed with relief. She was trapped and probably going to die, but for the first time in days, she was with Kieran.

Kieran whispered against her ear, his voice barely

more than a vibration. "For the love of God, why did you not just say 'yes?'"

Equally quietly, she answered him. "He would have had to kill me eventually."

His chest rose and fell in an exasperated breath. "I know that, but you would have had a chance for rescue before he figured that out."

She buried a giggle in his chest in spite of their grim situation. "The price is too high."

He still sounded annoyed. "What are you talking about, you pigheaded woman?"

She maneuvered until she could kiss his cracked lips. "What would be the point of surviving without the man I love?"

He did not reply, although he kissed her back.

The silence stretched between them for longer than she could bear. "I understand if you can't say it back to me. But I want you to know that you are the only man I will ever love, and I'm thankful to have the chance to tell you so before we die."

She swallowed a sob. "When I was afraid Barclay might have killed you already, all I could think was of how stupid I was not to have told you how I felt sooner."

He rested his cheek on hers. "I don't deserve you."

He still hadn't said he loved her.

To cover her pain, she sat up on the thin pallet. "I'd better get you untied. We have people out looking for you; perhaps someone has trailed Barclay here."

He adjusted on the pallet so she could slip behind him with a minimum of noise. Then he inhaled softly. "Did you say 'we?'"

Diantha told Kieran about the Greens' efforts to

find him as she patiently worked at the rope bind-
ing Kieran's wrists. After what seemed like an eter-
nity, the strands finally loosened. Once he could
free his hands, he eased the loops off and untied
her bindings.

He told her not to touch his leg bindings. "If Barclay wants the horses ready, he's taking us somewhere, which means they'll have to free my legs for
sure. If they see those ropes are tampered with,
they'll check our hands. Then we'll lose our one advantage."

After they stretched and rubbed the kinks out of
each others' muscles, they stretched out with their
arms around each other.

Kieran urged her not to give up hope. "We will
find a way out of this, love. If Archie knows, he's
rounding up help, and there's not a cannier man
at Duncarie. And once we get out of this mess, so
help me, I will spend my life making sure you never
have a moment's regret for marrying me."

He might not have said he loved her, but at least
he cared for her. Touched, she tightened her arms
around him and listened to her husband's beating
heart. She might not get another chance to do so.

By the time MacLeish shoved the panel back
they had retied each others' bonds so that they
could free themselves. The servant grabbed Diantha first, crudely running a hand over her breasts
in the guise of grabbing her arm. She gritted her
teeth and held her wrists together and prayed that
Kieran would not do something gallant and stupid.

Barclay, standing nearby with his revolver pointed
at them, barked at the man to let her be.

Luckily, enough shadows had gathered in the old building that their retied bonds were not obvious.

As Kieran had predicted, his feet were freed and they assumed his hands remained firmly tied behind his back. She had pulled the loose sleeves of his jumper down as much as she could to disguise his rope.

The two men shoved them outside, where two saddled horses waited. Barclay looked at Diantha and gestured to one of the animals with the pistol. "Mount." Keeping the pistol trained on her, he turned to MacLeish and ordered him to get Kieran on the other horse.

As she struggled to get into the saddle, her heart leaped into her throat. What if Kier's wrists came free in the process?

The bruiser shoved him onto the horse. With a grin, he turned to his employer. "What next, sir?"

Barclay lowered his pistol. "I have to tie off a loose end."

Without warning he lifted the gun again and fired. MacLeish's face froze in an expression of hurt surprise as the bullet entered his brain. Then the body collapsed onto the short grass. Barclay looked from Kieran to Diantha. "Shall we go?"

Her blood ran cold as he mounted behind her and then reached to gather the reins of Kieran's steed.

She gathered he had specific plans for them, since he could easily have killed the two of them along with his servant. She tried to make a place in her mind where she could think calmly, the way she had when her father used to beat her.

She looked around, still unsure of their location. The abandoned croft lay in a hollow with a band of evergreens on one side. They rode toward the trees. Under them, he led the group along a narrow path that climbed upward. The sun had lowered nearly to the horizon by the time they emerged. With a shock, she saw a road running through a glen at the foot of the promontory. They looked down on Norpen Glen.

She twisted around to face him. "Anyone on the road can see us."

He raised his eyebrows and smiled at her. "But who is going to be on this road now? Everyone is home for dinner. Except me, but I am officially looking for you." The smile widened. "Sadly, your bodies won't be found until Mother Nature has had time to destroy any evidence of foul play. But I swear I will give you an elaborate double funeral and the best monument money can buy.

He halted the horses and dismounted. "I'll be able to use the money you brought to the family."

They stood near the top of the promontory. On one side, a long slope led down into the trees, and eventually to the bottom. The other climbed to the top of the cliff she had seen on the way to Cariford. Other than a thick layer of bracken, the only thing that found a foothold on the slope above them was a bent tree at the cliff's edge.

As Barclay reached up to pull her off the horse, she glanced at Kieran over his head. Her husband brought his hands from his back with the rope gathered in one hand.

As soon as her feet hit the ground, she began to struggle, careful to keep her wrists together so their captor did not suspect he was in danger.

With Barclay's attention on her, Kieran dismounted. In a flash, he brought the rope down over his cousin's head and pulled the ends tight. Barclay's hands instinctively flew to the rope at his neck as his face grew red, then purple.

Then Kieran stumbled over a rock and his grip loosened. She saw Barclay reach inside his jacket.

"No!" She grabbed at his arm just as his hand emerged with the revolver. He backhanded her so violently that light exploded inside her skull. She collapsed. Through the ringing in her ears she heard a shot.

A scream tore from her throat. Barclay stood holding the gun pointing upward, calmly regarding Kieran where he had collapsed on his knees and one hand. The other clutched his side, over a rapidly growing patch of bloody jumper.

Barclay's eyes darted to where Diantha sat tumbled in the grass. As if luxuriating in the moment, he turned to face her even as his arm straightened to aim the gun at Kieran's heart.

Scrambling to crouch as best she could in her skirts, she clenched her teeth and all but growled, "Don't you dare." Her own voice surprised her, coming low and steady. She tensed, trembling as she balanced on her hands.

His eyebrows rose. "Don't I dare what?" Mocking laughter followed the contempt-laden words. "Believe me, fair cousin, I have plenty of time to wring your pretty neck and make it look as though your arrogant husband killed you."

Diantha stayed where she was. She didn't have the strength to fight Barclay if she stood upright, but if she stayed close to the ground, like a fulcrum, she might have a chance to knock him off his feet. If only she could get the gun.

She cast a glance at Kieran. Her heart nearly failed at the dark blood oozing through his fingers from the wound in his side.

Rage such as she had never known filled her heart. Not the blazing anger her husband provoked, but an icy wrath that gave her a fearful clarity of thought. No matter what happened to her, Barclay would pay for hurting Kier. Nothing else mattered.

"Don't hurt her. I beg you." Slipping to an elbow, her husband extended a pleading hand. "If you ever felt anything for me, leave her alone."

A burst of wind ruffled through their adversary's hair. Diantha gathered herself.

Barclay shook his head. "Sorry, cuz, but the only thing I ever felt for you was envy." The words had barely left his mouth when she launched herself at his midriff, grabbing him outside the arms. The gun fired once, a puff of vegetation flying up where the bullet entered the ground. Then she saw the weapon hit the ground. As she tried to kick it away, she heard her name being called, barely discernable through the blood rushing in her ears.

Her adversary tried to wriggle out of her control, but she grasped her wrist with her opposite hand to pinion him closer. She only had the strength to hold him for a few seconds, but that was enough to kick the gun away from Barclay's reach. Panting, she scrambled to her feet near the edge of the precipice. The last rays of sunset warmed her back and bathed Barclay in a golden light of false benediction. Winded, he bent over to catch his breath.

"You little bitch." He squinted at her, raising a hand to shade his eyes. Beyond him, she saw Kieran crawling toward them.

She did not dare shout at her husband to stay still and reduce the flow of blood. The longer Barclay focused on her, the better.

"You can't possibly think anyone will believe you." She inched backward as she gasped out the words. "Could someone with Kieran's sense of responsibility murder anyone, particularly his wife?"

He responded to her taunt, bracing his hands on his knees. "Even the best man can crack, and it seems he was devastated to discover that his wife had fallen in love with his cousin. Naturally I shall confess our shameful passion with the greatest reluctance." Catching his breath with disconcerting ease, he straightened and recovered his usual aplomb. "But it seems the better man won all the way around."

As she felt her way backward with her feet, the wind-blasted tree entered her peripheral vision.

Trying to appear relaxed, she took off her jacket and mopped her face with it. "I don't think so. Apparently you didn't notice where the gun fell while you were struggling with me."

He tensed and focused on her hands, hidden by the folds of cloth. "You must have grabbed it when you rolled on it. But I hardly think a mere female would have the nerve to pull the trigger, much less give me a fatal wound."

Her shoulders drooped. "You're right, I suppose."

She raised her eyes at his contemptuous snort. "But then I'm not the one holding the gun."

Whirling around, he found Kieran, still prone, but teeth bared in a feral grimace as he balanced on his elbows to hold the pistol she had kicked in his direction. One look at his blue lips told her something was dreadfully wrong, however.

"It's over, Barclay." She pointed to a pair of horses and riders galloping down the glen. "Too many people know you kidnapped us. Your story will never be believed." She pleaded with him. "Save yourself from the noose, at least. Help me get Kieran back to the manor."

He made a move toward his cousin only to freeze at the metallic sound of the trigger cocking.

"No! I'll be damned if you transport me to some hellhole. I've got one card to play yet!" With a wild burst of energy he hurtled toward Diantha, hands outstretched to grab her. He meant to use her life as a bargaining chip, she realized. Instinctively, she looped her jacket over the lowest branch of the tree and swung out of his reach.

His fingertips just grazed the skirt before he overbalanced and toppled over the edge. Landing on the opposite side of the trunk, she cringed as his scream of terror ended abruptly.

"Diantha! Oh God, no!" Kieran collapsed on his arms, nearly sobbing her name.

"Darling, shhh, I'm safe." She rushed to him, stroking his back and neck. "We're both safe now. Can you turn over for me? I must see to that wound." With his cooperation, she rolled him onto his back. To her alarm, he started to shake.

"Thank God the Comtesse didn't catch you." He made the jest through chattering teeth.

"Do be quiet, my love. Why ever are you shaking so?" She stood, and lifting her skirts, unfastened the billowing petticoat underneath.

"Shock. Need warmth."

Frantically she located a seam and ripped off a muslin flounce. Forming it into a pad, she bound it over the bullet hole in his flesh with another ruffle. Not knowing what else to do, she wrapped her arms around him and pressed close, covering him with her body and skirts. He tried to put his arms around her, but she guided his chilled hands to rest between her belly and his.

"Help will be here soon. Stay with me Kier, don't drift off."

"Don't want to." She forced him to converse with her until Archie and Billy Green reached them. By then, dusk had fallen and she had to guide them with her voice.

"My laird! Thank God, I thought it was you tha' fell." The grizzled man's face crumpled in the light of the lantern he carried.

"Don't be such a cawker, Green." Kier gasped out the words from the ground. "You didn't think I'd ever harm my lady."

The ghillie looked downright foolish. "Ye're both safe after all."

Diantha shook her head, unable to keep her voice from trembling. "Barclay shot his lordship and he's still bleeding." The lamplight showed the reddened hue of her makeshift bandage.

The brothers sprang into action. Using their pocketknives, they easily cut her petticoat into strips. Archie replaced her messy handiwork with a larger pad firmly tied over the wound with neat bandages.

"Billy, you ride back to the house, tell them what's happened." Archie frowned. "We'll have to put the laird on horseback and follow slower. Her ladyship can ride with him; I'll walk."

Diantha told them about Barclay's horses. "I can ride one of them."

She alternated between frustration and agony during the ordeal of getting Kieran on horseback, but pressed her lips together and helped where she could.

He barely nodded when she explained what they wanted to do. Watching him try to help their rescuers despite his pain and light-headedness wrung her heart. Billy mounted his horse and tore off down the road as soon as his brother had Kieran securely in his grip.

Picking up the lantern with one hand and taking the reins with the other, Diantha urged her horse down the trail.

Her awareness shrunk to just herself, Archie, and Kieran during the jolting horseback ride that returned them to the house. Her husband drifted in and out of consciousness while the ghillie held him upright and kept steady pressure on the wound. She had to grit her teeth to keep from urging the horses on, for she knew a faster pace would only make it harder to staunch the flow of blood. In the bobbing light of the lantern, she saw that despite the servant's efforts, more red stained the bandages.

As Kieran's periods of lucidity shortened, her insides twisted in fear. Even the sight of Doctor Andrews and Billy driving a wagon to meet them in the main valley did not comfort her, for her husband barely roused.

"Lay him down." The doctor helped ease the wounded man onto his back in the wagon. "Green, I'll need you at hand. My lady, help us cover his lordship as much as possible, and hold that lantern steady. We don't dare wait to get to the house." The four of them quickly arranged a warm blanket over Kieran's body and placed hot water bottles at his head and feet. Billy slapped the reins and the wagon jerked into motion.

"Keep that light steady!" The medical man barked the order as he searched his bag for the instruments he needed. With Archie's help, he poured alcohol over a steel probe and began to search for the bullet. Crouched next to Kieran's head, Diantha balanced the lantern in her hands and watched the grisly business as little as possible.

Her arms ached with the strain as the doctor carefully extracted the flattened piece of lead. Asking her to shine light on the wound, he examined it as best he could. "At least there don't appear to be any bone fragments."

After bandaging Kieran's wound, the doctor informed her that he had made what preparations he could at the house, and asked about Barclay.

Before she could think of a story to explain his absence, Archie gave an account of what little he had observed of the struggle, including Barclay's death. Doctor Andrews regarded her silently for a few heartbeats.

"Well done." He cleared his throat. "I believe I can think of something to put on the death certificate."

Chapter 17

They arrived to find the house in an uproar. Mrs. Menzies approached Diantha, wringing her hands. "Is it true about Lord Rossburn and Mr. Upton, my lady?" She jerked her chin to the ceiling. "Lady William disappeared into her room as soon as Billy Green brought the news, but I followed the doctor's directives to the best of my ability." She sniffled. "My poor Lady William."

Archie and Billy entered just then with two more ghillies, using the blanket as a litter to carry Kieran. Seeing the large bloodstain soaking through the thick material, the housekeeper shrieked in horror.

"For God's sake, ye miserable woman, stop your caterwauling and get out o' the way!" Archie shouted as they hurried up the stairs with their burden. Doctor Andrews, following closely, paused to speak to Diantha.

"I'll need you to sit with the elder Lady Rossburn. She is doubtless frantic with worry."

Diantha shook her head. "My place is with my husband!"

He waved her protests aside. "You have done more than your share to keep him alive, Lady Rossburn." He snapped the words out. "Unless you've dealt with violent injuries, which Archie Green has, you'll only be a hindrance in the sickroom now."

His brisk manner vanished. "I swear that if it should be necessary to summon you, I shall do so without delay."

She understood that he referred to Kieran's death. Her face stiffened as she fought back tears.

"Now do as you're told and let me try to save his lordship's life."

Lady Rossburn's maid opened the door to Diantha's soft knock. In her seat by the fire, Kieran's mother gripped the arms of her chair until the inflamed knuckles threatened to burst through her skin. Still, her voice remained steady. "Is there news?"

She carefully gathered the older woman into her arms as she briefly described the doctor's actions so far. Lady Rossburn nodded. "I have every confidence in Doctor Andrews and in my son's constitution." Nevertheless, the gnarled hands gripped Diantha's tightly until word came that her son would survive the night.

"Please, look in on my sister-in-law on your way to Kieran's room." Tears of relief, the first she had shed, glistened in her eyes. "She is suffering more than we are now."

Resisting the temptation to leave Iona to her fate, Diantha nodded and kissed the soft cheek before hastening out of the room.

No reply answered her soft knock on Iona's door. After several moments, she quietly twisted the handle. The door swung silently open under her touch. "Ma'am?" Dim light came from a pair of candles on a table by the bed. No sound came from the huddled figure partially hidden by the gauzy bed curtains. "I am so terribly sorry to disturb you—is there anything we can do for you?"

In spite of herself, pity for the woman's plight welled up in her heart. She approached her. "I cannot tell you how horrified I am at your son's death. I swear to you that I regret it more bitterly than you can imagine." She could not blame Iona for not wanting to speak to her, but could not keep herself from asking for absolution.

"May I at least send for your maid, or write to a friend to come and stay with you during this time?" She took hold of a cold hand and felt wetness on her fingers. Jerking it back, she nearly fainted. The dim candlelight revealed that for the second time that night, her hands were covered in blood.

"I can't faint here." Automatically, she staggered to the doorway. Keeping her hands hidden, she gained the attention of a footman.

"Please inform Doctor Andrews or Archie Green that they are needed in Lady William's room." Her mother would be proud of her calm manner, she reflected grimly. By the time the doctor rushed in, she had lit enough candles to reveal the body on the blood-soaked bedding.

He shook his head and lifted a lifeless hand with its slit wrist. "Bad business all the way around." Iona's slim fingers wrapped around a sterling silver razor. Drying blood picked out Barclay's monogram.

* * *

After quietly ordering a few trusted servants to clean up Iona's room, the doctor escorted her to Kieran's chamber. "Do not disturb him with more bad news, my lady. I was able to stop the bleeding, but he's not out of the woods yet."

Her heart contracted at the sight of Kieran lying motionless in the four-poster bed. His dark hair formed a stark contrast to his waxy skin. As she approached, she wondered if he had died as well. A dry sob escaped her. At the sound, he opened his eyes.

"Diantha." The thread of speech betrayed his weakness, but a smile flickered across his beautiful mouth at the sight of her. He extended a hand, barely able to lift it off the coverlet. "Come to me."

"Are you in much pain?" She moved to the bed and clasped it. Unable to resist the lure of the dark waves, she gently brushed a strand off his forehead.

"Andrews gave me a little morphine, but I wanted to see you before I nodded off." He awkwardly raised her fingers to his bloodless lips. "I can never thank you enough for saving my life tonight."

Gratitude, not love. To her horror, tears sprang to her eyes at the realization that despite his tenderness, he could not fully return her feelings. Diantha tried to blink them away, but not quickly enough.

"Crying?" His fingers tightened on hers but he could not maintain his grip. "My poor girl, you must have been terrified."

"I shall feel better once you're fully recovered." She forced her voice to remain tranquil. "But in order to do that, you must rest." He made an impatient noise.

"None of that, sir. You are going to rest until the doctor tells you otherwise."

"Termagant." The thick lashes fluttered closed as the morphine started to take effect.

"So it would appear. And on that note, I must leave." Needing to feel his skin, she bent to press her lips against his forehead.

Eyes still shut, Kieran smiled. "Don't go yet."

She could not keep her heart from turning over at the request, even as she recognized that it stemmed from residual shock at the evening's horrific events. "I think I must, before Doctor Andrews orders me out." She hid a yawn behind her hand. "Besides, the shocks of the day are catching up with me as well. I suddenly find that I can barely keep my own eyes open."

He turned to stare at her intently. "Stay here tonight."

She froze. "Here? With you?"

"Only if you want to." His gaze never left her face. "Please?"

Torn between her rapidly beating heart and her common sense, she sought the first refuge for her stormy emotions she could think of. "I'll speak with the doctor."

To her surprise, the medical man made no objection. "Best thing for both of you right now, and if you're with his lordship we won't need to find a nurse tonight."

And so, after changing into her nightgown, she found herself nervously tapping at his door. When he did not answer, she quietly turned the handle and peeked inside.

"Kier?" Her soft inquiry met with no answer. The

light from a single candelabrum showed him fast
asleep. She chewed her bottom lip. If he did not remember issuing the invitation tomorrow morning,
he would be vastly put out.

He stirred in his sleep, giving a grunt of pain. As
he tried to adjust himself into a more comfortable
position, she threw caution to the winds. Arranging
the pillows to provide the most comfortable resting
place for him, she slid between the sheets on his un-
injured side.

Almost at once, his fingers entwined with hers.

"Dina," he sighed. Moments later, she felt his
warm body relax completely as he slipped deeper
into sleep.

The next few days passed in a blur for Diantha.
The need for secrecy complicated the funeral
arrangements; fortunately she and Doctor Andrews
came up with a satisfactory story to tell Kieran's extended family. Barclay, it seemed, had been dazzled
by the sunset and lost his footing at the cliff's edge,
then his mother's heart had given way at the news
of his death.

"Which is the truth in a way, your ladyship."
The doctor relaxed in her sitting room, sipping
a glass of sherry, while Diantha arranged a fragrant bouquet from the gardens. New lines creased
the doctor's face as he changed the subject. "I
understand Lord Rossburn has asked to attend
the services?"

"He is concerned that everything should appear
as normal as possible. I fear he will collapse before
their conclusion." In a low voice, she stated the fear

growing in her heart. "Are you convinced he will make a full recovery? He is still so weak."

"Your ladyship has nothing to fear." He crossed the room to clasp her hand in both of his. "He lost a staggering amount of blood. If he'd been left much longer, his wounds would have been fatal." She shuddered, feeling the prick of tears in her eyes.

"There, now, don't cry. While he'll be weak as a kitten for some time, proper food and plenty of rest will restore him. You just take the same good care of him that you have been." He patted her hand.

"The worst thing is he doesn't even argue about being confined to bed." A wry smile twisted her mouth. "It's not like him."

"That depends on what I'm doing there." Kieran stood in the doorway, braced up by his valet. Still far too pale, a lively twinkle nevertheless animated his aqua eyes.

"*Kieran Moray St. Colm!*" Face burning, Diantha glared at him as Davison helped him to the divan. "You are disgraceful!"

"Well I know it." The doctor's chuckle relieved her slightly. "I've had that lad as a patient a good deal longer than you have, you know."

He picked up his medical bag and took his leave a few minutes later, after assuring himself that Davison had not disturbed any bandages.

She approached her husband uncertainly. He had appeared comfortable enough in his room.

"You needed a change of scenery?" She resisted the urge to brush an unruly wave of hair off his forehead. A shock ran through her as he caught her hand.

"My room was getting a bit oppressive." His hand gently squeezed her fingers. "And lonely." Diantha's heart fluttered at his words, but she was afraid to hope he spoke out of anything but boredom and solitude.

The next month followed the same pattern. Except on the day of the double funeral for Barclay and Iona, he spent hours in her company. During the days when he lacked the strength to do anything but lay down, she ran the household from her sitting room. At first the servants found it uncomfortable to discuss their duties in his presence, but as Lord Rossburn did not attempt to interfere, they adjusted.

Estate business proved a greater challenge. Riding out to oversee the property was out of the question in Kieran's weakened state. He tried to conduct business through reports and interviews with the bailiff, but Mr. Johnstone could not be everywhere himself.

"Why not use Archie Green?" Diantha made the suggestion after another endless interview that left both employer and employee frustrated. "He's trustworthy and respected by the tenants. Give him a position such as 'assistant bailiff,' perhaps, and pay him for it."

The two men looked at each other.

"Right under our noses the entire time." Kieran grinned ruefully.

"Indeed, my lord." Johnstone bowed slightly in her direction. "Her ladyship's proposal is most sensible, and very welcome."

"Her ladyship is as clever as she is kind and

lovely." Under the affectionate smile he bestowed upon her, she gulped and weakly thanked him for the compliment. Then, stammering that she needed something from her chamber, she promptly fled.

Pacing the floor of her bedroom, she berated herself for foolishness. In truth, she admitted silently, her husband's recuperation had been the sweetest time of her marriage so far.

She felt valued as never before in her life. He seemed to enjoy her company, allowing her to cosset him, asking her to read aloud in the evenings. He even insisted on sleeping with her every night, although sleeping was all that happened in the immense oak bed. She had discovered waking up with him to be even more intimate than the intense lovemaking they had shared previously.

A dozen times, she had been on the verge of bringing up the feelings she had revealed to him. Fear had stopped her, and the conviction that he could never return them. He might rely on her good judgment and care for now, but surely he would eventually seek some woman more interesting than she was.

Instead, she enjoyed his company and wrote of each day in her journal, so she could treasure the memory of this time in the years ahead.

Finally the night came when Kieran gathered her close in his arms upon retiring, kissing her deeply. Diantha pulled back. "Is this wise?"

He could hardly pretend not to understand her with the solid jut of his manhood hardening against her leg. "I don't care if it's wise or not. We haven't made love since before Barclay shot me."

She winced, even knowing that his cousin could never threaten them again.

He cupped her cheek with a hand and regarded her soberly. "You saved my life. Barclay planned that for months."

She shuddered. "How can you be so calm?"

"Because I survived. I'm here in one piece, at least mostly." Lying back down on his side of the bed, he propped himself up on an elbow. She tried to read his face. "And that's because you refused to abandon me, and nearly got killed on my behalf." Unnerved by the utter seriousness in his voice, she dropped her gaze to the vicinity of his chin.

"I would prefer that you not make love to me out of a sense of obligation." It pained her to force the words out as memories of his touch burned through her body.

"Dammit, Diantha!" Startled by the exclamation, she lifted her eyes to his. Only inches away, the raw intensity radiating from the blue green depths arrested her.

"I will be profoundly thankful for your courage every day of my life." A crooked smile tilted the corner of his mouth. "But I assure you my motivation tonight is overwhelming lust."

She regarded him suspiciously. "Promise?"

He burst out laughing. "Promise!" Tingles ran up her arm as his fingers traced the veins on the back of her hand where it rested on the pillow between them. "Most women would have been mortally offended should their husbands have said that."

"I've learned the value of a lusty husband." She

barely gasped out the words before he pulled her into a passionate embrace. He rained kisses on her face as one hand slipped beneath the fragile batiste of her nightgown to stroke the soft skin of her thigh.

With a groan of pleasure, she gave herself up to the liquid heat coiling through her body. Pulling him down to her, she returned his kisses almost frantically. When he buried his face in her neck to lick and nibble his way to her earlobe, her breathing turned ragged. His hand fumbled at the buttons of her nightgown, trying to unfasten them. With a rueful smile down at her, he deposited a hard peck on her lips before pulling back to use both hands. She chuckled and pushed his hands aside.

"Let me."

He watched, riveted, as she undid the top button. "Slower," he breathed. She arched a brow, but complied, fascinated by the way his breathing quickened as her fingers worked their way down the plaquet. He sat back on his heels as she eased the gaping neckline off her shoulders, clenching his hands where they rested on either side of the bulge in his silk pyjamas. The heat in his eyes ignited a fire in her veins and her urgency transmuted into languor.

Reaching out, he slowly exposed her breasts. Her nipples tightened under his gaze, but he did not touch her except to pull the material down her body. She ran a hand over his arm, lifting her hips as he freed her from the wispy material.

"Kieran?" She puckered her brow as he stared down at her. His hands stayed balled in her wadded up nightgown.

"I want to look at you." The huskiness in his voice betrayed his want.

She grinned in relief. "You have looked at me on numerous occasions." She clasped her hands behind her head, arching her back slightly. His eyes crinkled with amusement at her ploy, but he replied soberly.

"I want to take my time tonight." She shivered as he stroked her cheek, then followed the curve of her neck, then down to linger at the hard peak of her breast before continuing down to her waist.

"I trust you'll allow me to do the same?" Heart pounding, she sat up and loosened the tie at his waist. A surge of feminine power rushed through her as she felt his erection twitch beneath her hand. His breath rasped as she pushed him back onto the coverlet and pulled the silk down his long legs.

Completely naked, he made love to her as he never had before. He caressed every inch of her with his hands and mouth and invited her to explore his body in return. The barriers she had always sensed between them seemed to disappear as he brought her to climax with mouth and body.

Afterward, they lay silently in each other's arms for a long time, content. On the verge of sleep, the words of their marriage ceremony came to Dina's mind unexpectedly: "With my body I thee worship." She wondered if this is what that felt like.

The next morning she woke up alone in her room yet again. Disappointment overwhelmed her. She had thought the freedom of their lovemaking the night before signaled deeper feelings on Kieran's side. She curled into a ball and took a shaky breath. It had apparently signaled nothing more than a return to his normal routine.

Despite the late summer sunlight that streamed in when her maid opened the windows, she felt gray and lifeless. Listlessly she allowed Florette to dress her in a morning gown of amethyst twill. She refused to wear mourning in private for Barclay and his mother.

"Milady is not going to read her note?" The maid handed her a square of heavy vellum, addressed to her in her husband's slashing hand. As the maid straightened up the room, Diantha unfolded it.

> *Dearest Dina,*
> *Please join me for a picnic lunch today? Doctor Andrews has pronounced me fully recovered and I should like to celebrate. Meet me downstairs at 11:30. Wear a riding habit.*
>
> > *Yours,*
> > *Kieran*

Numbly, she folded the paper back up and moved to her desk to draft a reply. He wanted to take her on a private picnic? It sounded so promising, but she squelched her hopes ruthlessly. They had no guests, who else was there for him to turn to when he suffered from boredom?

Nevertheless, a few hours later she descended the wide stairway to the entry five minutes early, wearing a cerise serge riding habit that flattered her brown hair and blue eyes. Thoughts of her own appearance left her head when she saw Kieran pacing the floor, already waiting for her.

"You're wearing a kilt!"

"Clever of you to notice." His lips twisted into the lopsided grin that never failed to make her smile back. The severity of the ash gray plaid shot with green, blue, and yellow enhanced his stunning good looks. He wore a black jacket above the skirt with a crisp white shirt underneath. Another length of plaid was looped diagonally around his body and secured at the left shoulder with a badge. Diantha swallowed at the sight of his muscular calves, then glanced at his face. She had nearly started drooling on the man; how humiliating.

Kieran's eyes swept slowly down her body with a glint of appreciation that set her heart hammering. He offered his arm. "Shall we go?"

Outside, the groom threw her up into the saddle while Kieran mounted his own horse. Seeing her look about for servants to accompany them, he patted one of the two hampers slung behind his saddle. "I thought we might serve ourselves today."

"I should like that very much." She beamed at him as they set out. "Where are we going?"

"It's a surprise."

He refused to disclose their destination despite her lighthearted coaxing. The ride passed with laughter and teasing until they reached a meadow stretching in all directions. The scent of heather arose with every step the horses took. After helping her dismount, he stood for a long moment looking down at her with eyes gone serious.

She returned her husband's regard, wrinkling her brow, until he let go of her waist and stepped away to fetch the baskets. She frowned at his back, wondering if he toyed with her emotions on purpose.

"You could be of some assistance here!" The

smiling request came as Kieran turned, arms full, to face her once more.

Together they spread the tablecloth and unpacked the carefully wrapped china, glasses, and crystal. MacAdam's perfectionism did not permit him to provide an inferior meal, and they dined on potted salmon with toast points, cold chicken in cream sauce, cucumbers vinaigrette, rolls, butter, and cheese. They washed everything down with a bottle of white wine. Only the wild birds wheeling overhead and the steady breeze kept them company.

"However did you get MacAdam to prepare all this on short notice?" Diantha inelegantly licked a spot of crème anglaise from her index finger. Beside her lay a dessert plate with only a few crumbs of cake left.

In the noonday warmth, they had both removed their jackets, and she relished the sensation of eating in her shirtsleeves.

Across from her, Kieran lounged back on his elbows. Sunlight fell on his face and neck where he had unbuttoned his shirt. "Actually, I spoke to him about it a few days ago."

"How thoughtful of you." Touched and oddly shy at the idea that he had planned their picnic in advance, she ducked her head. "This is one of the loveliest afternoons I've ever spent."

"It's not over yet." Rising in one fluid motion, he held a hand out and assisted her to her feet. "There's somewhere else I'd like to show you."

"More surprises?" She brushed some dried bracken off the skirt of her riding habit. At his innocent expression, she rolled her eyes. "Very well, but it had better be as nice as this was."

She spoke in a tone of mock severity, but he answered soberly. "I hope you think so." His aqua eyes searched her face intently for a moment before he released her.

In the time they finished packing up the leftover food and utensils into their protective layers of straw and newspapers, the sun had shifted slightly to the west. Despite the warm afternoon, Kieran insisted they put their jackets back on. Picking up the carefully folded plaid from its place on the ground, he shook it out and rearranged it over his clothing.

Eyeing the woolen length, Diantha shook her head. "You're going to roast."

He shot a smile at her. "It's important."

"For what?" The smile widened to a grin as he shook his head and knelt to toss her into the saddle. After she mounted, she sighed. "Has anyone ever told you that you are a remarkably stubborn man?"

"It has been mentioned, yes." With a chuckle, Kieran climbed onto his horse and led them toward a hillock in the distance. Birdcalls and the buzz of insects filled the companionable silence between them.

As they drew closer, Diantha noticed that it seemed to be crowned with a ruin of some kind. She studied it as they approached along a barely discernable path through the heather.

"It looks like a Norman keep."

"It is a Norman keep. Or at least as close to one as we could build in the 1100s." Reining in his horse for a moment, her husband stared up at the crumbled walls. "One of my ancestors was a Norman knight who fled England after he crossed Henry I, during the reign of Alexander I of Scotland. After distinguished service to the chieftain, he married his eldest daughter and was taken into the clan." They started up the trail again.

Riding next to him, Diantha listened to the pride in his voice. "Fascinating. What was his name? Did they live happily ever after?"

"We don't know his original name. He took our name when he married." He paused. "It was probably an arranged match, but I'd like to think they were happy."

Their glances met and by mutual consent, they left this dangerous subject. Instead, Kieran told her the history of the old keep, how it had sheltered generations of Rossburns.

"You've studied it a great deal." Diantha looked up as they passed through what had been the outermost gate. Blue sky stretched above them through the collapsed arch.

"Exploring this place was my favorite pastime as a boy." He stopped his horse and she did likewise.

"With all this falling stone?" She shuddered as they dismounted near an enormous pile of rubble. Mefisto and Dancer immediately fell to grazing on the long grass. "It's a wonder you weren't killed then." She clapped a hand over her mouth. "Forgive me, I spoke without thinking."

"Please." He leaned over to touch her arm. "We're both alive, and safe. I don't want to think about Barclay and Iona, and I don't want you to. Today is for us." He held her hand until she gave a tiny nod.

"Besides, I never felt the least endangered here.

Perhaps the spirits of Rossburns past protected me." He bent to tether the horses.

"Or you were a heedless boy." After a shout of laughter at her tart remark, he drew her arm through his as they strolled among the remains of the bailey. He showed her the rocky outlines of several store-rooms as they crossed to the roofless great hall. He even coaxed Diantha up a set of stairs creeping along the wall to a sturdy section of rampart. After looking out at the vast view of the Highlands beyond, she sighed and turned to lean her back against the worn stones.

"This is splendid. No wonder you're drawn to the place."

"You surprise me. My father used to bring me here when I was a boy, but no one else in the family visits." He placed a steadying arm over her shoulder as a stronger gust blew against them. "Too remote, I suppose."

Below, she spied a nearly intact building with an arched doorway in it.

"What is that?" His gaze followed her pointing finger.

"Next on the tour." After he carefully led her back down the narrow stairway, they made their way across the keep.

At the threshold she stopped and peeked inside. "Amazing." She lowered her voice instinctively. "I wonder how it survived."

A line of window openings on each side allowed enough light to illuminate the stone altar under a Celtic cross carved into the back wall. A few clumps of grass thrust through breaks in the stone floor, but the chapel had suffered less decay than the rest of the keep.

"I like to think there's an element of divine intervention." She slanted a glance up at Kieran, but he spoke seriously. "It always seemed so restful in here."

She had to agree. The windows allowed fresh air and light in, but sheltered by the bailey walls, very few of the outside breezes entered. The warm air barely stirred.

Linking hands, they slowly approached the altar. Someone must have carved the cross with a great deal of care, she decided. She stepped forward to examine it more closely, but a hand on her arm restrained her. She looked at Kieran in confusion.

He in turn regarded her soberly. "I've wanted to do this since the night Barclay tried to kill me." Turning her to face him fully, he took her hands and tenderly kissed each in turn. He took a deep breath and looked into her eyes.

"I, Kieran Moray St. Colm, take thee, Diantha Susanne to be my wife. I promise to be a loving, faithful, and loyal husband to you as long as we both shall live."

Diantha gulped down a small sob. Another followed. He brushed the tears from her face with his thumbs. Finding her voice at last, she replied.

"I, Diantha Susanne, take thee, Kieran Moray St. Colm, to be my husband. I promise to be a loving, faithful, and loyal wife to you as long as we live."

She saw a track of moisture on his cheek when she finished. Slowly he unfastened the clan badge and lifted his plaid off. She stood immobile as he wrapped her in the woolen length, fastening it with the brooch. "Welcome to the family." He cradled her face in his hands. "My lovely, brilliant, foolishly loyal wife."

"My kind, beautiful, far too stubborn husband." The words scarcely left her mouth before his lips touched hers in the sweetest kiss they had ever shared.

"Our first kiss as true man and wife." He rested his forehead against hers.

"Actually, I thought that might have been last night." She hiccupped as a chuckle escaped her.

"You're spoiling the moment." Even as his chest shook with laughter, a warm drop fell from his closed eyes and rolled down her cheek. "I've wanted to feel this kind of love all my life, but didn't think it existed. And it nearly cost you your life before I realized I'd found it."

"I thought you wouldn't want me." She pressed her face against his chest.

"I will always want you." His lips brushed the top of her head. "More important, I love you. I will love you for the rest of my days and beyond." For long moments, they embraced loosely, letting the light and peace of the old chapel fill their hearts.

Finally, sliding an arm around her waist, he led her to the doorway. She stopped and looked back, wanting to remember every detail of what she would always think of as her true wedding day.

Shakily, Diantha stepped through the arch and searched fruitlessly in her pockets under her husband's quizzical gaze. "I don't suppose a kilt has any room for a pocket handkerchief, does it?"

Another chuckle escaped him. "I'm afraid not."

She mopped her eyes on her sleeve and took a shaky breath. "They do seem to be rather inconvenient garments."

"On the contrary, they can be remarkably useful for some activities."

She sniffed. "I hardly think there is sufficient time to raid any rival clans before teatime."

"That wasn't the activity I had in mind." She regarded him with a furrowed brow as a slow smile spread up to his eyes.

"Haven't you ever wondered what a Scotsman wears underneath a kilt?" Recognizing the wicked twinkle in those aqua depths, she gasped in indignation.

"Kieran! Are you telling me that you're not wearing—that you're completely—" She broke off as an entirely different emotion surged through her. "Really?"

He smirked at her. "Really. And I think I know where the lord's bedchamber used to be."

Books by Bestselling Author
Fern Michaels

___The Jury	0-8217-7878-1	$6.99US/$9.99CAN
___Sweet Revenge	0-8217-7879-X	$6.99US/$9.99CAN
___Lethal Justice	0-8217-7880-3	$6.99US/$9.99CAN
___Free Fall	0-8217-7881-1	$6.99US/$9.99CAN
___Fool Me Once	0-8217-8071-9	$7.99US/$10.99CAN
___Vegas Rich	0-8217-8112-X	$7.99US/$10.99CAN
___Hide and Seek	1-4201-0184-6	$6.99US/$9.99CAN
___Hokus Pokus	1-4201-0185-4	$6.99US/$9.99CAN
___Fast Track	1-4201-0186-2	$6.99US/$9.99CAN
___Collateral Damage	1-4201-0187-0	$6.99US/$9.99CAN
___Final Justice	1-4201-0188-9	$6.99US/$9.99CAN
___Up Close and Personal	0-8217-7956-7	$7.99US/$9.99CAN
___Under the Radar	1-4201-0683-X	$6.99US/$9.99CAN
___Razor Sharp	1-4201-0684-8	$7.99US/$10.99CAN
___Yesterday	1-4201-1494-8	$5.99US/$6.99CAN
___Vanishing Act	1-4201-0685-6	$7.99US/$10.99CAN
___Sara's Song	1-4201-1493-X	$5.99US/$6.99CAN
___Deadly Deals	1-4201-0686-4	$7.99US/$10.99CAN
___Game Over	1-4201-0687-2	$7.99US/$10.99CAN
___Sins of Omission	1-4201-1153-1	$7.99US/$10.99CAN
___Sins of the Flesh	1-4201-1154-X	$7.99US/$10.99CAN
___Cross Roads	1-4201-1192-2	$7.99US/$10.99CAN

Available Wherever Books Are Sold!
Check out our website at **www.kensingtonbooks.com**